Ham Bones

This Large Print Book carries the
Seal of Approval of N.A.V.H.

Ham Bones

Carolyn Haines

THORNDIKE PRESS

An imprint of Thomson Gale, a part of The Thomson Corporation

Detroit • New York • San Francisco • New Haven, Conn. • Waterville, Maine • London

A Southern Belle Mystery.
Thorndike Press, an imprint of The Gale Group.

Thorndike Press® Large Print Mystery.
The text of this Large Print edition is unabridged.
Other aspects of the book may vary from the original edition.
Set in 16 pt. Plantin.

LIBRARY OF CONGRESS CATALOGING-IN-PUBLICATION DATA

Haines, Carolyn.
Ham bones / by Carolyn Haines.
p. cm. — (Thorndike Press large print mystery)
ISBN-13: 978-1-4104-0282-0 (hardcover : alk. paper)
ISBN-10: 1-4104-0282-7 (hardcover : alk. paper)
1. Delaney, Sarah Booth (Fictitious charater) — Fiction. 2. Women plantation owners — Fiction. 3. Actresses — Crimes against — Fiction. 4. Single women — Fiction. 5. Mississippi — Fiction. 6. Large type books. I. Title.
PS3558.A329H36 2007
813'.54—dc22 2007032777

Published in 2007 by arrangement with Kensington Books, an imprint of Kensington Publishing Corp.

Printed in the United States of America on permanent paper
10 9 8 7 6 5 4 3 2 1

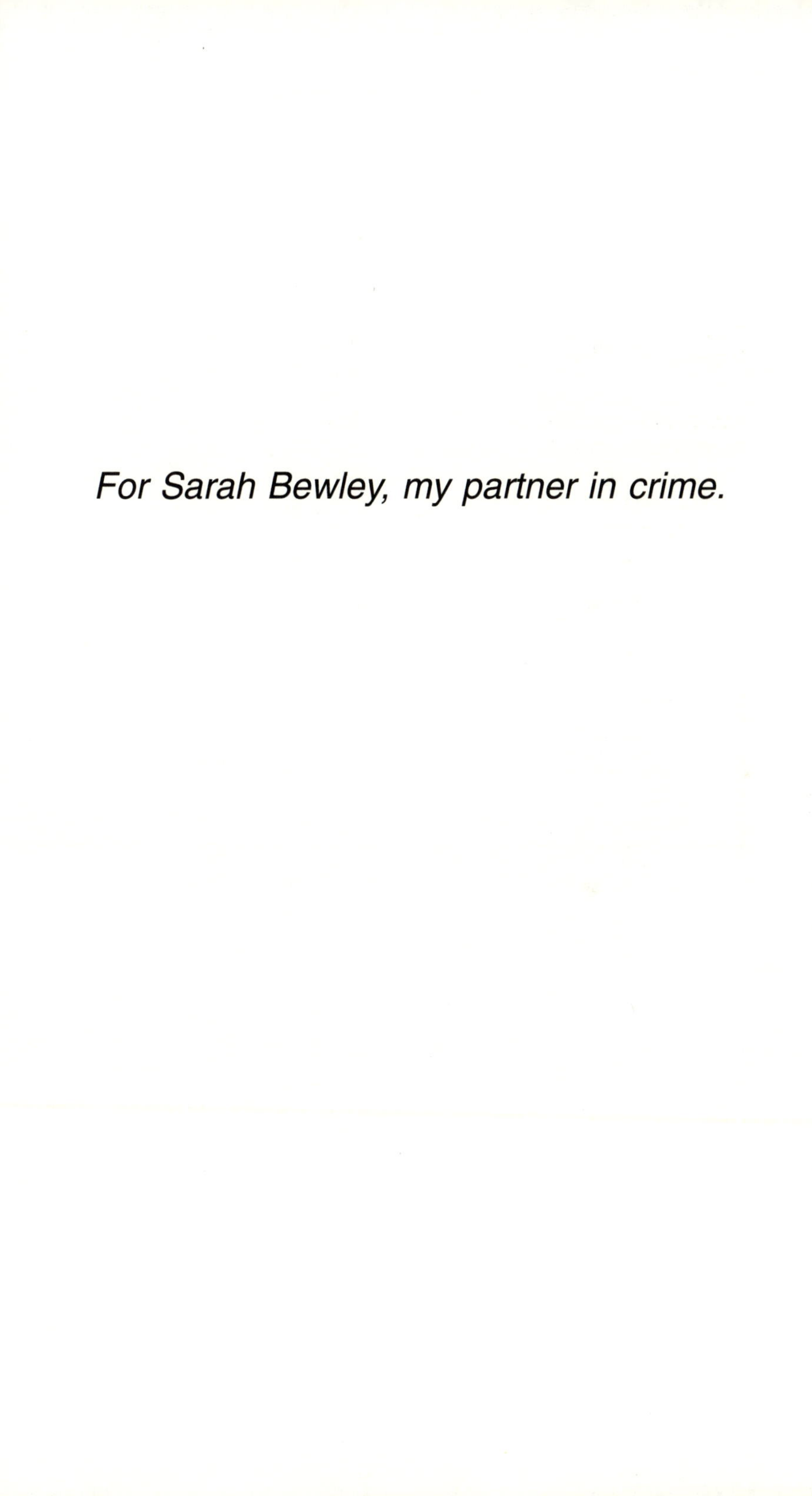

For Sarah Bewley, my partner in crime.

ACKNOWLEDGMENTS

So many people are invested in the Bones books and offer advice, ideas, and suggestions, but for this one, I have to credit one of my most loyal readers, Londa Pybus of Midlothian, Virginia, for the fabulous title. It was truly inspired.

Thanks go, yet again, to the Deep South Writers Salon: Gary and Shannon Walker, Susan Tanner, Stephanie Chisholm, Aleta Boudreaux, Alice Jackson, and Renee Paul. Over the sixteen years we've met as a critique group, we've read a lot of pages. Thank you for the constant care and hard work on behalf of my stories.

Special thanks to Dr. Fred Wells, who has a mind for fictional murder and a love of the Mississippi Delta.

My agent Marian Young is top-drawer. No writer could have a better advocate. Thanks also to Audrey LaFehr and the entire Kensington staff, especially the art department.

Chapter 1

When the cold January wind blows across the empty cotton fields, it's hard to remember the lush summer heat. Dahlia House has weathered more than a hundred and fifty winters, standing against wind and rain and war. Sitting on the porch, bundled in the new, red, polar fleece jacket that was one of my love's many Christmas gifts, I try not to let the fading daylight leave me blue. The holidays have come and gone, another season slipped away, a new year begun.

My resolution this year is to leave the past behind. Since the death of my parents, I've dragged my guilt behind me like a ball and chain. No more. Coleman Peters, the sheriff of Sunflower County, is recuperating from a gunshot wound to his chest and has filed for divorce from his psycho wife. By springtime he'll be a free man. I, too, must shed the things that bind me to a time and place that no longer exist. Divorce, a mere legal maneuver, is easy compared to severing memories.

Looking out on the brown fields that meet the gray sky on a distant horizon, I find it impossible not to think of the past. Only a year before I was in the Big Apple learning that my Big Dream wasn't going to happen. I would never tread the boards of Broadway as a leading lady. While my talent was a blinding star in Mississippi, I was barely a fizzle in New York City. I'd come home in defeat.

"I do declare, if there's one word that won't be allowed on the premises of Dahlia House, it's de-feat!"

I didn't have to turn around to realize who was speaking. Jitty, the resident haint of Dahlia House, had come to devil me in the broadest Southern accent I'd ever heard. It wasn't bad enough that I was suffering from SAD; now I was afflicted with SMG, sassy-mouthed ghost.

"Jitty, I'm not in the mood for your corn-pone rendition of Scarlett. Can't you see I'm sinking into a perfectly good funk?" I swiveled to take a gander at her. She had the annoying habit of skipping through the decades for her wardrobe. When last I'd seen her she was all Marie Antoinetteish. My jaw dropped several inches as I took in the layers and layers of pale pink tulle that swung on hooped petticoats. The dress was perfectly fitted to her nineteen-inch waist. With her wide-brimmed hat she looked like the unthinkable — an antebellum belle.

"Honey chile, you keep sittin' out here on the gallery mopin' about the past, you gone put the funk in dysfunctional." She snapped a fan open and laughed beguilingly behind it.

I rose to my feet. "Jitty, I've put up with hot pants and flapper fringe, poodle skirts and Trekkie suits. I've even been through French Revolution garb, but I draw the line at this" — I pointed at her dress — "mockery of my heritage!"

"You're the one who can't let the past go." She sashayed around the porch, her hoop skirts swinging to reveal ruffled pantaloons.

I was saved from a response by the sound of a tooting horn. Tinkie's new Cadillac cruised down the driveway. When I turned back to Jitty, she was gone.

The Cadillac stopped and Tinkie sprang from behind the wheel, her gaze sweeping over the drying garlands of cedar and magnolia leaves I'd used to decorate the porch.

"Christmas is over, Sarah Booth. It's bad luck to leave those decorations up." She snatched an end of a garland and pulled. Since her visit to Dr. Larry Martin had revealed that the pecan-sized lump in her breast was completely gone — vanished! — Tinkie had been a ball of fire.

"I'll help you with this," she said as she tore the greenery free of the house, "but then you'll have to help me."

"Help you what?" I was wary of Tinkie's deals.

She dropped the garland at her feet, her face alive with pleasure. "Finish the preparations for the cast."

"No!" I wanted no part of it. "When I left New York, I gave up all ambitions of hanging out with actors. I don't even like actors."

Her bottom lip protruded slightly in a pout that brought grown men to their knees. "Don't be that way, Sarah Booth. This is going to be wonderful. A New York production of *Cat on a Hot Tin Roof* is the biggest thing that's ever happened in Zinnia."

"And it wouldn't be happening now if a hurricane hadn't destroyed the entire Gulf Coast." It was true. The production had been booked into the Beau Rivage Casino and a category-five hurricane had devastated the coastline of Mississippi.

"I hate to benefit from someone else's

misfortune." She pulled another garland free of the balustrade. "They had to go somewhere, though, and we're fortunate that The Club had a stage and auditorium."

"Yes, what would the debutantes in town do without the facilities of The Club?" I rolled up the garlands she was destroying. Inside the door was a garbage bag for just this purpose, and I grabbed it and began stuffing. Tinkie was half-finished pulling down what had taken me two days to put up.

"You're just upset about Graf Milieu." She yanked a garland with such force that the tacks I'd used to secure it scattered over the porch.

"Graf is nothing to me." If I said it often enough, it would be true. In fact, I had no romantic feelings left for him, but I did have shame. He'd seen me defeated, running home from New York with my tail between my legs because I wasn't talented enough.

The sound of a loud bay drew both of our attention to the Cadillac. Sweetie Pie, my invincible hound, was standing on her hind feet, paws against the window, looking for Tinkie's little dust mop, Chablis.

"Where is your dog?" I asked. Tinkie seldom went anywhere without the Yorkie.

"I'm having her topknot layered and

glitzed. She has a seat for opening night. Chablis, in case you've forgotten, is a huge fan of Tennessee Williams."

I cast a sidelong look to see if she was teasing. Tinkie sometimes took it a little too far with Chablis, who was manicured, primped, and treated like a child prodigy. I loved the little rascal, but I didn't believe she cared for stage productions.

"I'm only kidding," Tinkie said as she grasped the last of the decorations. "But I am having a cocktail party at Hill Top on opening night, and I want Chablis to look her best."

"Right." I stuffed the last of the cedar into my trash bag and tied it shut. "So what, exactly, is it you want me to help you do?"

"The cast is due to arrive tonight. I want to have fresh flowers in the dressing rooms —"

"Dressing rooms?" I wasn't a member of The Club, but I'd been there plenty. There weren't any dressing rooms.

"Renata Trovaioli insisted that she must have her own dressing room, so while I was ordering new construction, I had one fixed up for Graf and Sir Alfred Bascomb. Can you believe it?" She clutched my hand. "Sir Alfred Bascomb is going to be here in Zinnia. He's incredible. I saw him in *Lolita*."

She looked like she was going to swoon.

"An incredible bore." I'd had one encounter with the Brit, and it had left me emotionally gutted. The man had looked down his hawkish nose at me and told me to get elocution lessons. "He doesn't find Southern drawls the least bit interesting."

"Did you see him in *The Gentleman Caller*? I mean . . ." Her hand went to her heart. "I cried for days!"

"Yeah, boo-hoo." The more she talked the more I knew I didn't want any part of her plans.

"Sarah Booth, did you really sleep with Graf? He's probably the most handsome man I ever saw. I'll bet —"

The question came out of the blue and struck like an arrow in my heart, bringing a kaleidoscope of images of the two of us as young lovers in the most fascinating city in the world. I held up my hand, palm toward her face. "Talk to the hand, Tinkie. My New Year's resolution is to leave the past behind me." I gave her a glare. "Graf is the past. No good comes of digging it up."

"You did sleep with him!" She arched an eyebrow. "I sure hope Coleman isn't the jealous type. Then again, he survived your fling with Hamilton Garrett V, and he *is* still married."

"Not for long. His marriage is a technicality." Coleman had filed for divorce in November. The case was slowly winding its way through the court system, and hopefully by spring he'd be shed of Connie and her insanity.

"Coleman hasn't been sleeping over here." She spoke fact. "The two of you haven't consummated your relationship, have you?"

I kept my gaze on the bag of Christmas rubble. "Coleman has honor. He doesn't want to start with me until he's completely free of Connie." I cleared my throat. "He was also shot in the chest, if you remember."

She shook her head slowly, her blue gaze holding mine until I looked away. "Honor is one thing, Sarah Booth, but to leave you all alone Christmas Eve. That's just plain stupid. He could sleep over and hold you. What's —"

"I haven't been alone." In another minute my blabbering mouth would be telling Tinkie my concerns — or even worse, all about Jitty. Tinkie would call the men in white suits. "I mean Sweetie Pie was with me, and Coleman came by. We built a fire, and we exchanged our gifts." What I didn't say was that he'd been careful to leave before our passions sent us upstairs to my bed.

"I hope you didn't serve him any of that fruitcake you made. After Virgie's deadly batch, I can't imagine ever eating fruitcake again."

"Coleman understands tradition. And fruitcake is the only tradition I keep at Christmas."

Tinkie's expression shifted to something close to pity and her blue eyes brimmed with tears. "I'm sorry, Sarah Booth. I know how much you miss your family."

I shrugged because I didn't trust my voice. I did miss my parents. Years hadn't dimmed the hurt, and the best thing to do was simply not to talk about it. "I'll help you, but only today. I'll take my car; I want to be home before the actors arrive."

"Don't trust yourself with Graf?"

The devil had danced away her tears. I couldn't help but smile. "I have no feelings for Graf except regret. I remember too well what a pompous ass he is."

"Then why won't you stay and welcome all of them?"

"Because I have a date with Coleman at eight." It was a lie born of pride. The trouble was that I hadn't seen Coleman all week. All I could do was pretend.

"Okay," she agreed. "I'll meet you at The Club."

■ ■ ■ ■

I grabbed the huge vase of American Beauties and started back into The Club. My back was killing me. I'd never thought I could be exhausted by hauling flowers and fruit baskets, but Tinkie had worked me like a field hand. She was a regular Patton at cracking out orders. I had serious sympathy for the numerous employees of The Club who fell under her regime. Oscar, as president of Zinnia's only bank and largest stockholder of The Club, wielded a big stick. Tinkie had borrowed it for this event, which had become her special baby. She was determined that Graf, Renata Trovaioli, Alfred Bascomb, and company would have every amenity a large city could provide. Zinnia would not be looked upon as a backwater.

I put the flowers on the dressing table especially crafted for Renata Trovaioli, a woman I'd once been an understudy for in a Marsha Norman play called *'Night, Mother.* Renata had been the worst kind of prima donna, and there wasn't a night that went by that I didn't wish she'd fall into the orchestra pit and give me my chance. I'd loved the play. Renata, though, was healthy as a horse. The only thing that might kill her would be a flying house from Kansas. I couldn't conjure one of those up, so I never had a chance to speak even a line of the play. Renata, on the other hand, won a Tony.

"Sarah Booth, quit daydreaming and put that vase down. I need someone to help me hang these pictures. They're only reproductions, but Renata is a huge fan of Van Gogh. I thought these would be homey." Tinkie held a painting of a vase of sunflowers with a frame that must have weighed ninety pounds.

"Could you hold it up there so I can see how it looks?" She pointed at a wall.

Hefting the painting with a small grunt, I lifted and lowered and shifted and eased until she declared perfection. "Hold it right there. I'll be back with a nail and hammer."

This work was far more difficult than pulling down a bit of garland. I'd make Tinkie pay.

When at last the picture was hung, I stepped back. "I'm going home, Tink. It's after six." I was starving and my shoulders were on fire. "Everything looks great." And it did. She'd done a spectacular job. The space looked like the backstage area of an elegant theatre. The lighting was flattering, the area for costumes plentiful, the sofas and chairs more comfortable than what I had at home. She'd blown through a wad of cash, but her plan was to auction off everything any of the actors touched. She'd recoup her outlay and make additional money for The Club's Hurricane Relief Fund.

"Is that — it couldn't be Sarah Booth Delaney!"

The baritone voice froze me to the spot. I closed my eyes and swallowed while Tinkie did her best sorority squeal.

"Why, it's Graf Milieu! Sarah Booth, turn around and look. It's really him!"

I knew it was him. I'd recognize his voice anywhere. I'd saved phone messages from him, simply to hear that rich, sexy voice. I spun around, pasting pleasant on my face. "Why, Graf, you look marvelous."

No hardship to say that. His dark hair was touched by gray at the temples, and there were a few additional character lines at the corner of his eyes, but the hand of time had touched additional handsomeness into perfection.

"Sarah Booth, you've never looked lovelier."

Before I could do anything, he swept me into an embrace. His lips, so warm and firm and tasting of peppermint, closed over mine. The kiss went from friendly to sexy in a nanosecond. "I've thought about you every day for the past year," he whispered into my ear. "The only reason I came to this godforsaken hole was to see you."

"Easy, Graf." I wiggled free of his arms. My heart was pounding, and I couldn't look at him. His words were vindication for an old, ugly wound. When I'd left New York, he hadn't made a single attempt to stop me. Not even a please. He'd remained silent as I picked up my last suitcase and walked out into a bitter winter day. He'd watched from the window as I'd gotten into the taxi. He didn't even wave.

Since I'd been home, he hadn't bothered to call. Not even once. Not even to make sure I'd gotten home safely. When I left New York, I left his sphere of awareness. Or so I'd thought.

"Why, Sarah Booth, you look pure flushed." Tinkie sucked in her bottom lip. It popped free and I heard a gasp behind me. Sir Alfred Bascomb stood only two feet away.

"I am flushed. With hunger." I strode away from Graf and Sir Alfred, heading for the hallway that would, eventually, lead to an outside exit. I had no use for either of them. "I'm going home, Tinkie," I called behind me. “I have plans.”

“In the arms of the great, big, handsome sheriff, who is still legally married,” she called after me, and I knew it was for Graf’s benefit. I heard her high heels tapping after me.

Betrayal stung me. “Coleman is your friend,” I whispered to her even though we were well out of earshot. “How could you?”

“Every cook knows an extra hunk of meat improves the stew.” She grinned. “Sarah Booth, Graf looked at you like a starving man would eye a T-bone.”

“How flattering. And how accurate. I’d be his next meal, and then he’d move on to dessert — if I were even slightly interested, which I’m not.” I put my hand on her arm. “Tinkie, you don’t know the history between us. He treated me poorly.”

The mischief fled from her eyes. “You’re right. I don’t know the history. It’s just that you’ve been so down lately. Coleman isn’t making you happy, and I thought a harmless flirtation with Graf might perk you right up.”

The problem was that Graf was never harmless. He could charm the knickers off the Queen Mother, and there was always a price to pay for being the object of his attentions. “Not a good plan. Let’s get this production up and running so these people can vamoose."

"Okay. No more meddling." She stood on tiptoe and kissed my cheek. "If you promise to laugh a little more."

"I promise." Anything to keep her from trying to set me up with Graf.

Renata Trovaioli swept into the hallway. Her hair was a tangle of Medusa curls and her ice-blue eyes were offset with kohl that gave her an exotic aura. "That stalking bitch is hanging around the front door. I was promised there would be security to protect me. She's going to kill me. She is! She's got a poster and is marching back and forth calling me a heartless killer!"

I had no idea what Renata was talking about, but Tinkie stepped forward to handle it.

"I'll call the sheriff." Tinkie whipped out her cell phone and began the call, as Graf and Sir Alfred came down the hallway toward us.

Renata's bosom heaved dramatically, and her hand fluttered as if she nearly fainted. "Someone, please! Help me!"

She slumped artfully into Graf's arms. As he looked at me, he rolled his eyes. While Renata's theatrics were annoying, they did give me a chance to slip out the door and depart.

As I stepped into the cold January dusk, I saw a petite woman with auburn hair and a huge sign. When she turned toward me, I could read the neatly lettered words.

"Renata doesn't brake for pets!"

I walked over to the woman. "You probably have every right to despise Renata, but I should warn you they're calling the cops."

"My name is Kristine Rolofson, and I've been arrested at every venue Renata has played since she struck Giblet and left her lying in the street, bleeding and in pain." Anger sparked in her eyes. "She's going to pay, and I won't stop until the laws are changed. She should've been prosecuted for leaving the scene of an accident."

"If you want to live to picket another day, you should leave." I pointed in the distance to the flashing blue lights. Coleman, Gordon, or Dewayne was on the way. Or, it could be all three of them. Even law officers weren't immune to the intrigues of celebrity.

Kristine lowered her sign. "She really called the police."

I nodded. "Renata is acting like you're a security risk."

Kristine laughed. "Right. I'm so deadly. She just doesn't like the bad publicity that comes with me."

I had an inspired idea. "Put your picket sign in my car, and I'll take you straight to Cece Dee Falcon, the reviewer for the *Zinnia Dispatch.* She's a close friend, and I'm sure she'd love to hear all about Giblet." My grin was wicked.

"Great." She tossed her sign into the backseat of my roadster, whistled up her dog, and both of them jumped in.

In less than a minute we were on the road to town and what I hoped would be a huge thorn in Renata Trovaioli's side.

CHAPTER 2

By eight o'clock, I was in my pajamas and under a fleece throw in front of the fireplace. My lie to Tinkie gnawed at my conscience. I had no date with Coleman, and hadn't seen him since New Year's Eve, when he'd given me a chaste kiss on the cheek and ducked out the front door as the ball was dropping in New York City.

His behavior had been puzzling at first. Now it was frightening. Coleman was a man who took his vows seriously, but I couldn't help but wonder if the gunshot — or Connie's shenanigans — had done something permanent.

Though we'd never acted on our feelings for each other — with the exception of a few kisses — I was afraid that somehow he felt as if he'd dishonored his marriage vows to Connie. Forget that she was a psycho bitch who'd tried to kill me. Forget that she'd tricked Coleman into staying in the marriage by pretending to be pregnant. Forget that her entire life with Coleman had been a lie. Connie had never been capable of the type of love that Coleman had committed to. Now I had to wonder if he would ever really be free of her.

I sipped the Jack I'd poured over ice and lifted my latest book. I was way into the preternatural adventures of Sookie Stackhouse when a vigorous knock on the front door almost made me jump out of my skin.

Coleman! At last he'd come to spend some time with me. I did a fashion check to be sure the snowflake pajama bottoms matched my top and hurried to open the door.

The blast of winter wind was nothing compared to the chill that raced through me at the sight of Graf Milieu. I tried to close the door, but he was quicker. He wedged in a foot and then slipped inside.

"We have to talk, Sarah Booth."

"No, we don't have to talk." There was nothing to say.

"I need your help."

"People in hell need ice water." It wasn't original, but it expressed my desire to help him perfectly.

"Renata is driving me insane."

I laughed. I couldn't help it. I'd heard that

Graf had become romantically involved with Renata about two minutes after I left New York. Good. Whatever Renata was dishing out, he deserved it.

"Stop it." He unwound his scarf, revealing his dimpled chin. "She's impossible."

"Perfect for you." I'd been so damn possible that it hurt me to remember.

"She's forgetting her lines. We've done this play a thousand times, and she can't remember her cues." Frustration rippled across his handsome face. The problem with Graf was that he was an actor. A superb actor. I never knew when he was telling the truth or when he was acting.

"That's not a problem I can help you with, Graf."

"But it is!"

Despite myself, I was intrigued. "How?"

"Would you be her understudy?"

The request was absurd. "You have some nerve. I left New York because you let me know that you didn't have any faith in me as an actor. Now you come here and ask me to be Renata's understudy. Are you insane?" The more I talked the angrier I became.

"It was never your acting ability I doubted, Sarah Booth. It was that you didn't believe in yourself as an actor."

"Get out." I had enough emotional turmoil in my life without him dredging up a past that was more than painful.

"At least hear me out." He brushed past me and walked into the parlor. "This is a great house. No wonder you came home."

I prayed that Jitty would appear in full belle regalia and run him back into the dark winter night. No such luck. Jitty was not a ghost to be summoned. I watched helplessly as Graf went to the sideboard and poured himself a Scotch.

"Graf, I'm going to call the sheriff if you don't leave."

"I'm surprised that Mr. Peters isn't here with you, all snuggly in those lovely flannel pajamas."

"Victoria's Secret isn't my game any more." I drew myself up to my full height. "I don't need subterfuge and artifice."

His laughter rang in the big room. "Well done!"

The room was suddenly too hot as the blood rushed to the surface of my skin. "Graf, I want you to leave."

Instead he took a seat in one of the wing chairs. "Not until you agree to be Renata's understudy."

I shook my head. "Positively not. I have a business to run. In case you haven't heard,

Delaney Detective Agency is a very successful enterprise and —"

"Your partner told me you were between cases."

Damn Tinkie! I'd strangle her when I got my hands on her. "The phone could ring any minute with another case. I can't afford to be tied up every night in some production."

"Don't you still dream of acting?"

He was Satan. "No. I don't. You made it clear enough that I didn't have the necessary talent."

Jitty couldn't move as fast as he did. He was in front of me, his hands on my shoulders, fingers warm through the flannel of my top. "It wasn't talent you lacked, Sarah Booth. It was conviction. You never gave it a hundred percent. You always held something back, in case you failed. The rest of it you had in spades — talent, beauty, a presence on the stage. All I tried to do was shake you up enough to make you risk everything."

"Stop it!" I shook free of him and went to the sideboard. I still had plenty of Jack left in my glass, but I went through the motions of freshening my drink. My mind was in a whirl. A year too late, Graf told me the things I'd needed to hear when I first went to New York. He was right. I'd always held a little back, just in case it didn't work out. Just a little bit to save my heart from totally breaking.

"Sarah Booth, the year you've been away has only added to your beauty. You've gained that confidence. I see it in the way you walk, in the way you look directly into my eyes."

Which was the one thing I didn't want to do at all. In Graf's eyes, I could see the past, and the glimmer of a future promise. I didn't want either. "I have changed, Graf. Enough to know that I don't want that life anymore. I'm a private investigator, and a dang good one. I make a difference in people's lives. I've come home to my heritage and my friends. This is what I want."

"A six-month gig in Hollywood could get you enough money to paint this old house and make a few necessary repairs." His glance swung around the room. "If you had a hundred thousand dollars to put into it, this could be a showplace."

"And if frogs had wings they wouldn't bump their asses." I walked to the door. "Please leave. I'm not interested. Besides, the last time I was Renata's understudy she never even had the sniffles."

He caught the whiff of my desire like a bloodhound on a scent. "It won't be like that this time. Renata isn't herself. I promise you. She can't remember her lines. It's getting obvious to everyone. I heard her talking with her brother about her forgetfulness. Even she knows it. Sarah Booth, Maggie the Cat is a part written for you. Tennessee Williams must have dreamed you when he wrote it."

He *was* Satan, come to tempt me with a long-ago dream that I'd had sense enough to put behind me. The truth was, of all the plays in the world, *Cat on a Hot Tin Roof* was the one I most adored. Maggie was a role both strong and weak, cunning and naïve. It was a test of an actress's skills. My idol, Elizabeth Taylor, had done the role justice, and it was a mark that any actor worth her salt aspired to.

"I have a real job." I pointed to the door. If I could just get him to leave, I'd be okay. I'd find some holy water and douse the house.

"What if I told you that Renata said you'd be even better at Maggie than her, but you'd never get the chance?"

"I'd say there's a lot of truth in that statement, especially the part where I'll never get the chance. She'd crawl out on that stage to keep me from getting there."

"But you want to be there!" His grin was

so bright I needed sunglasses.

"Go away. Please."

"I'll leave if you promise that you'll be the understudy. Just learn the lines and watch a couple of rehearsals. That's all."

"How did you get here?" My brain had suddenly begun to function. I walked to the door and looked out. Tinkie's Cadillac idled in the driveway. "I'm going to kill her."

"I was calling a cab. She simply gave me a ride. Everyone in town knows where you live, Sarah Booth. I would have found it on my own."

The window of the Cadillac glided down. Tinkie waved. "You'd be the best Maggie ever, Sarah Booth."

Before I could frame an indignant reply, her window closed.

"Do I have your word?" he asked.

A year ago I would have given my toes for a chance to play Maggie opposite Graf's Brick. Now it sounded like trouble. I'd grown wiser, but had I grown stronger, more able to risk? I'd never know if I didn't step onto that stage. "Okay."

He leaned down and kissed my cheek. "I can't wait." He opened the door and left, his footsteps on the porch reminding me that the past could be left behind, unless it walked right back in the front door.

■ ■ ■ ■

Keith Watley, the director, stood in the costume dock with his hands on his hips. "Big Mama, you're just not big enough! Bobbe! Bobbe, find the wardrobe girl and put more padding under that muumuu. I hire a hefty actress and she goes on Atkin's Diet. What am I to do?" He looked around the auditorium for someone to blame.

I sat in the back of the theatre and watched. Renata looked fabulous and fit as a fiddle. I'd wasted three very precious days waiting for the leading lady to fall sick. Unless I slipped a little salmonella into her salad, she wasn't going to miss a single performance.

"It's going to be wonderful!" Tinkie sat on the edge of the seat beside me. "I just wish the dragon lady would get a tiny bit sick. Just enough to give you a chance. I heard Renata and Graf arguing backstage. It's a good thing this isn't a love story or they'd never be able to pull it off. They hate each other."

Tinkie was happy as a clam with the inside gossip. "Two big egos do not a happy romance make." I slumped farther in my seat. I'd let my dreams rise up, and they were going to bite me on the butt. Jitty was right. I was still living in the past. My acting days were over, and I was foolish to spend my valuable time waiting for someone else to get sick. I pushed myself up. "I'm going home."

Tinkie tilted her head and glanced up at me. "What's going on with Coleman?"

"I wish I knew." I was tired of trying to make excuses for the fact that the man I'd given my heart to had abandoned me.

"I saw him in town this morning, and he doesn't look good." Tinkie rose and followed me from the auditorium as Keith sent us a death glare.

"You're breaking the focus of my actors!" he yelled at our backs as we made an escape.

"It's for the best," I told Tinkie. "If he yelled at me like that onstage, I might clobber him."

"He's a bit high-strung, but nothing you can't handle."

"What I could handle right now is a good case. I see nothing on the horizon for us." I was down in the dumps. The new year had started off with a big, wet fizzle. My love was absentee, my business was nonexistent, and my bills were mounting by the minute.

"The play opens Friday night. That's tomorrow. It's a seven-day run. After that

I'll be ready for a case, but I hope nothing happens before then. I've got my hands full with these people."

I couldn't help but smile. Tinkie had Oscar and her father for financial backup. I was the Lone Ranger. If I didn't get a case soon, I'd be at the Burger Shack flipping patties. "I guess another week won't sink me."

"What are you wearing tomorrow night? I found this incredible off-the-shoulder black dress." She rolled her eyes. "You can't wear jeans, so what are you going to wear?"

"I'll think of something." The truth was, I hadn't given opening night a single thought. If I wasn't on the stage, what difference did it make what I wore? I didn't have a date.

"Is Coleman coming with you?" Tinkie honed in on my bruise.

The doors to the auditorium burst open and Renata strode up to me. "I won't go on tomorrow night unless I have my lipstick!"

Bobbe Renshaw, the makeup artist, was right on her heels. "This shade is perfect with your coloring." She brandished a tube of red lipstick.

"I want my Almond Mocha Retreat." Renata glared at her and then turned to Tinkie. "Get my lipstick or the show is over."

"Certainly, Ms. Trovaioli." Tinkie spoke as

if Renata were a two-year-old. "What lipstick would that be?"

"It's a special brand made just for me at a shop in Memphis. Someone will have to run up there and pick it up."

I edged toward the door. I saw "gofer" written all over this, and I had no desire to be Renata's step-and-fetch-it.

"I'm not going anywhere," Bobbe said firmly. "I don't have a driver's license."

Tinkie turned to me. "I'm meeting with the caterers this afternoon. I can't go."

"Sorry, I have an appointment with Reveler." It was a perfect afternoon for a ride, and my horse was one thing that would pull me out of my blues.

"If I don't get my lipstick, I'm going home." Renata aimed the threat at the only one who would care — Tinkie.

She turned pleading blue eyes to me. Tears glistened in them, and I thought about all the work she'd done to make this happen.

"We'll find someone and pay them to go," I said.

"Fine," Renata said, her nose in the air. "If that lipstick isn't here, and it isn't the proper shade, the curtain won't rise. That would please you to no end, wouldn't it, Sarah Booth? You've always been jealous of me." Renata's pale eyes were ice daggers.

"It's difficult to be jealous of someone whose career depends on a tube of lipstick."

"You stole the tube I had, didn't you?" She snatched at my purse.

"That's ridiculous." Tinkie stepped in. "Sarah Booth hasn't been near your dressing room, and besides, she wouldn't take your lipstick."

For all of Tinkie's stalwart defense of me, she was misinformed. I had been in Renata's dressing room to deliver the fresh roses Tinkie had ordered. It was a daily standing order — two dozen red beauties — until the play closed. Since I'd been doing errands for Tinkie, I'd been the one to take the bouquet into the dressing room. Now, though, wasn't the time or place to correct Tinkie, even though Bobbe Renshaw cut me a knowing glance.

"Defend Sarah Booth all you want," Renata said. "When the play fails to open, she'll be to blame."

I'd had enough. Memphis was a couple hours away, and it would be worth going just to get away from Renata's ceaseless harping. "I'll go get your lipstick, just to shut you up."

Tinkie's smile was worth whatever it was going to cost me. I was doing this for her, not Renata.

The leading lady pulled a card from her purse. "They sell this shade to no one but me. You'll have to give them my card before they'll give it to you."

"How exclusive." I refrained from rolling my eyes, but just barely. Taking the card, I stared into Renata's perfect face. She was a great beauty, but there was something plastic about her expression. Perhaps it was the lack of warmth in her eyes. Whatever, she'd lost the facile expressions of her youth and had become hard and brittle. She was only thirty-seven, but I could see the hardness of her future. Gloria Swanson in *Sunset Boulevard.* If I worked at it, I could almost pity her.

"Get it right." She dismissed me with a wave of her hand. "Since you had no talent on the stage, Sarah Booth, perhaps you'll work out as an assistant."

"Did it ever occur to you, Renata, that if you don't get your precious lipstick, I'll open the show in your stead?" I'd hoped to harpoon her, but she only chuckled.

"The dream of the understudy. Fetch the lipstick, dear, and stop wasting all of our time with your futile dreams."

It wasn't the sting of Renata's words that forced me to walk away, it was the look of pity on Tinkie's face. I realized then that

Tinkie knew more about my rusty dreams than I'd ever believed. She knew, and she hurt for me. I had to get out of there before I decked Renata Trovaioli and ruined all of Tinkie's hard work.

CHAPTER 3

Standing outside the cosmetic shop on a busy Memphis street, I forced myself not to rip open the hermetically sealed lipstick. The old man who'd run the shop — a crank who looked like Ebenezer Scrooge — told me he didn't keep samples of the colors, so I had no idea what Almond Mocha Retreat looked like. It had to be something pretty special for Renata to have such a fit over. Then again, she could have a hissy fit over the sequin count on a gown. She was that kind of gal.

Tapping the lipstick against my palm, I fought against the urge to rip it open and write Renata's name coupled with obscenities on the sidewalk. Only my friendship with Tinkie saved the lipstick. I got in my car and turned toward home. Renata would have her Almond Mocha Retreat, the curtain would rise, and Tinkie could bask in the success of the production. I'd seen enough during the rehearsals to know it was a superb rendition of Tennessee's work.

Although the playwright had never lived in Zinnia, he'd spent plenty of time in the Mississippi Delta. He would be proud that his work was being performed by such a talented cast. Despite the fact that she had the personality of Godzilla, Renata was a spectacular actor.

As I crossed the mighty Mississippi, my cell phone rang. Tinkie checking up on me for sure. I answered in a fake Japanese accent.

"Sarah Booth?"

Coleman's voice sent chills down my spine. "Sorry, I assumed it was Tinkie."

"We need to talk."

Four little words that could stop a perfectly healthy heart. "Sure. When?"

"I have to go to Jackson this afternoon."

"What's in Jackson?" As if I didn't know. Connie Peters was institutionalized in the Bridge, an upscale mental ward. I suspected that Coleman was footing the bill, but I'd never asked. He had to assuage his guilt in the way that worked best for him.

Coleman opted not to answer the question. "Tomorrow is the opening of *Cat on a Hot Tin Roof.* Would you like to go with me? Maybe we can talk after the play."

That would leave me in torment for only twenty-six hours. "Sure."

"Good. I'll pick you up about six. Maybe we can have a cocktail at The Club."

"Perfect." I put the cell phone away and gripped the wheel with both hands. Something was definitely on Coleman's mind, and I didn't think it boded well for our relationship. I'd deliberately left him alone to deal with his feelings about Connie. He carried a lot of guilt about her mental condition, though Connie had always been half a bubble off plumb as far as I could tell. In high school she'd been the Energizer Bunny or Gloomy Gus. There was never that happy balance. Bipolar would be my uneducated guess. Since it was chemical, Coleman couldn't assume the blame, no matter how hard he tried. And he was trying hard.

The truth was, he was trying much harder to feel guilty over Connie than he was trying to have a relationship with me. There was also the nagging fear that his wound wasn't healing properly.

My own spirits sank even lower as I drove through the empty cotton fields toward home. My life was a void. Any minute I could step into the chasm and completely disappear. Only Tinkie, Sweetie Pie, and

Reveler would notice.

I pulled into Dahlia House as dusk was settling. Perhaps I should have gone by The Club and delivered the lipstick, but I wasn't up to verbal sparring with Renata. I'd let Tinkie take it in the morning. It was too late for a ride, but I went to the barn to feed Reveler. The cold weather had made him frisky, and he reared and bucked as I gathered his feed.

Horses are herd animals, and I wanted to get him a companion. While a goat might work, I had my eye on a beautiful little mare at Lee's place. She was a half sister to Reveler and shared his good nature and common sense, but I'd have to break several big cases before I could take on another mouth to feed.

Sweetie Pie met me in the barn as I was finishing. Her tail wagged furiously in greeting, and she gave one low, sweet, hound-dog howl. Jitty had another greeting entirely as I stepped through the back door.

Her dress was rich green velvet, and before I could stop myself I hurried into the parlor to make sure the curtains were still in place.

"Fiddle-dee-dee," she said. "Don't get your panties in a wad. I haven't pulled down the draperies."

"And it's a good thing."

I had forgotten that her costumes came from another plane altogether. The ghostly seamstress who'd constructed this concoction must have used fifty yards of lush velvet and a half-mile of satin trim. "Panties in a wad isn't exactly a saying from the pre–Civil War era. Scarlett didn't wear panties." I eyed the liquor cabinet but decided that Jack on an empty stomach was begging for a hangover.

"You look like someone stole your lunch money."

"You look like a Cecil B. DeMille production." I matched her tit for tat.

"Where's that lawman?"

The one thing I didn't want to do was explain Coleman's whereabouts to Jitty. It wasn't that she didn't like him. She just wanted me in the state of nuptial bliss. Until the divorce came through, Coleman wasn't a good prospect to put me there.

"I'm going to —" The phone rang and saved me from a spur-of-the-moment lie. I picked it up and answered.

"Put on your best miniskirt and let's go dancing." Graf's voice was a rough purr.

The one other thing I didn't want to do was stay in the house moping about Coleman and arguing with Jitty. Heck, there was hardly room for her dress and me. "Sounds like a plan."

"I'll pick you up at ten when we finish rehearsals."

"I'll be waiting."

Jitty didn't follow me to my room, and I bathed and dressed in privacy. Her absence worried me a bit, but I figured she was dancing the Virginia Reel with some Rhett Butlerish ghost. I intended to tap my toes to a far different sound. Super Chicken was singing at Playin' the Bones.

Not caring that I might appear too eager, I was on the porch when Graf arrived. He kept the conversation light on the drive and through dinner. When Super Chicken took the stage, I'd forgotten how much fun it was to dance with a man who knew all my moves.

"What did you do to Renata today?" he asked after we returned to the table for more drinks.

"Not nearly as much as I'd like to."

"She was fit to be tied for the whole rehearsal." He leaned close and his breath touched my ear. "She said she was afraid you were going to try to kill her so you could get on stage."

"Right. That's my plan." Around the club couples were dancing to a sexy tune. I was glad Graf and I were sitting this one out. My body had a mind of its own when it came to hot music and men.

"She told everyone that you were out to get her."

"She'd better worry about Kristine Rolofson. That woman has a reason to kill Renata. Imagine, hitting a dog and then driving away to let it die on the side of the road."

Graf's finger tucked the hair behind my ear. He leaned in so close his lips touched my lobe as he spoke. "Renata doesn't like dogs."

"Renata doesn't like anyone." I got up. Playing with fire would only get me burned. It wouldn't warm the cockles of my heart. Only Coleman could do that. "I'd better head home, Graf. It's a long day tomorrow." I reached into my purse and withdrew the lipstick and charge slip. "But you could give this to Renata. I picked it up for her in Memphis."

His left eyebrow arched. "You picked it up for her?"

"Is there an echo in the room?" When a Daddy's Girl repeated a question, it worked. Graf was merely being sarcastic. "I charged it to my credit card, so here's the slip so she can reimburse me."

His laughter was warm as we stepped into

the cold night. He put his arm around me and pulled me close, just as I noticed Deputy Dewayne Dattilo coming in with a date. Dewayne's kicked-puppy look turned red-hot with betrayal. Coleman's deputies were loyal to a fault.

I turned to Graf and whispered that I was cold. He pulled me closer. Let Coleman stew on that!

It took only long enough for me to get seated in the car to regret my actions. I wasn't a high school kid; I was supposedly an adult. Yet I was acting like a hormonal teenager trying to make an uninterested boy jealous. Great. Move over in the loony bin, Connie, I'm about to book a room.

Now I'd simply have to live with the consequences of my actions. I'd admit the truth to Coleman when I saw him. I'd tell him that his absence had hurt me, and that I'd struck back in a truly childish action, using Graf, who deserved such treatment, but nonetheless I didn't want to be the one dishing it out. By the time that train of thought ended, I was exhausted, and Graf pulled in front of Dahlia House.

"I'd love it if you invited me in for a nightcap."

I didn't remember him being so blunt. Then again, we'd been lovers for nearly two years in New York. Perhaps subtlety was only necessary for a first conquest.

"I'm in love with someone else." It was time to be a grown up.

"You loved me, once."

"Once upon a time is for fairy tales, Graf. What we had wasn't real. I thought it was. I wanted it to be. But it wasn't. Nothing about my life in New York was real except the disappointment and the fact that I didn't have the talent to make it on Broadway. Those are the only truths I brought home with me."

"I never thought you'd be a bitter woman, Sarah Booth. I'm sorry for the hand I've had in making that happen."

I wasn't bitter! I was a realist, and he was an egotist. Take a lesson from the past, Sarah Booth! "Good night, Graf." I got out and walked into the dark and empty house.

During the week of rehearsals, I'd prepared my dresses to be Maggie the Cat. Since it was unlikely that Renata wouldn't finish a week's run in Zinnia, Keith Watley hadn't allocated any funds for an understudy wardrobe. No matter, I had my own inspiration. My mother's dresses, though a bit snug in the waist and bosom, were perfect for the part. I was holding them up on hangers, wondering how I could get them into Coleman's truck without an explanation, when his knock came at the door.

Brazen was the choice I made. "Coleman, please put these dresses in the truck." I handed them to him at the door without an invitation to enter.

He hung them in his truck, and when he got back to the door, I handed him a drink and ushered him inside. "Let's have a drink here, where we can talk alone. What did you want to tell me? That I'd make a perfect Maggie the Cat?" I played it for humor because my heart was thudding.

"The play has sort of been the last thing on my mind."

Looking into his eyes, I could see that. Panic struck me. He'd come to break up. The sadness was there, just behind the intelligence. "What's been the first thing?"

"They're going to operate on Connie. There's a tumor. In her brain. It might explain her behavior for the past few years."

My knees jellied and I found myself sitting on the horsehair sofa. Of all the things I'd expected, a brain tumor wasn't one of them. "Shit."

"I've been at the hospital talking with the doctors. It's a very dangerous operation, but it's her only hope of regaining her old life."

Regaining her old life. I pondered the many things that could mean. "When is the surgery?"

"Next Monday." He cleared his throat. "I realize with Graf Milieu in town you undoubtedly have better things to do, but will you go with me to the hospital while they operate?"

"Yes." I spoke without a second's thought. Whatever I could do for Coleman, I would. "Graf is nothing to me, Coleman, except for a few good memories and a lot of pain. Once I thought I loved him, but that was a long time ago. I was a different person then."

He looked away. "The only person I've ever loved is you. No one else has even come close."

Could I feel any more like a cad? "I'll be ready to leave whenever you say."

"Thank you." He kissed the top of my head. "Once this is over, Sarah Booth, I want us to talk about the future. I have to find out what's going to happen to Connie. Right now she's still my wife. I have an obligation."

It was why I loved him, and why I despaired. "I understand." I did, but I also hated it.

"Let's go to The Club. I want to imagine you on the stage."

"If Renata would drop dead, I'd have my chance."

Coleman was chuckling softly as we walked out the door.

The Club was spectacular. Tinkie had outdone herself, and the "little black dress" she'd picked up was nothing less than Prada. Coleman got me a Jack on the rocks, and as he walked toward me I realized I'd never seen him in a tux before. He cut a handsome figure, right down to shoes so brightly polished I could see my reflection.

"You two make a handsome couple," Cece Dee Falcon, the society editor at *The Zinnia Dispatch,* said as she came up to kiss me on both cheeks. "Coleman, I was wondering if you'd dumped Sarah Booth. I haven't seen the two of you together at a single Christmas party."

"Sarah Booth won't get away from me that easily." Coleman wasn't the least bit flustered.

"You'd better treat her right." Cece gave him a look that said she meant business. "She has friends in high places, you know."

"Are you writing the review?" I wanted a change of topic.

"Indeed. I went backstage to interview Renata and she slammed the door in my face. I'd say unless she develops a new attitude, she isn't going to do well in Hollywood."

"Hollywood?" I'd been around The Club on and off all week, and I hadn't heard a word about Hollywood. "Renata has a movie deal?" It was almost more than I could bear. "What, they're refilming *Bride of Dracula*?"

Only Coleman appreciated my humor.

"I'm interviewing Graf." Cece had lost interest in me completely. Her gaze had caught Graf's lean, handsome figure moving across the room. Though Cece had once been Cecil, she still had impeccable taste in men. Graf was mesmerizing as he worked his charm on a bevy of Daddy's Girls. Their response was a high squeal of pleasure in perfect five-part harmony. They must have practiced that for months in the Ole Miss sorority house. Cece didn't even hear them. She was moving toward Graf. "I'll find out about the movie deal with Renata. My understanding is that Graf got the deal, and Renata is a tagalong." She was gone.

"Graf certainly works on women." Coleman's tone was lighthearted, but there was a hint of worry in his eyes.

"He used to work on me." My past with Graf would be the talk of the town, but I could look at Graf objectively now. He was extraordinary, in physical detail. But the perfect exterior hid a flawed heart.

"Are you sure that's past tense?"

Oh, the thought of tormenting Coleman with jealousy. It flitted through my mind, delicious and awful. "I'm sure it's the past tense." Coleman obviously knew of my dancing with Graf the night before. "I'll be very glad when this production is over and gone from Zinnia. My New Year's resolution is not to live in the past. Graf is the past. Acting is the past."

"I wish I could see you on stage." Coleman let his finger trace my jawline. "I regret I never got the chance to see you perform."

Tinkie appeared at my elbow. "Sarah Booth, could you check the dressing rooms and be sure the fresh flowers are there?"

"Sure." I kissed Coleman's cheek. "I'll be right back."

Everything in the dressing rooms was perfection, including the tube of Almond Mocha Retreat set prominently on Renata's dressing table. I'd just returned when Tinkie tapped a crystal goblet with a spoon. "Everyone, please take your seats. The show starts in five minutes."

Coleman and I were front and center. Tinkie had reserved the seats for us. The auditorium was full, and I was happy for Tinkie.

When the curtain came up, I was transported into the world of Big Daddy. Sir Alfred was stupendous, but it was Graf as Brick, hobbling about on his crutches, that held the audiences' attention. And Renata. Whatever her flaws as a human, she was mesmerizing on the stage.

The curtain for intermission came down at the end of the first act. Tinkie had decided on two intermissions in the hopes of selling even more booze. It was a great idea. Coleman and I were in the drink line when a scream shattered the laughter. Bobbe Renshaw came running into the room, a makeup towel in one hand and a brush in the other.

"It's Renata! She's dead!"

Chapter 4

Coleman pushed through the stunned drinkers and hurried toward the dressing room with me right on his heels. A horrible, self-centered thought zinged through my brain — at last I was going to get to be on stage. I almost veered away to Coleman's car to get my dresses when I got hold of my galloping ego and reined it in. God, I was as bad as Renata had ever dared to be. Then again, I wasn't hypocritical enough to shed crocodile tears for a harridan I loathed.

The sight of Renata, on the floor of her dressing room, sobered me. She really was dead. This wasn't just theatrics on her part, which deep down in my heart I'd expected. She was on her back, her eyes wide open but filmed with death. Her lips were a bright terra-cotta against her pale and lifeless skin. In her hand was the tube of Almond Mocha Retreat she'd been so determined to have. At least she'd died with her lipstick on.

"Sarah Booth!" Tinkie gasped as she said my name.

"What?" I looked around. Tinkie wasn't a mind reader. She couldn't have known what I was thinking. She pointed at the mirror where letters in terra-cotta spelled out, "Burn in hell you heartless bitch!"

"She was murdered!" Tinkie's eyes were moon-sized. "Someone killed Renata Trovaioli. Oh, my God! Who would do such a thing?"

All eyes turned to me. The moment dissolved as Graf burst into the room and went down on one knee beside the body. "Renata! Renata!" He grasped her hand and held it. Bobbe, the makeup artist who'd discovered the body, stood in the doorway sobbing.

A petite woman pushed her way into the room, and I recognized Kristine Rolofson. In her arms she carried a small reddish dog. She put the dog on the floor and it immediately went over to Renata, growled, and hiked a leg. Tinkie swept it into her arms just in time to avoid a seriously embarrassing moment. She handed the dog to Kristine, and Coleman stepped between all of us and the body.

"Everyone out!" Coleman pointed to the door. "This is a crime scene, and it's already been contaminated enough. Tinkie, get Doc Sawyer over here right away."

"He's around somewhere. He was in the audience." Her voice trembled, but she kept her composure. Tinkie was always great during a crisis. She'd saved my life more than once.

"Get him in here and get everyone else out. Find someone to stand by the door! No one except Doc is allowed in this room." Coleman was in charge and snapping out orders.

I eased to stand beside him as Cece swept through the door. Before Coleman could stop her, she snapped a photograph.

"Cece, that's enough. This is a murder scene and you shouldn't be here."

"Murder?" Cece arched perfectly groomed eyebrows. "Maybe she had a heart attack." She made a face of surprise. "Oh, I forgot, she didn't have a heart."

"Tasteless, Cece. The woman is dead." Coleman grasped her shoulders and started to ease her from the room.

"She might have died of natural causes or an accident," I pointed out, following them out into the hallway. I started to add that we should check for falling houses, but I could see Coleman was in no mood for the sick humor of me or my friends. Someone had died in Sunflower County, and he took it very seriously.

Tinkie returned and Coleman pulled her aside. “Who might want Renata dead?” he asked.

“Just about everyone who ever crossed her path.” Tinkie shuddered. “She was one of the most disagreeable people I’ve ever met.”

“But was there someone in particular? Someone who would gain from her death?”

Keith Watley swept into the corridor outside the dressing room. “Sarah Booth! Sarah Booth Delaney!” He was yelling my name like it was a fire drill.

“She’s here.” Tinkie motioned him over to the doorway to Renata’s dressing room. “What’s wrong, Keith?”

His gaze fell on me and all others were excluded. “Get into costume. The show must go on, and you’re replacing Renata.”

“No!” I tried to sound shocked and disappointed, but I couldn’t conceal the delight. Hey, it was the rule of showbiz. The show went on, no matter what.

“We need costumes!” Keith was looking around wildly. I could never wear Renata’s things. She was an official zero and I was five sizes bigger. “You can’t go on in jeans! No woman with class wore jeans in the fifties.” His face was red with stress.

I cleared my throat. "I have something in the car." My mother's dresses. Thank goodness I'd brought them.

"You do?" Tinkie and Cece said in unison.

"I was a Girl Scout." I held up my fingers in the official sign. "I'm always prepared."

"For the death of the leading lady?" Coleman's tone was unreadable.

I looked at the closed door to the dressing room. I'd behaved callously at Renata's death. I didn't like her, but I shouldn't have gloated. I was tied to the lipstick and of all the people in Zinnia, I was the only one who stood to gain by her death. I wasn't in a place where I should be cracking wise.

"Certainly not for Renata's death. She just didn't seem interested in the role any longer. I thought she might decide not to perform the whole week." Even as I spoke I knew I sounded defensive. "I wanted to be ready in case she *quit.*"

"Has Renata ever missed a performance?" Coleman asked softly.

"I don't know." My tone was cold. He was my date and he was grilling me like I was Jack the Ripper. "And furthermore, I don't care. I need the keys to your truck." I held out my palm. When Coleman placed the keys in it, I stormed down the hallway and into the cold night to retrieve my dresses. I wasn't sorry Renata was dead. I couldn't make myself even pretend to be. I hadn't killed her, and I wasn't going to miss my chance to be on the stage opposite Graf, no matter how black it painted my motives for murder.

I heard footsteps behind me and could tell by the quick tattoo of spike heels that Tinkie had come outside. I was a little agitated at her, too. I kept walking, knowing my long stride would force Tinkie to jog in her heels.

"Sarah Booth!"

I stopped and turned to face her. "What?"

"I've called Oscar. Listen, I don't want to panic you, but I think you should call a lawyer."

The fright on her face convinced me that she wasn't needling me for the fun of it. "Why? I haven't done anything."

"I believe that. I know you couldn't harm a fly. But I do think Renata has been murdered. You're bound to be a suspect, if not the prime suspect. Think about it."

"That's hogwash. My date was the sheriff of Sunflower County. How silly to think I'd slip from his side and kill Renata. Besides, she looks like she had an aneurism or a heart attack or something like that. There wasn't a mark on her that I could see."

Tinkie dug the toe of her shoe into the concrete and wouldn't look at me.

"What? Was she shot? Stabbed? Tell me."

She took a breath. "Coleman thinks she was poisoned."

I stumbled back against his truck and leaned on the cold metal fender for support. "Shit."

"You can say that again." She bit her lip and shook her head. "I'm afraid you could be in serious trouble, Sarah Booth."

I got the dresses from the truck and started back inside.

"You're not going on the stage, are you?" Tinkie grasped my arm.

"Of course I am. If people are foolish enough to think I killed a woman so I could be on stage for a few minutes in Zinnia, Mississippi, I won't disappoint them." It was the most ludicrous thing I'd ever heard. If I'd wanted to kill Renata for some stage time, I would have done it in New York City, a town where theatre mattered.

"Please reconsider, Sarah Booth. Think how it will look."

"Think what will happen if I don't. The show will close."

"I don't care. You're more important than a show."

Her words slowed me, for a split second.

"I'm going on, Tinkie. I want to. I need to get this behind me."

She sighed and her grasp on my arm loosened as she fell into step beside me. "I think you're nuts to do this, but if you must, I'm with you all the way."

The applause was better than I'd ever dreamed. Graf and I stood center stage, flanked on either side by Sir Alfred and the rest of the cast. The auditorium reverberated with the clapping and foot-stomping and whistles. Graf's hand exerted excited pressure as we took our fifth bow.

At Keith's direction we hustled off stage, and in the wings Graf pulled me into his arms. "You were fabulous!" His face told me he wasn't lying. "Whatever you've been doing this past year, Sarah Booth, it's paid off in spades. Everyone in the audience couldn't take their eyes off you."

His words soothed the scars my New York debacle had left on my ego, and I took even more satisfaction in his embrace.

Keith Watley hustled into the wings, a smile a mile wide on his face. The director flung his arms open and clasped me in a bear hug.

"Sarah Booth," Keith said, laughing, "where were you when I cast Renata? You're the ultimate Maggie the Cat. Had she not died, I'd never have seen your talent."

His words reminded me that I'd gotten my golden moment at the cost of Renata's life, and suddenly the applause was hollow. I'd been cold and brutal about her death, because deep down inside I wanted my chance on the boards. She'd been a bitch, but that didn't excuse my selfishness.

"I need some water." I felt faint. The excitement, the reality of my desperate need — all of it had combined to make me feel light headed.

As I started toward the dressing rooms, I faltered. I couldn't go in there. The kitchen was the best place. I could get a drink of water and avoid the crush of people who were pouring backstage to congratulate the cast and crew. Something I'd craved all of my life now unsettled me. I wanted to go home. I wanted to have a moment to explain to Coleman that I was sorry that Renata had died. And I did hope it turned out to be some medical problem, something that would point the finger of blame at no one. Especially not me.

The lipstick on the mirror spoke of murder, but it wasn't necessarily so. Someone could have written the message and it might have shocked Renata into a coronary. Who knew, and it was pointless to speculate until Doc Sawyer had performed an autopsy.

The staff at the kitchen gave me a warm welcome and a stool at one of the stainless-steel counters. Trays of pink shrimp and crab claw tarts whisked through the door, along with slabs of roast and ham, chicken salad, tiny sandwiches decorated with peppers and chives. All beautiful and no doubt wonderful. My appetite had fled, and I was glad to be in the kitchen with people who ignored me as they went about their jobs.

I had five minutes to myself before Tinkie found me. She looked at me with proud awe. "I am amazed, Sarah Booth. And afraid. After that performance, I don't think we'll be able to keep you in Zinnia for long. New York is where you belong."

Her words frightened me. This year was supposed to be about letting go of the past, not falling back into it. "Don't get the cart ahead of the horse, Tinkie. And speaking of horses, it would be mighty hard to have Reveler in New York City." I gave her a grin even though I felt awful.

"Everyone is looking for you. You have to come out of the kitchen."

"No, I'm happy here."

"Half the town is talking about you. You have to acknowledge the performance."

I considered. "Where's Coleman?"

She looked down at her shoes. "He went into town with Doc and the body. He asked me to give you a ride home."

Right. "Did he see any of the show?" I hated myself for asking.

She shook her head. "No. He was back here with Doc and he never left the body. Something about chain of evidence."

He was only doing his job, but it still left me feeling cold and unwanted, especially in light of the questions he'd been asking before he left.

She sighed. "I still think you should go out and accept the congratulations. You did a stupendous job, Sarah Booth. I would think you'd want to enjoy the glory."

"Not tonight." I just wanted to go home and crawl into my bed and sleep. Tomorrow, in the light of day, I'd feel more like confronting the cause of her death.

As Tinkie and I walked across the parking lot, she put her arm around my waist. "Do you think we'll get the case?" she asked.

"What case?"

"If Renata was murdered, there'll be a big case. High profile. It would be good for the agency."

"As long as we have a paying customer," I said, getting into her car.

Dahlia House was dark when Tinkie parked in front of the porch.

"Shall I come in with you?" she asked.

"You have a party at Hill Top. I've been selfish enough getting you to drive me home. Go and play host."

She frowned. "I'm worried about you." She touched my cheek. "You're pale and cool."

"I'm tired. You have to admit, it's been a harrowing night. Performing is exhausting to me. It never came naturally, which is probably why I don't have any real desire to do it for a living."

"Really?"

I could see the hope in her face. "Really. I don't want that life anymore, Tinkie. This business tonight was fun. It scratched an itch that's been bothering me for a long, long time. Now I'm not a failure anymore. That's all I really needed — to do it and succeed. Now I can truly put it behind me."

"But you'll finish the show?"

"Of course. If Keith wants me to, I will."

"But you won't run away to Hollywood with Graf?"

I laughed and it sounded real, even to me. Maybe I was an actress. "No. Not Hollywood, and certainly not Graf." But her words had opened a hole in my heart where

Coleman was concerned. He could have taken the body with Doc and returned to see me home. I understood chain of evidence, but once the body was delivered to Doc for the autopsy, he had no need to stay with it.

"I'll come by in the morning with Cece's review."

I got out and waved as Tinkie headed down the driveway. As much as I loved her, I needed to be alone for a while to sort through my feelings. I had lied to her about Hollywood. With the tiny success on the stage of The Club, my ambitions were reborn. I wanted to be an actress. A star. Time was running out, too. At thirty-four, I didn't have a lot of good years left. Hollywood wasn't kind to aging women. In a way, Renata had died at her peak, which wasn't all bad — as long as she wasn't murdered. And in order to sleep, I had to believe that her death was from natural causes.

As soon as I opened the front door, I knew Jitty was awake and waiting. She stood at the staircase, the most beautiful red dress I'd ever seen swirling about her ankles. I couldn't pull my gaze off her dress, which looked vaguely familiar.

"How does it feel to be swept off your

feet?" she asked, giving a little shimmy that set the dress rocking. "Nothin' like bright lights and applause, is there?"

Somehow, Jitty knew my every move. "It was a vindication." I tried to brush past her and head for my bed, but her skirt filled the staircase.

"I thought you was lettin' go of the past."

"Not everyone operates by your set of rules, Jitty. Maybe this is how I'm letting go of the past."

"By struttin' around on the stage and knowin' you were born with a talent?"

I'd never hoped to hear Jitty admit that I had a talent. That in itself was another tiny helping of vindication. "I do have talent. When I was in New York, what I lacked was nerve."

"And comin' home to Zinnia, you found that."

"Can I please just get some sleep?"

"Gone be hard to sleep with that guilty conscience." She pressed her skirt aside with her hands.

I saw my opening and darted past her on the steps. "Why should I have a guilty conscience? I haven't done anything wrong."

She floated up the steps after me. "You wished that woman dead."

"I've wished a lot of people dead. No one

has ever obliged me before. Why should I think that Renata keeled over because I wished it?"

"Because maybe she did."

That stopped me. And it made me furious. "You and Coleman, what is it? Both of you have teamed up to make me feel bad about something I had nothing to do with. Sure, I took her place in the cast. I don't regret it for a minute. I learned something valuable about myself — that I can act. That I have talent, that I could go back to New York if I wanted to —"

Before I could finish my tirade, Jitty began to fade. The dress was a mesmerizing red swirl as she departed.

"You come back here!" I hated it when she slid out of a conversation just because she was losing. "Jitty!"

But she was gone. And then I remembered the dress. Scarlett had worn it when Rhett swept her off her feet and carried her up to their New Orleans wedding suite for a night of blissful sex.

I climbed the steps slowly. Jitty's point was well made even in her absence. Ego was cold comfort on a January night.

CHAPTER 5

The rapping on my front door — incessant and loud — finally woke me. I'd had trouble going to sleep, and as I forced my eyes open, I realized bright morning sunlight was flooding through my bedroom window.

"Bam! Bam! Bam!" The rapping turned into pounding. I got out of bed and hurried to the door. Whoever it was sounded desperate.

"You've got to read this!" Tinkie thrust a newspaper in my face as she raced into the house and toward the kitchen. "I need coffee! Maybe even a Mimosa. We should celebrate or pack up and flee! You decide." I took the paper and followed in her wake. She'd conveniently turned it to the page with a blaring headline, "Hometown Girl Wows the Audience."

Living in New York, I'd fantasized about picking up the *Times* and reading a review of my work. This wasn't New York, and it was the *Zinnia Dispatch* with a review written by a close friend, but nonetheless, I felt chills race over my body as I read Cece's delicious words.

I was halfway through when I hit the part about Renata's death. Cece hadn't tempered her thoughts with kindness toward the deceased. She called Renata a prima donna and noted the play was vastly improved by her absence.

"Had Ms. Trovaioli not died so inopportunely, the audience would never have been treated to Ms. Delaney's performance. Perhaps the Angel of Death is a better critic than any of us knew!" Cece wrote.

"Holy shit." I sat down at the table and let Tinkie put the coffee on. She always made it too strong, but I needed a jolt of something.

"Holy shit is right. Cece just gave you the definitive motive for murder." She turned the coffeemaker on and faced me. "Tell me one thing, Sarah Booth. You didn't leave Coleman's side all night, did you?"

Of course I had. Why would anything be simple like that? "I went to the bathroom. I went to the kitchen to count the bottles of champagne chilling. I took some gifts to Renata's dressing room." I shrugged. "Nothing criminal in those things."

"Except it gives you opportunity. You have motive. Now if there's means, you'll have the three elements of murder." Tinkie didn't look happy.

"Coleman knows I didn't harm Renata."

The doorbell rang, and I hurried to answer it. Cece would be impossible to live with after her review, but I couldn't wait to hug her. When I swung the door open, I stepped back in surprise. Coleman and Dewayne stood on my front porch, and neither of them looked happy.

"Tinkie just put some coffee on. Go in and have a cup." I stepped back, aware that I was still in a pair of pink flannel pajama bottoms and a thermal shirt. "I'm going to run upstairs and change into some jeans."

"Sarah Booth." Coleman stepped into the house and grabbed my wrist. "You're under arrest for the murder of Renata Trovaioli. Anything you say can be used against you . . ." He continued with the Miranda warning as I stood speechless in my foyer.

"What in the hell is going on?" Tinkie rushed through the parlor and came to stand by my side. "Coleman, what on earth are you doing?"

"Dewayne, put Sarah Booth in the car." Coleman stepped between Tinkie and me. "Stay out of this, Tinkie. Let justice take its course. The best thing you can do is call a good lawyer for Sarah Booth and then see a bail bondsman. I'll speak to the judge and see if she won't let Sarah Booth free on a small bail."

"What are you talking about? Let Sarah Booth go!" Tinkie reached around him and grabbed my elbow. "Take those handcuffs off her this instant! Stop this foolishness, Coleman! This is the woman you love!"

Coleman removed Tinkie's hand from my elbow. I was still too stunned to gather my wits. I was being dragged from my house in a pair of PJs and no shoes. The reality finally dawned on me and I applied my brakes. Dewayne looked at Coleman for guidance.

"I didn't kill Renata." I wanted to slap Coleman's carefully controlled face for making me say such a thing. "Why would you think I did?"

Coleman's expression was stony — the same as when I'd answered the door. "Renata Trovaioli was poisoned with cyanide."

"Big deal. Where would I get cyanide, and how would I get her to take it? In case you've forgotten, Renata didn't exactly like me. She wouldn't eat poison just because I asked her to." I could feel the heat rising through my body. I was madder than I'd ever been in my life. Mad and betrayed — a bad combination.

"The poison was administered in a tube of lipstick." Coleman stared into my eyes as he spoke. "A tube of special lipstick that you picked up for Renata in Memphis."

If Reveler had kicked me in the gut, I couldn't have been more surprised. "Lipstick? There was poison in the lipstick?"

"Don't say another word." Tinkie slipped around Coleman and put her finger on my lips. "I'll get a lawyer for you, and I'll get the bail. Just don't say another word, Sarah Booth."

"But I didn't —"

"I know, but it doesn't matter. Do the smart thing and shut your mouth."

I clamped my lips shut with an audible sound.

"At least let her change into some clothes," Tinkie said. "This is absurd, Coleman. She isn't going to run off. Let her wash her face and get properly dressed."

He nodded and Dewayne unlocked the handcuffs. Tinkie took my elbow and guided me toward the stairs. "Take a quick shower," she whispered. "They'll wait, and you'll feel better."

Good hygiene was Tinkie's answer to almost anything. In this case she was correct. I wanted a shower, clean clothes, and brushed teeth, because as clean as Coleman kept the jail, it still wasn't a place I wanted to perform my morning ablutions in.

When I came down, dressed and scrubbed, Dewayne signaled for me to hold out my wrists. My gaze was locked with Coleman's as Dewayne snapped the handcuffs shut. There was nothing Coleman could do that would ever make up for this moment. Nothing. He could have come alone and taken me back to jail without all this formality and fanfare. He could have told me he was sorry, that he knew I was innocent but that the law demanded a certain protocol. The route he'd chosen, though, was the most publicly humiliating for me.

When I stepped onto the porch I was met by a strobe flash from a camera. Gavin, the hairy-legged reporter with shoes that ate his socks, stood in my driveway with a camera. He popped off another shot before Coleman threatened him into running away. Still, it was too late. My fantastic review in this morning's issue of the *Dispatch* would be replaced by a photograph of me being led to jail like a murderer.

Dewayne put his hand on the top of my head as he assisted me into the car. Gavin rushed up and took another shot. I thought for a minute that Coleman was going to strip the camera from his hand, but he did nothing. Nothing.

"I'll be there soon," Tinkie whispered through the back window that was opened a crack. "I'm calling Harry DeLa Bencher, the best criminal lawyer in Memphis. I'll get the bail money, too."

The reality of my plight hit hard. "Tinkie, I don't have enough money for bail. Dahlia House is mortgaged to the hilt. There's nothing valuable here. My car is an antique." The only things of real value were Reveler and Sweetie Pie, and that made me realize I hadn't seen my hound all morning.

"Find Sweetie!"

She nodded. "I'll take good care of her and the horse. Don't worry about a thing."

That was easy for her to say. She wasn't the one being dragged off to jail on a murder charge by the man to whom she'd given her heart.

Bitter irony is sitting in a cell talking to a defense lawyer with the last name DeLa Bencher. With each passing second I felt worry wrinkles take hold in my face.

"You're predicament is serious, Ms. Delaney." He pushed horn-rimmed glasses up his patrician nose. His face didn't have a single line or wrinkle. I couldn't be certain if that was because he was young or because he was a sociopath with no conscience and therefore didn't worry.

"It may look serious," Tinkie said, pacing the corridor outside my cell, "but Sarah Booth is innocent. Surely you can prove that."

"Innocence and guilt aren't my concern." Harry gave Tinkie a look of pure surprise. "Facts and evidence are what I need. Emotion never won a case."

"I'd feel a lot better if you pretended to believe me." The sound of keys jingling drew my attention to the door that separated the jail from the sheriff's office. One last smidgen of hope that Coleman would come and unlock my cell still lived in my heart.

"A good lawyer never invests emotionally, Ms. Delaney. I can assist you best as an impartial advocate."

"How much is this impartiality going to cost me?"

"Never you mind, Sarah Booth," Tinkie spoke up. "Oscar and I are taking care of Mr. Bencher's fee."

For the moment. But that bill would come home to roost. Tinkie was my friend, not my protector. It wasn't her responsibility to pay for my legal fees.

The sound of shouting came from the sheriff's office. I could hear Coleman, but the other voice, male, I couldn't identify.

When the door flew open and Keith Watley dramatically swept toward my cell, I knew exactly what had happened. The director had finally heard that his leading lady was in the slammer for murdering his prior leading lady. Keith was having rough luck in Zinnia.

"Sarah Booth, the provincials have gone insane!" Keith stuck his arms through the bars and waved them until I stood and let him hold my hand. "I have a rehearsal scheduled for three this afternoon, and that buffoon of a sheriff says he won't release you until a bond hearing."

"We're working on it." Tinkie stepped forward.

"What morons these people are!" Keith pulled my hand through the bars and brought it to his lips. "They are too dull to see talent when it shines in front of them."

"They aren't concerned with Sarah Booth's acting ability," Tinkie cut in. "They think she's a murderer."

"Rubbish! Sarah Booth is a gentlewoman. She's dramatic, not homicidal."

Tinkie rolled her eyes. "If she needs a character witness we'll be sure and call you."

Before I had a chance to pipe up, the jail door opened and Coleman stood silhouetted in the doorway. He held a paper in his hand as he came toward us. "This is a search warrant for Dahlia House and your car." He handed it to Harry. Without another word, he turned and walked away. The door closed behind him, leaving silence.

"Well, he's certainly acting like a total prick." Tinkie's face was pale.

"He's acted like a jerk the entire time." My heart was breaking, but I was too mad to show it.

"He's acting like the law in Sunflower County," Harry said. "No more and no less."

"You can say that." Tinkie pointed one manicured finger in his direction. "But he's slept with Sarah Booth and he's acting like a total pri—"

"I have not slept with Coleman." My statement came out like metal on cement.

"You haven't?" Tinkie was puzzled.

"I have not." If Coleman was going to treat me like a killer, I didn't want everyone to think he'd been privileged to taste my favors.

"Good." Harry stacked his papers and stood. "It would be a conflict of interest."

"Tell me about it," I murmured.

"I'll see you at the preliminary hearing." Harry picked up his briefcase and yelled for someone to let him out of the cell.

With Tinkie and Oscar's help, I bonded out by early afternoon. When I got to Dahlia House, Gordon Walters was just packing up his gear. Tinkie had driven me, and she confronted him.

"Well, I guess you didn't find a single thing." She put her hands on her tiny hips and tapped her foot, the chic leopard print going up and down like a big cat's tail.

"You know I can't talk to you about what we found." Gordon was in a hurry to skedaddle.

"Then you did find something." Tinkie moved so that she was between him and his patrol car.

"Tinkie, you know I can't talk about that."

"You'd better start talking. You know Sarah Booth didn't hurt anyone."

He cast a look at me as I stood on the front lawn. I felt violated. My home had been invaded and inspected by Coleman's henchmen. Not even Coleman himself. He'd sent Gordon to do his dirty work.

"I have to go." He started past Tinkie, but she wasn't to be so easily thwarted. She grasped his arm.

"What did you find? We have to know."

Gordon looked into her eyes, seemingly transfixed. "Nothing in the house. It was the car."

We all swiveled to look at my roadster, parked by the side of the house. "What did you find?" Tinkie's grip must have increased because Gordon looked down at her hand on his arm.

He sighed. "There's some white powder in the trunk. Coleman sent some of the state poison experts over to check it out. Based on the smell, they seemed to think it was potassium cyanide."

I felt the need to vomit. The sickness hit me hard and violently, and I staggered to the steps to sit down. "Poison?" I managed to ask.

"Cyanide is a poison. We found it in the trunk, Sarah Booth." This time his gaze searched my face, trying to read guilt, I supposed.

"I never had any cyanide. I wouldn't even know where to get it." I forced myself to my feet. "You have to believe me, Gordon. I didn't do this."

"It sure stretches the imagination, Sarah Booth. But the evidence doesn't lie. That's why Coleman sent me over to do the search instead of coming himself. He didn't want folks saying that he let his feelings for you taint the evidence."

"Then he expected to find evidence." That stung, and my already weakened gag reflex threatened again.

Gordon shook his head. "This is killin' him, too. My advice is that you come up with a way to explain how that stuff got in your trunk." His face brightened. "Maybe you were hauling pesticides or something. I don't know much about poison but that might be the answer."

"I haven't hauled anything like that in my trunk." I felt as if I'd been gutted.

"If Sarah Booth decided to kill Renata, she wouldn't be so stupid as to leave traces of the poison in her car." Tinkie put her hands on her hips. "This is absurd."

"I'm not disagreeing, Tinkie. But you two had better come up with some good answers." Gordon was as glum as I was.

Tinkie straightened to her full five-two height. "You can bet we'll do that and more. Sarah Booth didn't harm Renata or anyone else. She's being framed! And we're just the detectives to prove it!"

I held onto Tinkie's bold words as I stood in the wings at The Club waiting for my cue to enter the stage. Tinkie had been kind enough to arrange a different dressing room for me — actually, Graf had swapped out with me. And he'd done his best to try to talk to me, but I avoided him and everyone else. Backstage, in the kitchen, in the ladies' room, in the audience — the whispers were everywhere. Most people viewed Renata's demise as a tragic misfortune. A few who'd met her on a personal level might think the great karmic wheel had crushed her by the weight of her own bad behavior. And then there were a handful of people who thought I'd really killed her for the chance to play Maggie.

"Don't think about anything except the play." Graf came up behind me and put his arms around me, hugging me back against him. "When we're on the stage, the only reality is the role we're playing. It has to be that way or it won't work. Here is the only place you're safe, Sarah Booth."

What he said was true, and it was something I'd just learned the night before, when I'd first replaced Renata. As soon as I walked onto the stage, I'd forgotten everything but the challenge of bringing Maggie the Cat to life. All of my worries, concerns, and grief had fallen away, leaving only the art of creating a whole new person by action and voice. It had been all consuming, and I lusted to feel it again.

"I'm ready, Graf." I eased from his arms. Tinkie had tried to convince me not to perform. She said if I didn't take the stage, there was no motive for me to kill Renata. Maybe she was right, but I wasn't giving this opportunity up, not even to prove myself innocent. I knew I hadn't done anything. Why should I give up the chance of a lifetime?

Graf's fingers laced through mine. "I'm going to help you prove you're innocent." He brought my hand to his lips and kissed lightly above my knuckles.

His words were balm on an ego left scorched by Coleman's lack of belief in me. "Thank you, Graf. I don't know what you can do."

"I have my own suspect." His lips grazed the sensitive curve of my ear. "Kristine Rolofson. I think she's been working up to killing Renata for a long time. She realized the play would close after this week, and she found a way to kill Renata."

"In revenge over hitting her dog?" I loved Sweetie Pie, but poisoning a person was a serious crime.

"I think so." He stepped closer so that I could smell his mysterious aftershave. "Even better, I have evidence."

"Evidence?" This was much better.

"After the police left Renata's dressing room, I found dog piss on the floor of her closet."

"Wow." I was completely underwhelmed.

"And I have a witness who saw Kristine slip into the dressing room during the first act." His smile told me he knew this was much better information.

"You really have a witness?" Oh, let it be true. That would be something incontrovertible. Coleman couldn't shrug it off. Someone else was in Renata's dressing room other than me.

"I do. And I'm going to make sure she goes to the sheriff's office to make a statement. She's a bit reluctant right now — doesn't want the focus to shift to her. But I'll talk to her."

"Thank you, Graf." From that heartfelt moment, it was easy enough to raise my face for the kiss he offered. It was so fast, and so natural. Graf believed in me and knew I'd never hurt another person. When his lips demanded a deeper kiss, I yielded. I closed my eyes and kissed him back, shutting out all thoughts of Coleman and the pain that followed close on the heels of his name.

A throat cleared behind us, and I slowly came to my senses. Keith wouldn't really care that Graf was kissing me. The tension would add another level to our performance, and Keith was smart enough to know that.

The clearing noise came again, and I eased out of Graf's arms to turn and face Coleman. He stood not three feet away, his face flushed and his eyes cold.

"I came to wish you good luck, Sarah Booth. I missed your performance last night so I thought I'd catch it tonight. Somehow, though, this wasn't the show I expected."

He disappeared into the darkness of the backstage area.

I'd hurt him, but I didn't feel a bit better. Not about him or about myself.

"Places everyone!" Keith bustled over to us. "The curtain goes up in fifteen seconds!"

Chapter 6

The applause was deafening. Graf held my hand as we took our bows. If Coleman was in the audience, I'd missed him in the few quick glances I was able to take. Good enough, then. He'd charged me with murder and then got huffy when he found me kissing a man who believed I was innocent. If he couldn't figure that one out, he was hopeless.

Instead of hiding in the kitchen, I was at the front of the line when members of the audience came backstage to congratulate the cast. The rumors were all over town. Folks were painting me to be an egomaniacal killer, and I sure wasn't going to act like I was afraid of the gossip. I shook hands and smiled, bold as a hungry harlot.

"Why, Sarah Booth, you were marvelous." Betsy Gwen Collier, better known as Booter, grasped my fingertips in the sorority girl's handshake. She smiled up at me. "I think it was well worth killing Renata to get a chance to show off your talent. I wonder, will they have theatrical performances in prison?"

I leaned down conspiratorially, "You have a booger hanging from your left nostril." She rubbed furiously at her nose with the back of her hand as the line forced her forward.

Harold Erkwell, a former suitor and good friend, merely kissed my cheek as he passed. His eyes, normally an ice blue, told me that he was sorry for what I was going through. The line moved on.

The minutes dragged as I listened to the compliments and the snide remarks from my fellow townsfolk. At last I saw a chance to slip away. I made it out the side exit and into the night. I'd barely had time to think about the cigarettes I'd given up when the door opened.

Graf was silhouetted in the rectangle of light. He saw me and strode over. "You were even better tonight, Sarah Booth. Listen, when this show is over, I'm headed to Hollywood. I have a contract to do a movie with Paramount. It's a marvelous script, and Renata had the female lead. It's a perfect character for you."

"Hollywood?" The offer was incredible.

Actually more than I could take in. "You want me to go to Hollywood and be in a movie with you?" I wanted to be sure of what he was offering.

"Yes. That's exactly what I want. We have something together, something special. As good as it is on stage, imagine what a camera could do — the intensity and close-ups."

"That's a sweet offer —"

"I'm not being sweet." He grasped my hands and held them against his warm chest. "This is my big chance, Sarah Booth. Probably the last chance I'll have to move from the stage to the silver screen. As much as I love Broadway the money is in movies. We could do this together. They were paying Renata a million dollars. You're an unknown, but once they see you . . ."

I didn't hear any more. A million dollars. For a movie. Flash images danced through my head — the deed for Dahlia House in my hand, Dahlia House with a new coat of paint, a glistening white fence around Reveler's paddock, a new Hermes Steinkraus saddle, money in my billfold.

"Sarah Booth!"

"What?" I returned to the moment with a crash. Graf had been steadily talking and I'd been in a dream world.

"As soon as the play ends, we need to fly to Hollywood and arrange a screen test for you."

"You're serious." I was amazed.

"As a heart attack. This could be the biggest thing that's ever happened to both of us. The chemistry we have together — if it translates to the screen, we could be Tracey and Hepburn. Imagine, a house on a cliff with the Pacific pounding below. A warm bed, our bodies together." His palm cradled my cheek. "I'm in awe of you, Sarah Booth."

"She won't be going anywhere." Coleman stepped out of the dark. "She's charged with murder, and she can't leave Sunflower County."

"That sounds exactly like something a redneck sheriff would say," Graf drawled. "Hell, I could have killed Renata. So could every member of the cast. Or how about Keith? He hated working with her with a dedicated passion. Ask any member of the crew. He's threatened to kill her a thousand times. Or what about that makeup girl, Bobbe Renshaw? Renata cost her a great job in New York with ABC. Bobbe could have stayed in the city with her young son and husband. When Renata lied as one of Bobbe's references and said the girl was a thief, ABC withdrew the job offer. If anyone had reason to kill Renata, it was Renshaw. And she had access to Renata's makeup a lot more than Sarah Booth."

In the dim light spilling from the open door, I could barely see Coleman's expression. What I did see made me furious. "After all that's happened between us, you seriously think I killed a woman." I stepped up to him and slapped him hard across the face. "I loved you, Coleman. The only thing I'm guilty of is being the biggest fool in the state."

I walked back into The Club, leaving both men in the night.

Jitty paced the kitchen, the full skirt of a green-sprigged dress swinging into the cabinets and chairs. I was transfixed by the size of her tiny waist, made evident by a dark green sash. "You really think Coleman will put you in the slammer?" Jitty asked.

I was worried. Coleman's behavior had cut me to the bone. As bad as heartbreak might be, the possibility of going to jail was even worse. I'd eventually recover from a broken heart — I'd done it before — but thirty years in jail wasn't something that time would mend.

"Sarah Booth, that man has been nothin' but trouble." She put her hand to her throat where an exquisite cameo rested in the hollow. "Then again, most men are trouble."

She put her hands on her hips and stood to face me. "Out of all the men in Sunflower County, why did you settle on Coleman Peters?"

Now that was a question I'd asked myself a number of times. In the year I'd been home, I'd had more than one chance to have a good man, but Coleman had stolen my interest. Dahlia House and the land had been a stronger pull than Hamilton Garrett V and Paris. Part of it, though, had been Coleman. He'd been a married man, and even though I'd thought we could never be together, I hadn't been able to completely forget him. Now that he was getting divorced, I'd allowed myself the fantasy of seeing a future together. More fool, me.

"Well, talking to you is like talking to a wall!" Jitty took a deep breath and her breasts almost spilled from the lowcut gown.

"I think that dress is only suitable for evening wear." I scrutinized the cap sleeves that attached to the off-the-shoulder neckline. "It's January, Jitty, and you look like you're headed to a barbecue at Twelve Oaks on a hot summer day. I think you're seasonally deluded."

"Throwing insults at me won't change the

pickle you've gotten yourself in, Missy. And I am going to a barbecue. You forget, where I reside it can be any season, any year."

"I thought we were going to stay out of the past." I let my gaze sweep over her attire, hoping to taunt her. I didn't want her to leave. Once she went, I'd be all alone with my thoughts, and they were exquisitely unpleasant.

"Throw a party, Sarah Booth. Have a barbecue." She reached behind her and produced a picture hat. When she placed it on her head, I almost sighed at the vision she made. One eyebrow arched as she spoke. "Dahlia House was meant for parties."

"Why should I have a party for people who think I'm a murderer?" The idea of trying to entertain people was enough to send me the rest of the way into a full-blown anxiety attack.

"The whole town is talkin'. Folks think you killed Renata. Think what Scarlett would do."

"You're right!" She was, in a twisted kind of way, brilliant. "Scarlett would rub their noses in it." I had an inspiration. "Remember that candy lipstick Daddy used to buy for me! I haven't seen any for years, but I'll bet I can find it on eBay!"

Jitty's smile told me I was on the right track.

"I'll play it to the hilt." The idea had taken on a life of its own. "I'll invite the cast and crew. A strike party when the show closes. I'll invite Coleman, too. And I'll have candy lipstick as dessert."

"That's the spirit. Now make your guest list. I've got places to go and people to see."

Jitty began to fade. As much as I wanted to keep her with me, I didn't say anything. She had her own afterlife to live. I was stuck with mine.

Two a.m. found me sitting at my computer. Instead of sweet dreams of a film career, my mind had clung to the image of Coleman in the parking lot telling Graf that I couldn't leave Sunflower County because I was a murderer. Or murderess, depending on a person's semantic preference. I didn't think it mattered to Coleman what gender tag he put on the word. Judging by his conduct, he really believed that I'd killed Renata.

I tried not to dwell on that and attempted to turn my mind down another trail by researching what I could find on Bobbe Renshaw. Graf had confided in me, even though he hadn't yet told the authorities, that he'd seen Bobbe exiting Renata's dressing room just before the intermission. And there was the dog urine in Renata's wardrobe closet. Kristine was equally high on the list of potential killers. Now, though, I wanted to know Bobbe's background.

After a few tries on different search engines, I found far more than I'd anticipated. Bobbe had graduated from UCLA with a degree in film history. Somehow, she changed the direction of her life and become involved with makeup.

A little more reading, and I found why she'd changed her interest. She'd dated the lead singer of a rock band, C-4, a group known for theatrics. In one song, "Reptile Boy," Danny Joe Batson was attacked by a man in a mask carrying a chain saw. As blood spurted across the stage, Danny's arm would fly into the audience. Then, in a miracle of healing, Danny would regenerate an arm and begin to play again. The makeup had been high-class and demanding. Bobbe had shown a talent for it.

Scanning through the photos of Bobbe with the band, I saw a different person. She was still the same tall, elegant girl, but in the photos she was smiling and hugging Danny Joe's waist. In another photo she was holding the fake arm in her mouth like a dog. The fun was sick but infectious. In a final photograph, Bobbe and Danny were getting married. Bobbe was pregnant and in the bloom of health.

I compared the pictures on this Web site to the woman I'd met at The Club. Bobbe was still a beauty, but the smile had disappeared.

Bobbe's bio carried her forward to the off-Broadway musical *Stomp,* and then she'd hooked up with Renata and followed her for the past two years. New York, Atlantic City, Reno, and Mississippi. The photographs depicting the travelogue showed a woman with more and more unhappiness in her face.

If Graf had been telling the truth about Renata blocking Bobbe's job at ABC, then Bobbe had good cause to kill Renata. Danny Joe and C-4 were living in New York City. The job at ABC studios would have been much easier on Bobbe than being on the road.

Sighing, I turned the computer off. It was nearly four a.m. I had another performance at eight p.m., and if I didn't get some sleep, I was liable to fall off the stage. Crawling under the covers, I let my hand drift down the side of the bed to rest on Sweetie Pie's head. My hound was loyal and loving. She never let me down. Why couldn't Coleman be that way?

I drifted into sleep where Coleman and I were standing at an altar. The minister held a Bible.

"Take the ring and place it on her finger," the minister instructed. "Repeat after me. With this ring, I thee wed."

But it wasn't a ring Coleman pulled out of his suit jacket. He snapped the handcuffs around my wrists and turned to the minister.

"Marry her? Why would I marry her? I'm taking her to jail on a murder charge."

I woke up with sweat beading my face and my heart racing. When I looked at the clock, it was just after six. I'd been asleep for little more than two hours.

It wasn't enough, but I sure wasn't going to try again after that nightmare. I got up and began to think about my day. I'd become my own worst enemy. Instead of being proactive, I was moping around, depressed, with my feelings hurt. What I had to do was begin to find the person who'd killed Renata. If Coleman was going to try to pin the murder on me, then I had to find out the real killer.

And I had to do it soon.

I could feel everyone staring at me as I

walked into Millie's Café, Tinkie at my side. She slowed at a table where Booter and two friends had stopped eating their naked salads to stare at me.

"You've been to both performances of *Cat,* Booter." Tinkie picked up a piece of spinach from Booter's salad bowl and chomped it. "I didn't realize you were such a culture vulture. When we were at Ole Miss, didn't you flunk Art Appreciation?"

"I don't recall." Booter was unfazed. "What I remember about Ole Miss was how every fraternity boy in the school wanted to be my sweetheart. Compared to that, my memories of art appreciation dim a bit." She batted eyelashes an inch long. "I guess being unpopular, you have completely different memories."

Tinkie's smile had something feline in it. "I know what you mean, Booter. When I heard that the entire Ole Miss football team, including the B string, bragging about shaking your pom-poms, why, I just realized what a wallflower I was with only the president of the Greek system for my homecoming date. How I survived without having my name and phone number on the boy's bathroom walls, I'll never know."

Tinkie selected the plumpest olive from Booter's salad and popped it into her mouth. "I adore Greek salads, don't you?" She took my elbow and steered me to the back table where Cece and Millie were waiting. I'd called a powwow of the smartest women in the state of Mississippi. During the sleepless night, I'd determined to fight back.

"Sarah Booth, could I have your autograph?" Cece held out a paper napkin. Beside her, Millie laughed out loud.

"Don't look so glum, Sarah Booth." Millie whipped out the *National Enquirer.* She was an avid fan of that rag and the *Star.* "Look! You're a bona fide star! You're on the cover!"

Indeed I was, in a clinch with Graf taken when we were onstage. Even though I knew it was a play, I was transfixed by the way we stared at each other. It was downright passionate — filled with love and longing and hate.

"You're going to be a big star!" Millie got up and went to the counter for two more coffee cups and the pot. "Jimbo in the kitchen is fixing you up a piece of fresh apple pie, à la mode. My treat."

My gaze had just found the headline above my picture, which read, "Graf and old flame suspected of murder." Below that was a picture of Renata taken several years earlier. "Star dies of poisoning" was the headline for her photo. I almost missed the tiny picture of the shaggy red dog, but the headline caught my eye. "Giblet the Miracle Dog tells why Renata Trovaioli needed to die!"

Great, the dog was giving interviews. I turned to the page listed. Whatever the dog was saying expressed the sentiments of his owner. As far as I knew, no one had seriously looked at Kristine Rolofson as a possible killer. And God knows she had a motive. She'd devoted her life to making Renata pay for the hit-and-run of Giblet.

"I've already read that," Millie said. "It was awful. Little Giblet was trotting down the street. He went every morning to the deli and picked up coffee and a Danish for his owner, Kristine."

"I know you three are crazy about dogs, but really!" Cece wasn't pulled in by the canine-interest story. "How did the dog pay for the coffee and Danish? I've been to New York, and I never saw a deli owner putting up with that."

Millie rolled her eyes. "Kristine had an account at the deli. She paid by the month or week or whatever!" She turned back to me. "The little dog had just picked up the sack with the coffee and Danish and was headed back to Kristine's apartment when Renata came flying down the street going at least ninety miles an hour."

"There was a witness who clocked her speed?" Cece shook her head. "Sounds like —"

"Kristine herself was sitting on the steps of her building waiting on Giblet. But she wasn't the only one. Another person saw Renata. She got the license plate of the car and actually reported it, but the police wouldn't do a thing because Giblet was only a dog."

"Only a dog," I repeated.

"At any rate, Kristine saw the accident and was able to get Giblet to the vet immediately. After extensive surgery and much pain and suffering, Giblet was saved. When the police wouldn't prosecute, Kristine went directly to Renata. The only thing she wanted was an apology. Renata slammed the door in her face!"

Tinkie had been silently following the conversation. Her brow furrowed as she spoke. "There's no doubt Renata was a heartless bitch. There's no doubt she deserved to die. What we have to prove is that someone other than Sarah Booth killed her!"

A commotion at the front of the café

caused all of us to stop talking and look up. I held a forkful of delicious apple pie in midair as I watched an extremely handsome man walk through the tables.

We weren't the only people who'd stopped talking and eating. Booter rose slowly from her chair as if magnetically drawn in the wake of the man, who was making a beeline for our table.

His gaze swept over the occupants and settled on me. As he drew closer, I could see the tension in his face. Hazel eyes zeroed in on me as he advanced, and I had a sudden feeling that no matter how handsome the package, I wasn't going to like what he had to deliver.

"Sarah Booth Delaney?" he said, standing to his full height of over six feet.

"Yes." I wasn't about to back down to a stranger. "What can I do for you?"

"Go to prison for the rest of your life." He spoke loud enough so that everyone in the café could hear. The place was completely quiet. Even Jimbo in the kitchen had stopped chopping things and was listening.

"What are you talking about?" I lowered the apple pie to the saucer.

"You killed my sister, and I'm here to see that Renata is avenged." He looked around the café. "I want everyone here to know that this woman is a murderer. I'll spend the rest of my life making certain that she pays for the heinous crime she committed."

CHAPTER 7

Cece rose to her feet. I stood, too, sensing that I might need to restrain her. She was always ready to jump to my defense, but I didn't want to see her arrested while defending my honor.

"I have one thing to say," Cece said. She stood completely motionless.

"What would that be?" Anger simmered in the man's eyes, and his voice was a dare.

"You are one handsome hunk of man!" Cece tilted a shoulder. "I'm Cece Dee Falcon, society editor of the *Zinnia Dispatch.* I'd really like to . . . interview you."

"Cece!" Tinkie and I spoke in unison.

"Oh, calm down." She stepped around us so that she was beside Renata's brother. "If I have a few moments with Colin Farrell, here, I think I can make him understand that you're falsely accused, Sarah Booth." She smiled up at him. "I'd sure like to give it the old college try."

"You're the person who wrote that awful review."

Cece frowned. "That might have been my assistant."

"Cece!" Tinkie and I spoke in unison again.

"Oh, hush." She shook a finger at us. "And mind your own business." She turned to Renata's brother. "What's your name, shu-ga?"

"Gabriel Trovaioli." His anger hadn't dissipated at all.

"Gabriel, I'd be glad to hear your side of the story, but I have to tell you, Sarah Booth wouldn't hurt a fly. Not even an insect like Renata."

I wanted to knock Cece upside the head. She wasn't helping matters at all.

"My sister called me the afternoon she died." He turned angry eyes on me. "She told me she was afraid Sarah Booth Delaney would kill her."

"What?" I didn't believe it. I hadn't even been near Renata. "That's ridiculous."

"She said you were desperate to get on stage and that you and Graf had rekindled your love affair. She said you'd kill her and that Graf would try to cover for you."

"That's a pretty serious accusation." Millie held a coffeepot in one hand and looked as if she might throw it. "If Cece would quit thinking with her crotch, she'd point out that slander is a serious charge."

Thank goodness for Millie. She wasn't immune to a handsome face, but she didn't let a good-looking man addle her brain.

"I didn't hurt Renata," I said crisply.

"Like you'd admit to killing her." He iced me with his gaze.

"Mr. Trovaioli, I didn't like your sister. She was an arrogant woman with a mean streak a mile wide. But I didn't kill her. I didn't even wish her dead."

He studied me. "You are good," he finally said. "She said you'd been working on your acting, and you're convincing enough."

My appetite was completely gone. Everyone in the café had stopped all pretense of eating. Booter and her table full of DGs watched with unadulterated pleasure. "I'm not acting. I'm innocent. At least of hurting Renata in any way."

"She warned me that you'd deny it. But I have proof."

That was impossible. There wasn't proof because I hadn't done anything.

"What proof?" Tinkie rose and came to stand behind my shoulder.

"Ms. Delaney works fast. She's already booked for a screen test in Hollywood next week, as soon as the play closes."

I was as stunned as Millie, Tinkie, and Cece. They all turned to look at me with varying degrees of amazement.

"I haven't scheduled any screen test, and even if I had, it isn't evidence that I killed Renata."

"You're busted, Ms. Delaney. Paramount Studios. Director Federico Marquez has ordered the test." He acted as if he held the smoking gun.

Graf hadn't even bothered to wait for me to agree. He'd gone on and scheduled my screen test. On the one hand, it showed his faith in my ability. On the other hand, it made me look guilty as sin. Denial was the river I chose to swim. "I can't help what arrangements Graf has made. I didn't agree to any screen test."

"Then you're turning it down?" Gabriel asked.

It was like a tennis match. Heads swiveled from me to Gabriel and back to me. "I don't know." I spoke firmly. "Since I didn't know about this screen test, I have to think about it."

"Excuse me." Cece picked up her purse that matched her purple suede heels. "I just have the scoop for my next story. Sarah Booth has screen test."

"You can't print that!" I made a grab for her elbow and missed.

"Of course I can, dahling."

"Cece, I don't know if I'm going to take the test or not."

"Of course you will." She smiled at me and winked at Gabriel. "But even if you don't, it's still a great story."

She walked out of the café with everyone watching. The door closed and I turned to face Tinkie. "If she prints that, it'll make me look guilty."

"You already look guilty," Tinkie said. "That's why we have to get busy." She handed Millie a twenty and blew her a kiss. "We'll be back."

She took my elbow and marched me past Gabriel, who settled at our empty table. As I walked past the front window, I saw Booter headed for him. If he had any doubts about my guilt, he wouldn't by the time Booter finished with him.

Tinkie headed out of town and I was too depressed to ask her where we were going. Circumstantial evidence was piling up around me like kindling around Joan of Arc. The most solid evidence was the poison found in my car. I still hadn't figured that one out. How did it get there? The only poison I'd ever hauled in the Roadster involved killing fire ants. That was a far cry from cyanide.

"Why would Renata tell her brother that you were going to kill her?" Tinkie didn't look at me as she asked the question. Her gaze was on the four-lane that headed north to Memphis.

"I have no idea." I spoke stiffly.

"Did you threaten her, Sarah Booth?"

At first the question cut me deeply, but I held myself in check and thought through my answer. Tinkie knew I had a temper, and she knew that Renata worked on my control. It wasn't such an unreasonable question to ask. I might have threatened Renata. "No."

She glanced at me, and her right hand patted my shoulder. "I know you didn't kill her, I'm just trying to get a handle on all of this. You've got to admit, it's strange that her brother would show up and say she feared that you were going to hurt her."

"How do we even know what he says is true. He might have heard that I was a suspect and decided to add fuel to the fire. Or maybe he killed her and is using me as a scapegoat!"

Tinkie sucked on her bottom lip. It gently popped free of her teeth in a manner that made men weak with desire. "I don't think that sounds right. Why would he pick you?"

"Maybe Renata bad-mouthed me." That was about a ninety-nine-percent probability.

"That's good." Tinkie smiled. "She realized you had more talent, so she decided to smear your name to everyone she knew."

Even as Tinkie said it, I knew it was stretching a point. "Maybe. But what difference does it make why she did it?"

Tinkie took a deep breath. "Because Gabriel will go straight to Coleman, Sarah Booth. You don't think he came all the way to Zinnia to have a scene in a café, do you? He's here to see you put in jail."

"Great." That was exactly what I needed. One more person wanting my hide. I slumped in the seat. "Where are we going?"

"To the cosmetic store where you got that lipstick. If the poison wasn't on the lipstick when you picked it up, then someone had to put it on it afterward. It'll help us track down the killer when we decide before or after."

Tinkie was brilliant. Thank God she was on the case or my future would be toast.

"Tell me the address and then you take a nap. You have to be ready for the stage tonight."

"I didn't tell Graf I would have a screen test."

She lifted her chin a tad. “Sarah Booth, he’s offering you a chance at your dream.”

“If any of it’s real.”

“You and Graf had a special magic on the stage. If a camera can capture it, I think —”

“I don’t know if that’s my dream anymore, Tinkie. I have a life here, a business. A home with Sweetie Pie and Reveler.”

“I know. Just don’t pass it up without thinking about all of it. You can make a lot of money in Hollywood. You wouldn’t have to stay out there forever.” The car zipped through the empty cotton fields, headed north faster than the speed limit.

“I haven’t said no, but I haven’t said yes. And just for the record, I wouldn’t agree to anything without discussing it with you, partner.”

“I know that, Sarah Booth. That’s why I knew Gabriel Trovaioli wasn’t speaking the truth.”

I closed my eyes and settled against the plush leather seat of her Cadillac. In less than an hour we’d be in Memphis, and I did need the rest. Between stage anxiety and being charged with murder, I wasn’t sleeping well.

The shop was tucked into a row of boutiques in an artsy part of downtown Memphis.

When I'd gone to get the lipstick, I'd hardly noticed. I'd been so furious at Renata's imperious demands that I'd been blind to the quaint beauty of the area. Traffic was thick, but Tinkie found a parking place only a block away. We walked to La Burnisco Salon, an umber stucco front with a black and white awning over the beveled glass door. Inside, glass counters like those found in a jewelry shop showed displays of cosmetics. The precious jewels of La Burnisco.

The elderly man who'd waited on me wasn't behind the counter. A tall, elegant blonde eyed us from behind the counter. She dismissed me instantly and focused on Tinkie.

"May I help you?" she asked, and I wasn't included in the question.

"Is the manager in?" Tinkie smiled.

"Yes." The blonde's perfect face gave nothing away.

"May I see him?"

"You're looking at her." She didn't smile.

"Okay." Tinkie's tone was terse. "I want to see the elderly man who was in here three days ago and sold my friend a tube of lipstick."

She didn't flick so much as an eyebrow. "There's no elderly man working here. Not today. Not ever. Old men wouldn't sell many cosmetics." What passed for a smile touched the corners of her mouth. I was convinced she'd botoxed herself into permanent facial paralysis.

"Look, my friend picked up a tube of lipstick. A special order for Renata Trovaioli. A man sold it to her."

"Not at this shop."

Tinkie stepped as close to the counter as she could get. "I don't know what kind of scam you're running here, but I want to see the old man."

At last the blonde looked at me. "Is she on medication?"

That was the final straw. Tinkie did a side step and maneuvered behind the counter before the blonde could blink. Tinkie rushed to the door at the back of the shop and flung it open. In a split second she disappeared from sight. I'd never seen Tinkie move so fast or so determinedly.

The blonde sauntered to a telephone, picked it up and dialed three numbers. I didn't have to be psychic to know she'd called the police.

"I'd like to report a robbery in progress," she said. "La Burnisco Salon, 122 Alva Street. Yes. This madwoman is ransacking my shop." She hung up and looked at me. "I suggest you get your friend and get out of here before the cops arrive."

"An old man sold me a tube of lipstick. Almond Mocha Retreat. For Renata Trovaioli. I picked it up right here. He was standing right there. You can't —"

"My name is Laura La Burnisco and I'm the sole owner of this business. I create all of my own cosmetics, and though I have an A-list of clients, Renata Trovaioli is not one of them. I have no idea where you think you were, but it wasn't this shop." She pointed to the door where Tinkie had disappeared. "Get your friend and leave before you end up behind bars."

"Tinkie! She called the cops." I rushed back to find Tinkie examining a storage room. There was no one else in sight.

"Let's get out of here." I grabbed her arm and began to pull her to the front door.

"Are you sure you came to this shop?" Tinkie turned in all directions. "There's no place an old man could hide."

"I came here. I got the lipstick from an old guy who looked like he belonged in a Dickens novel. Muttonchop whiskers, curly white hair around a bald spot, rimless glasses perched on his nose." I remembered him completely. In vivid detail.

"Are you sure, Sarah Booth?"

And with that question, I wasn't any

longer. I'd been so angry and hadn't paid attention. Could I have gone to another shop, a place where Renata's lipstick had been poisoned? Tinkie read my face, and hers showed concern.

"Let's talk about this somewhere else." This time she took my arm and led me out the door and onto the street. We were pulling away when the cops arrived, sirens blaring.

"My credit card will show the purchase." I suddenly felt better. I'd charged the lipstick to my card knowing I'd be reimbursed.

"Thank goodness." A little of the tension left her face. "How could you not remember the lipstick shop?"

"I do remember it. La Burnisco. 122 Alva Street. I remember the black and white awning, and the stucco front. The color was so rich. I remember that." But as I spoke we passed several shops nearly the same color. Two of them also had striped awnings. It was part of the historical décor.

"Tinkie, I came to Memphis and got that lipstick for Renata. I didn't open it."

"I believe you, Sarah Booth. You don't have to convince me. It's Coleman and a jury I'm worried about."

In my mind I saw twelve Sunflower Countians sitting in the jury box ready to judge me. It wasn't a comforting prospect.

"Where would I have come up with a tube of lipstick called Almond Mocha Retreat? The exact shade Renata asked for. I couldn't have produced that in a couple of hours' time. And you know Renata, had it not been the right shade and the right tube, she would have thrown a hissy fit."

"That's true. As I said, Sarah Booth, I believe you."

"But you don't think anyone else will." I could see it in her expression. She drove without looking at me, and when I saw the glimmer of a tear in the corner of her eye, I realized she was worried about me. That, more than anything else, frightened me.

"What am I going to do?"

"*We're* going to get to the bottom of this." She hesitated. "Sarah Booth, what's going on between you and Coleman?"

"I wish I knew." Normally I'd try to hide the fact that I'd been dumped. I was too dejected to even try to disguise my dismay.

"He filed for divorce. I checked."

Leave it to Tinkie to get the facts, but this wasn't only about Renata's murder. "There's something wrong with Connie."

Tinkie tapped her toe. "We've known that for months. But that doesn't explain why

Coleman is acting so bizarre. I know he doesn't believe you killed Renata."

I kept my voice steady and my eyes dry, but it took an act of will. "Connie has a brain tumor. They're operating today and I was supposed to go with him for the surgery."

"You didn't refuse, did you?"

The question hung between us as we crossed the Tennessee-Mississippi line. It was a long time before I spoke. "He never even called me. Coleman may be jealous of Graf."

"Does he know about your past with him?"

"He knows Graf and I were lovers. There's no telling what else has been passed on to Coleman."

"That could account for his peculiar conduct."

"There's no excuse for thinking the woman you love is a murderer."

"We don't know Coleman thinks that." She took the highway that led to Dahlia House so I could prepare for the play.

"If he didn't think it, wouldn't he say he didn't think it?" I was exasperated.

Tinkie glanced at me, a withering look. "What do you expect, Sarah Booth. He is a man, isn't he?"

Chapter 8

As we pulled into the driveway of Dahlia House, I sat upright. A patrol car was parked at the front door, and I knew Coleman hadn't come for a social call. Coleman was in Jackson. With his wife.

I considered asking Tinkie to turn around and leave, but I needed to get ready for the play. As we cruised to the front of the house, I saw Gordon Walters leaning against the patrol car.

When I got out, he walked over, a slight flush touching his cheeks.

"Ms. Tinkie, Sarah Booth, how are y'all doing?"

Gordon had never been one to sit out in the cold without good reason, which concerned me.

"What's going on?" Tinkie asked.

"The sheriff asked me to come by and remind the two of you that Sarah Booth is the main suspect in a murder."

"Like I'd forget that," I snapped. "What's wrong with Coleman? Has he completely lost it?"

Gordon looked like I'd asked him to reveal his most intimate secret. "I don't know." He spoke barely above a whisper. "I honestly don't know, Sarah Booth, but I'm worried about him. He hasn't eaten or slept. He acts like a bear with his leg in a trap, and he took off about an hour ago and didn't say where he was going."

"And you stood out here in the cold to tell me that?" I didn't believe it for a minute.

"Sarah Booth!" Tinkie frowned at me.

"She's right," Gordon admitted, the flush once again touching his olive skin. "Coleman sent me to tell you that as a person charged in a murder case, you're not supposed to leave the county. That means no more trips to Memphis."

Two things struck me as audacious — the first was that Coleman had sent someone to remind me of my felonious state, and the second was that Coleman would attempt to order me about as if . . . well, as if I were charged with murder. That more than likely meant that I had broken my bond by traipsing off to Memphis with Tinkie. The truth was, I hadn't honestly considered myself a suspect so all the rules and regulations given in a spiel by the bail bondsman had gone in one ear and out the other. Tinkie put a cold hand on my wrist.

"Gordon, I simply didn't think. I just don't consider Sarah Booth a serious suspect."

"I know." Gordon almost dug his toe in the shell driveway as he hung his head. "Technically, I should arrest her for violation of bond, but I won't do it. I know she didn't hurt that actress."

"Thank you, Gordon." All of my anger dissipated in a puff of cold wind. I was left shaking. "I never considered that I was violating my bail. Tinkie and I were trying to solve the case."

He nodded. "Sarah Booth, Coleman knows that. He sent me here to warn you not to leave the county again."

"He should never have charged me in the first place." I put my cards on the table. "He knows I'd never hurt anyone. Not even Renata Trovaioli."

"You're the best suspect and the person charged. He has to hold you to the letter of the law, Sarah Booth. Surely you can see that?" He was almost pleading.

"No. I don't see it." My anger had returned. "I don't see it at all. How can he charge me with a crime he knows I didn't commit? That's just wrong and you know it."

Gordon looked to Tinkie for help. "If he hadn't charged you, everyone in town would have gone around whispering behind your back. Because folks know how he feels about you, there would never have been an end to the suspicions and whispers. It would have been that Coleman let you get away with murder for the rest of your life. He didn't want that for you. He knew that would have driven you out of town and away from him."

Tinkie put her perfectly manicured hand up to her mouth. "Oh, my God. That's the most romantic thing I've ever heard."

"Stop melting!" I gave my full attention to Gordon. "He sent you here to tell me all of that?" I was so mad that my voice trembled. "He should have told me himself, the coward."

Gordon stepped back against the blast of my fury. "Of course he didn't send me here to tell you that. Are you insane?" He held up a hand. "Don't answer that!"

"Sarah Booth, what is the world is wrong with you?" Tinkie put a restraining hand on my arm. "Gordon is trying to help, and you attack him."

"Why didn't Coleman come to tell me

that himself?" I thought something in my chest was going to split. My heart. It was breaking.

"I'm handling the case," Gordon said. "That's why I'm here."

I tried hard to draw a deep breath, but it was impossible. My head was spinning and now Tinkie's restraining hand became one of support as she felt me wobble.

I sought a sensible question and finally found one. "How did you know about Memphis?"

Gordon didn't bat an eye. "Dewayne followed you. We figured you were going to the cosmetic shop, but we had to be sure."

I'd never seen the tail — because I hadn't expected one.

"Have you spoken with the owner of La Burnisco?" Tinkie was working the case instead of nursing hurt feelings.

Gordon nodded. "I was there yesterday. They claim to know nothing about Renata Trovaioli's lipstick. The owner said she'd never had an older man working for her, not even in a part-time capacity."

Which was exactly the same thing Tinkie and I had discovered, but a new flush of anger took me at the thought that Gordon hadn't done better than I had at grilling the blonde. "You believed her?"

Gordon gave me a look that made me realize I'd hurt his feelings again. "I didn't believe or disbelieve her, Sarah Booth. What she said runs counter to your statement, but there has to be an explanation that doesn't involve you putting cyanide in a tube of lipstick. You obviously got the lipstick somewhere, so why would you make up a place that actually exists and could be checked?"

"I'm sorry, Gordon." It was my turn to blush.

"They have a book at La Burnisco. Every person who buys cosmetics signs the book." He never dropped his gaze. "Your name wasn't there."

"But I signed it. The old man insisted. I told him the lipstick wasn't even for me, that I was just picking it up, but he insisted that I sign it." This was getting crazier with each new twist.

"Do you remember any other names on the book?"

"I signed at the top of a blank page. There weren't any other names." I knew then the old man was part of an elaborate frame. How did he get in the shop, though, without the blond barracuda's knowledge? "I bought that lipstick at La Burnisco from an old man who looked like Ebenezer Scrooge." I had a recurring flash — and not a hot one. "My credit card will show the purchase!"

Gordon shook his head. "We've checked that already. There's no charge for lipstick from La Burnisco on your card, Sarah Booth."

"But that's impossible!" I turned to Tinkie. "I gave Graf the slip with the charge on it to give to Renata so I could be reimbursed. The stupid lipstick was a hundred and fifty dollars!"

"I know you gave Renata the lipstick, but I never got the charge fee. Renata told me before you came back from Memphis that she would personally take care of reimbursing you."

I couldn't believe this. The charge had to be on my credit card. The old man had run my card — I'd watched him. "Was there a receipt in Renata's things?"

"No." Gordon spoke softly. "That's not even the worst of it, Sarah Booth."

"Oh, shit." I needed a drink and sofa to fall onto. "Come inside." They followed me into the house, and I went straight to the cut-glass decanters on the sideboard in the parlor. Out of the corner of my eye I saw a flicker of movement in the dining room and knew Jitty was listening in. I poured a drink for me and Tinkie and offered Gordon some iced tea. When we were all seated, I nodded for him to tell me the rest.

"We went to Sheffield's Feed Store."

His pause was dramatic and I motioned him to continue. Sheffield's was where I bought Reveler's grain. Neil "Bad Boy" Sheffield owned the store. I'd known him since high school, when he'd taught me how to dirty-dance. He was an irresistible charmer who made me feel like a million dollars even when I went in the store wearing paddock boots and cut-off shorts, an ensemble guaranteed to make Tinkie's well-groomed hair stand on end.

"The clerk there, Nancy Bulgarelli, said you were in the store last week trying to buy poison. Said you needed it for raccoons in your feed room."

My perplexity must have shown on my face because Gordon waved a hand. "The problem is that Nancy has no reason to lie."

"I don't have raccoons in the feed room and even if I did, I wouldn't poison them."

"Sarah Booth would never hurt an animal." Tinkie was incensed at the suggestion. "That's the biggest tub of hog slops I've ever seen."

When Tinkie gets to talking about hog slops, things are on a dangerous slide. "Why would Nancy tell such a whopper?" I asked the question aloud, but it was mainly for my consumption. Nancy was a fifteen-year-old high-schooler with big blue eyes, a lingerie model's figure, dimples, and a ninth-grader's obsession with boys, but she was a sweet kid.

"She admits she didn't get a good look at you. She was stocking shelves on a ladder. She said you came in wearing a big gardening hat, went behind the aisle with the insecticides, and asked about strychnine pellets."

"I never did any such thing." I swirled the ice cubes in my drink. "I'm beginning to see a definite pattern here, and it reeks of a setup. The person who really killed Renata has been working for at least a week to pin this on me."

Gordon rose and handed me the empty tea glass. "That's exactly what I think, Sarah Booth. The problem is we have to prove it, and Nancy won't budge off her story."

"If she didn't get a clear view of me, why does she think it was me?" I'd have a talk with Nancy. She worked afternoons, and she'd be at the store the next day. I wouldn't have to leave Sunflower County to find her.

"She said you mentioned Reveler and that you left your phone number for Neil to call you when he got back from picking up feed in Clarksdale."

Up until that point, everything Gordon had said had served to anger me. When Reveler was mentioned, I felt as if someone had opened the door on a freezer and blasted me with icy air. Tinkie felt it, too. She slowly stood, her face so pale that her coral lipstick looked too dark.

"Whoever is doing this to Sarah Booth knows way too much about her life."

"Who might that be?" Gordon asked.

I thought of the people who might hate me, and there were a few names on the list, but none of those people would think to kill Renata and pin it on me. Except for someone in the acting company.

I looked at Tinkie and her mouth silently formed the word "Graf." Neither of us spoke it, though. "I don't know," I said. Meaning that even if I suspected Graf I wasn't going to say so.

"Coleman has made a list, and Graf Milieu is at the top of the list. Of course, he can't openly pursue that, Sarah Booth, because you've made it obvious that you have feelings for Graf and folks are already talking. To try to shift the focus to him would have folks saying Coleman is protecting you and trying to get rid of his competition."

"So what if that's what folks say?" I'd never known Coleman to flinch before public opinion. He did what was right, not what was popular.

"It's not for him, Sarah Booth. He's looking out for you. You're the one who'll have to live with the outcome of all of this."

Tinkie came over and put her arm around my waist. "He's right, you know. Coleman's playing it by the book so that no one will ever be able to say you did it and got away with it."

That was cold comfort.

The Club's auditorium was filled to capacity, and at least fifty unticketed people were standing outside, hoping for admittance. Keith was beside himself with glee, and he was running all around the auditorium acting very much like a Nazi commandant.

"Sarah Booth! Sarah Booth!" He screamed my name as if he didn't know exactly where I was.

Bobbe finished blotting my makeup, and I started to slip from the chair when she touched my shoulder. "I need to talk to you."

The look in her eyes told me she was afraid of something. "After the show?" I asked.

She nodded. "Don't tell anyone."

"Okay." I wanted to question her more, but the makeup room door flew open, and Keith stood there, panting.

"A reporter from New York is in the audience. He wants to talk to you after the show."

I glanced at Bobbe and saw her face fall. "I have a commitment already."

"Sarah Booth, it's *Broadway Bound.* You have to do the interview."

He looked so desperate. "Keith, you've had Broadway hits, why is this so important?"

"Just do it, please."

"Fifteen minutes. That's all I have." Bobbe gave me a nod of agreement before she slipped from the room.

"I didn't want to say in front of Bobbe, but this whole thing with Renata's murder and all has created such publicity." Keith ran a hand through his thinning hair. "I've gotten calls from London and Tokyo and even Sydney. It's becoming an international incident. If they don't put you in prison, you'll be a huge star, and I'm the one who discovered you! My career will soar!"

"Thanks, Keith. Glad to know I got here on Renata's corpse." I brushed past him and went to the wings to take my place. Somehow, all of the glamour had evaporated from being on stage. Now, it was really going to be work to put on a performance.

I made it to the final curtain with a pounding headache, and when Keith showed up backstage with a rotund little man with a tape recorder and notepad, I gave the interview, running through my routine denials of guilt in Renata's death. At last, though, I walked back to the dressing room to find Bobbe.

She was sitting in her makeup chair, tears running silently down her cheeks. When I closed the door firmly behind me, she turned to face me.

"All I ever wanted was to be at home with my family. That isn't a crime."

"Certainly not."

"We had an argument the morning she died. Several people heard it. I knew she'd screwed up the job at ABC for me, and I let her have it."

I took a seat on the stool that was normally her seat. "I shouldn't have to point out that I'm the one charged with Renata's murder, not you. You don't have a reason to cry."

"As soon as they figure out you didn't do it, I'll be the prime suspect."

Bobbe was a beautiful girl, who looked as if she should be in front of the cameras, not backstage. I watched as she wiped the tears from her cheeks. "The sheriff will look at everyone, but it's becoming clearer and clearer to me, Bobbe, that someone in this company did kill Renata. Graf saw you coming out of her dressing room right before the fatal intermission. He hasn't told the sheriff, but he will." Especially if the heat was turned up on him.

She turned away. "I didn't kill her, but I sure as hell wanted her dead."

"Well, that's not a crime. Everyone who worked with her wanted her dead." That wasn't an overdramatization, either.

"I put that lipstick on her lips." She faced the makeup table and picked up a tray of lipsticks. "You know, I thought it was such a lovely shade that I was tempted to try it on myself."

"Thank God you didn't!" The idea was appalling.

"My fingerprints are on the tube. Once they figure you didn't do it, how long will it be before I'm in the crosshairs." She sobbed. "I don't have friends down here. I don't have money for a lawyer. What will I do?"

I put my arm around her. She'd been on the road with the show for nearly thirty-six weeks without a break to go home. As I patted her back, I slid my cell phone from my pocket. "What's your home number?"

"You can't call Danny!" She grabbed at the phone, knocking it to the floor.

"What's wrong?" I was more surprised than anything else. She obviously missed her husband and child, and I was only going to call them down here to be at her side during a crisis.

"Don't get Danny down here. If he starts drinking and running his mouth, he'll only make it worse."

I nodded, understanding at last that life with a rock star could sometimes be rocky.

"What can I do to help?"

"Promise me that if I am accused, you'll take the case and prove me innocent. I'll pay you, somehow."

"Don't worry about the money, Bobbe. If you're charged, Tinkie and I will do all we can for you."

Her smile was tentative. "God, why couldn't you have been with the show all the time? That stupid bitch made it so much harder than it had to be. I hate her. I'm glad she's dead."

And though Bobbe's smile was warm, my heart felt a sudden chill.

Chapter 9

Dahlia House was cold and foreboding, as if the weather reflected the condition of my heart. What should have been a week of triumph left the taste of ashes in my mouth. I was good. Damn good, on the stage. I sipped my celebratory Jack Daniel's and listened to the merry tinkle of my ice. Though the fire in the parlor fireplace crackled brightly and I'd turned on every light in the downstairs, nothing could block the fact that I celebrated alone.

Hamilton would have carpeted the floor with rose petals for my arrival.

Harold would have gently sucked my thumb and ignited the twinkle lights that set my heart aflutter.

Scott Hampton would have penned a blues song about my performance as Maggie the Cat.

The faces of the men from my past swept before my closed eyelids like an album of dead possibilities.

I'd settled on Coleman. I'd let his Dudley Do-Right attitude and unspoken promises lure me into love. I'd checked the answering machine before I made a drink. There was no call from him, no word on Connie. He was as alone as I was — and it served him right!

Though it would have been a sacrifice, I would have given up the stage to be with him during his time of strife. Nobody said it better than David Allen Coe. If Coleman's needs were great, I would've lain with him in a field of stone.

What he didn't understand was that I had needs, too. Success brought its own share of gnawing anxieties. Either Coleman didn't realize it, or he didn't care. A dream that'd been nurtured, worked toward, and brutally battered, had finally come true for me. I needed someone to share the success. God, I needed his arms around me to anchor me to Dahlia House and Zinnia and Sunflower County, because I felt myself beginning to slip away just like Jitty faded.

In my mind, I could clearly see a house on the Pacific bluffs, surf pounding against the rocks, the perfect weather warming my face. Reveler stood in a beautiful barn, unbothered by flies and mosquitoes or humidity. Sweetie sniffed the ground around the small farm, happy to be a California hound. With her ears, she'd be a natural at surfing. It could happen, and the images tantalized me with possibilities.

Around me was the home I'd known as a child. My New Year's resolution was to give up the past. At first, I'd viewed my dream to be an actress as the past I was meant to leave behind, but what if it was this older past, this past of ancestors and wood worn smooth by the steps of dead generations? What if . . .

"Jitty?" I called her, knowing she wasn't a ghost who answered summons. I needed her, though. I needed someone.

"Jitty!"

A shimmer of light floated into the parlor and Jitty materialized in black widow's weeds. A heavy veil covered her face, and I couldn't see the expression in her eyes.

"Who died?" I asked.

She lifted the veil, and the gentlest smile touched her face. "You'll have to tell me that, Sarah Booth. It could be me."

"That's impossible. You're already dead."

"I'm here only as long as you need me."

I'd never considered that Jitty's existence was so strongly linked with my own destiny. Actually, it was too terrifying to think about, but I had to ask.

"If I left Dahlia House, would you stay here?"

"All alone, in an empty house? What would be the fun of that?" she asked.

"This is your home." I almost choked on the word, overcome by a wave of sadness that body-slammed me.

"Four walls and a roof don't make a home, Sarah Booth. I'm here because of you."

"If I left here, would you . . . disappear?" *Die* wasn't exactly a word I could make myself say.

"I honestly don't know." She was stiller than I'd ever seen her, a black figure hovering at the edge of the rug.

"Coleman has broken my heart," I confessed.

She nodded. "Some folks can see a train wreck comin', Sarah Booth. Others have to wait for the steam, crash, and broken bones."

I would fall into that category. Jitty had warned me about Coleman. So had Tinkie. And Cece. And Millie. The list went on. But I hadn't listened. Instead, I'd listened to my heart, a stupid muscle that knew how to do only two things — pump and break.

I cleared the lump from my throat. "The

show closes this Thursday. If I'm not in jail, I'm going to Hollywood with Graf and take a screen test." I didn't realize my mind was made up until I said it aloud.

"Dreams are hard to come by, Sarah Booth. Especially ones that come true. To turn your back on a dream would be foolish, and God knows, I'd like to see you stop that track record here and now." Her smile took the sting out of her words.

"Why do you think Coleman stopped loving me? I know it was real. I didn't make it up or dream it. It was real. What happened?"

She came forward and perched on the arm of the sofa. Her dress was truly exquisite. The low-cut neckline, edged in black, made her skin creamy, a buttery caramel. "All along ever'one tole you, he's a married man. You just wouldn't listen."

"He accused me of murder. That doesn't have a thing to do with his marital status."

"Think it through, girl. Use your head for a change."

I tried. "What?"

"On the surface it may not, but Coleman is smart. And one thing about him, he's a man of honor. You're the logical suspect in this murder. He had to come down on you like a ton of bricks. He didn't have a choice.

Now he can't afford to call you or even talk to you casually, for fear someone will say he gave you information or evidence to help you prepare your defense. Whatever else he may have done, he's lookin' out for you right now. He's doin' the honorable and noble thing."

Her words cut deeper than a strap. My head knew she was right, but my heart hurt too badly to accept her explanation. "I need him here, holding me, telling me that he knows I'm innocent. That's what I need from him." I went to the sideboard and made another drink.

"He has needs, too."

"I don't believe it. You're defending him!"

"You won't listen because you want what you want. He's giving you what you need, even if you're too pigheaded to see it."

"I want arms to hold me, and I want someone to see me as talented and not a failure. I want kisses —"

The knock on the door was unexpected, and for a moment I thought my powerful wanting had made Coleman materialize right on my front porch. I rushed past Jitty to answer the door. Standing in the cold blast of air was Graf Milieu.

He didn't bother to ask; he simply stepped inside, swept me into his arms and kissed me with such passion that I couldn't stop myself from melting.

His arm reached beneath my knees, and he picked me up, kicking the door shut as he started up the stairs with me.

"Graf, I —"

"Don't talk. Don't try to stop this. It's what we both want. What we both need." He kissed me hungrily again and took the stairs.

Graf went unerringly to my bedroom. He put me on the bed, his hands already at the buttons of my shirt before I could stop him.

"Wait."

The one word sounded too loud in the room.

Graf's fingers stopped their work, and he looked me dead in the eye. "I want to make love to you."

"Do I get a vote?" I swung my legs to the floor and stood. I had to move away from him while I still had some mental powers. Graf's passionate kiss had rekindled the fire of the past. I'd been deeply in love with him. And he'd been deeply in love with himself — I had to remember that.

I'd changed, though, and it was possible that Graf had changed, too. Possible, but only time would tell. I wasn't about to jump out of the emotional frying pan into the fire.

"You kissed me back, Sarah Booth. You want this, too."

Direct, as ever. "I was feeling sorry for myself, Graf. The man I've been in love with has other obligations. I'm alone tonight, and I wanted someone to share my success. You walked in the door, bringing all of the past behind you."

"It's not the past I'm offering, Sarah Booth. It's a future. A real future. This time next week we'll be in Hollywood. The studio will be licking your feet. In a week, you'll have a contract. In a month, you'll be filming. In a year, you'll be a star!"

I was on the fast track, according to Graf. I can't deny that his words soothed my ego. I'd never realized how deeply I'd been wounded by my theatrical failure. Graf could talk all night about me, and I would love it.

"I have a life here, Graf. Obligations. Personal relationships. It isn't just about me."

"Isn't it?" He looked around. "You can close up this house tomorrow. We'll send money back to have workmen spruce it up, give it the love it needs."

"I have a partner in my PI agency."

He shook his head. "Who can carry on alone, or she can find a new partner. Tinkie has proven she's capable of rolling with the punches."

I paced the room. "I have a horse and a hound."

"They have grass and kennels in California. That's a weak excuse."

I swallowed and continued pacing. The only thing left holding me here was Jitty. A week ago, Coleman would have been at the top of the list, but he didn't even warrant a PS position. I'd never be able to explain Jitty to Graf.

"I'll think about it."

"Think about it?" He was incredulous. "What happened to the young woman who stayed up 'til three in the morning rehearsing for a bit part with no pay?"

"She grew up." I was surprised at myself, because it was true. Somewhere in the past year, I had grown up.

"Sarah Booth, you can't turn your back on this."

"I'm not saying that I will." I took his arm and led him to the stairwell. I didn't want to stay in my bedroom. Avoiding temptation isn't my strong suit. I'd grown up — a lot — but I wasn't infallible.

"When will you let me know?"

"Graf, let's just finish the play." I edged him down the stairs and into the parlor. "I have a lot of things to work through here."

"It's that sheriff." He looked around as if Coleman might jump out from behind the sofa.

"Partly." I wasn't going to lie, either.

"I can't believe this!" He put his hands over his face as if he literally couldn't look at me.

"Do you want a drink?"

His hands dropped. "Sure. Scotch would be great."

His moment of high drama had failed, but that was no reason to turn down a drink. I fixed his Scotch and freshened my Jack. Curling in a wing chair, I pointed to the sofa. "I need to talk to you about Renata."

"It was over between us a long time ago." He sighed. "It was the damn play. We had to work together each night. You can't imagine the hell it was."

He was wrong; I could. Renata would have punished him each night because their love had died. I wasn't interested in Graf's love life, though. I had to be certain he didn't know anything about her death.

"Graf, did she ever mention anyone who might want to hurt her?"

"Other than the crazy dog woman, and Bobbe Renshaw, and Keith and Sir Alfred, because she was outshining him, of course, and me, for the same reason, and the sound system guy. And the lighting guy. Oh, yeah, the head caterer in Reno." He put his drink down and threw up his hands. "Renata thought everyone was out to get her."

I sipped my drink. "Someone went to a lot of trouble to set me up." I told him about the person who'd gone to the feed store to buy poison.

"Someone impersonating you?" He leaned forward, concern etched into his forehead. "That really makes you look guilty, you know."

"So guilty that if I don't find out who did this, I won't be going to Hollywood. I'll be going to the women's prison for a long, long time. I don't think they'll let me out to do films."

"What can I do?"

He looked so genuinely worried that I felt a pang where my heart cracked just a little more. Coleman should be sitting here with me, worry on *his* face. My heart might snap and pop, but with each new pain, it was hardening toward Coleman. Soon, he wouldn't have the power to hurt me anymore.

"You were . . . close to Renata once," I prompted. "Someone must really have hated her to poison her. I don't think it was someone from Zinnia. No one here knew her except as a famous actress. The killer had to come from her past."

He swirled the ice in his glass as he thought. "That sounds logical, but I honestly can't think of anyone. The technical people on the show have come and gone. Renata was hard on them. She was demanding and ungrateful and difficult. They'd quit and move on to less stressful jobs. None of them would come to Zinnia to kill her."

"What about . . . romantic partners?"

He stood up and went to the fireplace. His face was blocked from my view. "In the last year, Renata changed. She simply wasn't interested in romance. It was like a switch flipped." He turned, his face in shadow and the fire crackling behind him. "It was overnight. I never understood what happened."

Graf was vain and preoccupied with himself, but I could see Renata had hurt him. I knew what it felt like when someone grew suddenly cold — like a switch had been flipped. That was the exact description of Coleman's behavior toward me.

"I'm sorry. You really loved her, didn't you?"

He cleared his throat. "I loved her talent and her passion for the stage. There were times I didn't like her at all. Beneath that, though, she was professional and extremely talented. I did love that."

"After you two broke up, there wasn't anyone else?"

"Not to my knowledge. And I assure you, Renata would have rubbed my nose in it good and hard." He drained his glass and walked to the sideboard. His hands were elegant as he made the drink. I couldn't help but admire how each movement was clean, defined. He was made for the stage. Or the screen.

Yet I had the sense he was hiding something from me. "Did you have other involvements?"

He didn't look up. "Yes."

I hadn't expected such honesty.

He picked up his drink and faced me. "I was hurt, and I lashed out by picking up women. I let Renata know that I wasn't alone and wouldn't ever be. Here in Zinnia, she kept throwing your name up at me, taunting me with innuendos."

I was more curious as to why he'd told me the truth, so I asked. "Why are you being so honest?"

"Once the finger of blame moves from you, it might swing in my direction. If I have to hire you to take my case, I don't want to start off with a lie."

And I'd vainly thought it was because he didn't want us to start up a relationship on a lie. Would I never learn? "Was there any reason you'd want Renata dead?"

"Absolutely not."

There was the sound of tapping at the front door. Tinkie. What in the world would bring her out this late after the schedule she was keeping at The Club and trying to help me solve the case?

I excused myself and opened the front door. Tinkie was huddled in her fake leopard fur, hopping from foot to foot. "Let me in, I'm freezing," she said as she brushed past me. "I know Graf is here and I don't care if I'm interrupting something."

She went to the parlor and straight to the sideboard. I heard ice tinkle into a glass. "The olives are in the refrigerator," I said.

"Thanks." She hurried through the dining room and into the kitchen and returned with the jar of jalapeño stuffed olives and proceeded to make a vodka martini.

She took a long swallow and blew out her breath. "That's much better." She looked from Graf to me. "Planning your film debut?"

I shook my head. "We're talking about Renata. About her past, and anyone who might have hated her enough to kill her."

"Have you heard from Coleman?" she asked.

I shook my head, wondering why she'd bring him up in front of Graf. One minute she was throwing me at Graf and the next she was tossing Coleman between us.

"I spoke with Gordon." Her voice was quiet, my first hint that something was seriously wrong.

"And?"

"They operated on Connie. The tumor was larger than they anticipated."

My mouth and throat went numb. "How bad?"

"She hasn't regained consciousness. Coleman is staying with her tonight in the hopes that she'll wake up."

"What's the prognosis?"

"The doctors really don't know. The tumor isn't malignant. It's a matter of how much damage was done before it was caught."

"How is Coleman holding up?" I glanced at Graf, who had the good sense to remain silent.

"Stoic. You know Coleman."

I'd offered to be there with him. I should be there with him, but he'd made it clear I wasn't part of his life.

"I'm going to Jackson," Tinkie said. "I stopped by to tell you. Someone needs to be with him now, and I don't know that he has anyone."

"I'll get my coat." I was already moving across the room when her words stopped me.

"You can't, Sarah Booth. You can't be with him. You can't leave Sunflower County. You can't jeopardize his reputation by showing up at the hospital where his wife may be dying."

Tinkie didn't mean to be cruel, but her words were like a slap. I was momentarily stunned.

Tinkie drained her glass, put it on the sideboard, and came to put her arm around my waist. "I'll call you as soon as I know something. I'll tell him you wanted to be there."

She stood on tiptoe, kissed my cheek, and hurried into the cold, trailing the rich fragrance of Opium.

CHAPTER 10

Somewhere along the line, Graf had learned patience. He kissed my cheek and left on Tinkie's heels. I was alone, and this time I didn't want to talk to Jitty.

I paced the parlor, prowled the kitchen, scuttled around the upstairs, and finally dressed and went outside in the cold. Reveler called a greeting as he caught sight of me and cantered up. I gave him the carrots I'd brought and led him into the barn. The moon was full — the light plenty bright to see as long as I stayed to roads I knew and kept a sensible pace. It would be bitter at first, but we'd all warm up in a matter of no time.

Sweetie bayed and barked and otherwise signaled her pleasure as I mounted. I wanted a look at my home in the silvery light of the moon, while I pondered my debt to the land.

The current trend was a lack of attachment to land. I'd seen families who'd farmed the same acreage for eight generations sell out and end up with asphalt for a super store covering the soil that had once sustained them.

The Delta had few enough trees left in places, but a shady oak or a loaded pecan was nothing to a developer. If I moved away from Zinnia, what would become of Dahlia House?

Maybe a garden club would turn it into a historic home, like the beautiful places in Natchez. The problem with that is tourism was nonexistent in Zinnia. Preservation is a costly hobby.

I could keep the estate and hire workers to maintain it — as Graf suggested. An empty home on empty land. My fingers tightened on the reins.

Now the fields were barren, the last crop turned under. Soon the huge machines would crawl across the acreage with fertilizer — another whole issue to worry about. But the land grew things like no other land. It was made to grow. So what if I allowed it to return to a natural state. Dahlia House would slowly decay among the tangle of vines, a sad but dignified death.

All of that on the condition that I'd make enough money to pay off the mortgage on

Dahlia House. If I didn't get the murder charge removed and get back to work, the bank would own Dahlia House and I'd have no say whatsoever in her future.

Tired of my morbid behavior, Reveler picked up the pace. We'd come upon a clear, sandy path that went all around the cotton fields. The weather had been dry, and the footing was excellent as we trotted through the bright winter night, turning back at last to Dahlia House, where the front lights bid me welcome.

By the time I got Reveler untacked and rubbed down, it was nearly three a.m. Sweetie had gone in and out of her doggy door a dozen times, letting me know that she'd worked up an appetite. She could eat her weight in groceries and never gain an ounce.

Reveler was good and cooled out when I gave him a small portion of grain, and I went inside to scavenge for me and my hound.

The answering machine was bare of calls, so I knew Tinkie had no news on Connie. I made a peanut butter sandwich and hot chocolate for myself and gave Sweetie some leftover roasted chicken. We settled in the kitchen for our feast, and I'd just taken a huge bite when the phone rang.

"Hello," I mumbled.

"Connie just woke up," Tinkie said. "She recognized Coleman, so that's a good sign."

"That's good." I fought the peanut butter that stuck to the roof of my mouth.

"Are you crying?" Tinkie asked.

"Uh-uh. Peanut butter."

"It's four a.m.!" Tinkie was outraged. "What are you doing eating peanut butter at this time of morning. Keep it up, and you won't fit into your mother's clothes for the rest of the play."

I looked at the sandwich. Peanut butter was a good source of protein. It wasn't so bad. I took another, small bite. "Okay, I'll throw it away."

"Good. Now let me tell you about Coleman. He looks like death warmed over. I'm really worried about him, Sarah Booth. He acts like a zombie."

I thought my heart had grown hard toward the man who'd broken it, but Tinkie was making me feel bad for Coleman. "I'm hurting, too," I pointed out.

"You're eating PB and J. Coleman looks like he hasn't eaten in a week."

Oh, poor him. "Look, I'm not in the mood to hear how hard Coleman has it."

There was a long silence. "That's good, because he's transferring Connie to the hospital in Zinnia so he can return to his duties. Since you don't care about him anymore, that shouldn't bother you a bit."

"Right. He and Connie can do whatever they want."

"And you and Graf are tripping off to Hollywood, right?"

"Maybe." She was making me mad and pushing me into a corner where I didn't want to go. If she kept it up, I'd be packed and gone by Sunday morning.

"Well, good then."

I could hear the hurt in her voice. "Hold on a minute. I'm not certain what I'll do, but I'm not doing anything with a murder charge hanging over my head."

"If it weren't for that, you'd go, wouldn't you?"

For all that Tinkie wanted me to have my dream, she was feeling a little abandoned. Finding Graf at Dahlia House had brought it all home for her. "I honestly don't know. I don't know what to do."

"I don't want to stop you, Sarah Booth, but I don't want you to go!" She was almost wailing.

"I haven't made any plans," I confessed, "but we'll work it out together."

"I'm coming home. Coleman is staying for the ambulance to take Connie in the morning."

"Wouldn't it be better to get a hotel room and wait until daylight to drive?" I asked. Tinkie sounded tired and upset.

"I don't want to wait."

Well, that was a Daddy's Girl's prerogative. "Be careful." I replaced the phone and finished my sandwich. Licking the grape jam from my fingers, I headed up to bed.

I awoke Tuesday morning when the sun was high in the sky. It had to be nearly noon, and for a moment panic touched my heart. Sweetie never let me sleep late. Nor Jitty. Then I remembered that Sweetie was tired from our midnight ride, but I had no idea why Jitty was being so considerate.

My thoughts were on Coleman and Connie as I bathed, dressed, and prepared for my day. I was absolutely numb — and I wanted to keep it that way. My future was at stake, and I intended to clear my name.

First on the agenda was a trip to the feed store. Neil Sheffield would tell me what he knew, and soon Nancy would be in to work. As a work study student, she got out of high school early.

The day was cold and bright, and I bundled up in an old sweatshirt and a heavy jacket. Knit hats had a ridiculous habit of shooting off my head, so I opted for a beautiful magenta scarf that my Aunt Lou-Lane had knitted for me when I was in college. Like my parents, she now slept in the family cemetery. As I wrapped the warm knit around my ears and throat, I gave her a silent thanks.

Sheffield's was a hopping place. Farmers from fifty miles around came to buy seed and fertilizer, feed and supplies. Neil was a handsome man with an easy grin and a quick humor. His knowledge of blues music was legendary, and he kept a state-of-the-art sound system in the feed store, playing the Mississippi greats like Muddy Waters and B.B. King.

I picked up some vitamins and hoof treatment for Reveler as I waited for my turn at the counter. I hoped for a moment alone.

When old man Barnaby had paid for his two bags of chicken scratch and left, I stepped forward.

"Sorry to hear about your troubles, Sarah Booth." Neil shook his head. "I know Coleman knows better. What's wrong with that man?"

"I don't know, but I need to talk to you about Nancy."

"I heard she said you came in to buy poison. I wish I'd known what she intended to say, because I would've stopped her."

His kindness made me feel better, even if we both knew he couldn't have stopped anything. "I never asked for poison, and I wasn't here that day."

"Neither was I. I'd gone up to Clarksdale. Nancy admitted she didn't get a good look at you. She *assumed* it was you because you talked about Reveler and the hound."

"Did she express any doubt to you?"

He sighed. "Just the opposite. I think I questioned her so closely it made her stubborn. Now she's determined to say it was you. I'm sorry. I was trying to help."

This wasn't good news. "Would you care if I spoke with her?"

"Not at all." He checked his watch. "She'll be here in five minutes or so. She's a punctual girl."

True to his word, the buzzer sounded when the front door opened and Nancy stepped into the store. She took one look at me and headed for the restroom in the back.

"Nancy, I'm not angry!" I went after her. I had to catch a break in this case and fast. "I just want to ask some questions."

She turned around. "And I want to ask you one. Why are you trying to make me out as a liar?"

Now it was my turn to start. "I'm only

trying to find out the truth."

"Then tell it! You came in and asked for poison. We didn't have it, and you left."

I took a deep breath. Getting angry or frustrated wouldn't do any good. Nancy wasn't lying; she'd been played and now her reputation was on the line. I had to win her over in an effort to counter the damage she'd dealt me.

"I believe someone came in here and *pretended* to be me. I know you saw me — or at least someone who looked a lot like me. That person meant for you to believe it was me."

My reasoned words at least had her thinking. She was a pretty girl. I'd made it a point to know she was the oldest of five kids and an absentee father. She wasn't a person who liked her word questioned because responsibility defined her.

"You were wearing a big old gardening hat." Her tone was stubborn.

I nodded. "I don't own such a hat. In all the times you've seen me here in the store, have I ever worn such a hat?"

"Usually you look like you've been cleaning the stalls — T-shirts and paddock boots. Never anything as nice as that hat." She was nodding.

"The voice sounded like mine?"

She dragged her bottom teeth across her upper lip. "Enough so I didn't think any more about it."

"And I asked for some poison to kill raccoons?"

"That 'bout made me fall off the ladder. I've heard you talk about animals before, and you'd never hurt one. Not even a raccoon."

Thank God, she was thinking now. She'd inched back off her story and begun to look for another interpretation. I pressed my point home. "If you can say that *maybe* that person wasn't me, do you think you would know her if you saw her again?"

Her eyes closed. "I'm not sure. I just caught a glimpse of her cheek."

I pulled the photographs of Kristine Rolofson and Bobbe Renshaw from my purse. I'd found them on the Internet, and though the quality wasn't professional, the prints were good likenesses of the women.

"Neither of them," she said with teenage certainty.

"How can you be so sure?" I forced myself to be calm.

"Well, if it was one of them, they wore a wig 'cause the woman who came in here had hair the same color as yours. I saw it curling out from beneath the hat."

Great. I put the pictures away. Both women could easily have access to a wig. And most likely, they'd destroyed the hairpiece. "Thanks, Nancy." I picked up my purchases and headed for the roadster, no closer to finding the truth than I had been.

The Sunflower County Courthouse contains the sheriff's department as well as the chancery and circuit clerks and their courtrooms. The serious business of felons is carried on upstairs, while divorce court proceeds on the lower levels in a smaller addition that had been tacked onto the building in 1974.

I'd hoped that Coleman's divorce proceedings would take place in that courtroom. Not likely now. I went to the sheriff's office, praying that he was still at the hospital with Connie. I needed to ask Gordon some questions about forensics in the case. I could have waited for Tinkie, but I was tired of waiting, tired of hoping someone else could unknot the tangle of my life. I'd played the shocked and innocent victim for too long; it was time for me to be an investigator.

"What about the lipstick tube?" I asked as I walked in the door.

Gordon looked up from a report he was

typing. "I'm not sure I'm supposed to give forensic evidence to the accused." He reached for the phone, but I was quicker. "Don't call Coleman. It'll only make it harder on him. If you don't tell me, Tinkie will just come in and get the info, and she'll tell me."

He looked doubtful.

"You know I didn't do this, Gordon. All I'm asking for is the stuff my lawyer will get anyway."

Shuffling through the papers on his desk, Gordon pulled out a sheet. He scanned it. "The lipstick contained enough poison to kill a person if it was licked off the lips."

"How in the hell would I get the cyanide into the lipstick in the first place. It would have had to have been mixed into the ingredients while it was being shaped."

Gordon nodded. "That's a problem. La Burnisco denies that this lipstick even came from their salon. They have no record of your purchase, Sarah Booth."

"I gave the receipt to Graf to give to Renata so I could be reimbursed. It has to be among her things." What a complete fool I'd been. The killer had probably picked it up off her dressing table, destroying the only physical thing that might back up my story.

"The DA can make a good case that you

produced this lipstick all on your own."

"Right, me and my little chemistry lab at home. What about fingerprints?"

"On the tube itself there are Renata's and Bobbe Renshaw's. No one else's."

"Have you spoken with Bobbe?"

"I'm going to see her after lunch."

"The cast and crew will be leaving in three days." The noose of time was tightening around my neck.

Gordon finally looked me in the eye. "I don't think so, Sarah Booth."

"What do you mean?" There would be no holding Keith Watley in Zinnia. He had bigger fish to fry and in his opinion, the only frying pan was in New York City.

"Coleman put me in charge of the case. With Connie so sick and all . . ." He cleared his throat. "Anyway, I'm in charge, and I'm not about to let my most prime suspects leave town."

My heart thudded. "You really believe one of the cast or crew did it?"

"Makes a lot more sense to my way of thinking, Sarah Booth. Let me line it out for you the way I see it." He was grinning big now, and I was, too.

"You didn't like Renata, and you wanted to play the part of Maggie. But in seven nights, those folks would be gone, and you'd be back in your life. If you still had the itch to be a Broadway star, I think you'd be in New York still trying."

Gordon's assessment of me made me proud. It's always interesting to see the picture someone else paints. "Thank you, Gordon."

He held up a hand. "On top of that, Renata might have pissed you off, but not enough to kill her. There are others in the cast and crew that she's done terrible things to. Like Renshaw and Milieu — they truly had reason to kill her."

I wasn't about to concur or disagree. I didn't want to shift the finger of blame from me to some other innocent person, and I didn't have the facts to begin to speculate.

"Go on, please."

"The most damning evidence is the lipstick and the poison in your car. You don't have any way to explain the lipstick with physical evidence, but the truth is, Renata asked for that particular lipstick and directed you to the store to get it. Nancy from the feed store called up and said she was having second thoughts about that being you who came in and asked for poison."

God bless Nancy!

"So the case is weakening?"

He nodded. "You're still charged, and I

don't have enough to drop the charges, but let's just say I'm continuing to investigate."

"Thank you, Gordon." I wanted to kiss his cheek but knew better. I looked around the office and felt a serious bolt of pain in my heart. Why couldn't it be Coleman who was standing here, telling me the reasons why I couldn't be guilty of murder?

Gordon picked up his hat. "Got to go, Sarah Booth. In the future, it would be more professional if Tinkie was the one who stopped by to chat."

"You got it," I said as I walked to the door.

CHAPTER 11

Tinkie waited until the show was over to drop the Connie-bomb on me. She'd insisted we drive to Clarksdale to eat at Madidi, a lovely upscale restaurant. I thought it was a long ride for a celebratory dinner and drink, but she wanted to get me alone in a very public place where I couldn't howl at the moon.

We'd finished our meals, and she had her cosmopolitan and I had a vodka martini. Around us, groups were dining and laughing. I recognized several sorority girls from Ole Miss. They'd aged with grace. Most were mothers, but their trim figures didn't give it away. They looked as sleek and hungry as New York models — the diamonds glittering on their ring fingers the symbolic designer label of an excellent marriage. I had to give it to the DGs on elegance. They had it in spades, and Madidi was the perfect place to show it off.

"I spoke with Coleman this afternoon," Tinkie said as she studied the pink perfection of her drink.

"I wondered what you were up to." I hadn't heard from Tinkie all afternoon. I'd assumed she was working on the case against me.

"Connie has no memory of any of her actions from the past year."

Anger bubbled in volcanic measure. "How freaking convenient!"

All around us the laughter stopped as people turned to look at me. While Tinkie could pass in this crowd, I was a definite outsider, and I was acting like one.

Tinkie put her hand on my wrist. "When they took out the tumor, they had to remove some healthy tissue. Or it could be that the tumor destroyed —"

"Tell me Coleman isn't buying this?" I couldn't believe what I was hearing, or the expression on Tinkie's face. She believed that Conniving Connie was actually telling the truth. This was the woman who'd faked mental illness, faked pregnancy — all to keep Coleman from leaving her. If he believed her now, he deserved to be saddled with her for the rest of his life.

"He doesn't believe Connie, but he does believe the doctor."

There it was. After the months of waiting, I was still standing alone as Coleman struggled in the web of Connie's deceit. I took a deep breath. "Fine."

"Sarah Booth, if Connie doesn't remember, can he hold her accountable? The doctor said the tumor might've made her behave so erratically."

"Tumor, malice, jealousy, vindictiveness, desperation." I ticked them off on my fingers. "What difference does it make? She did terrible things to him and to me."

"I think Coleman would rather be burned at the stake than lose you."

"He has a really funny way of showing it. Hey, I've got the perfect solution. Coleman can turn me over to the grand jury for a true bill on a murder charge. Then I can be tried and sent to prison, and he and Connie can live happily ever after. How's that?"

She patted my arm, and when I tried to withdraw it, she held on with grim determination. "I'm not the enemy here."

"You're just the messenger, I know. Next time let Coleman do his own dirty work."

Tears filled her eyes but didn't fall. "I'm sorry, Sarah Booth. I am. For you and for him."

"Save it, Tinkie. I made a bad decision. I made several of them. But I'm only thirty-four. If I don't go to prison for the rest of my life, I can make different choices."

She squeezed my arm. "I didn't want to tell you this, but I wanted you to have the facts. So when you make your choice about Hollywood, you can make it fully informed." She blinked the tears back and took a big swallow of her drink.

This wasn't Tinkie's fault, and I was treating her awful. She'd come to tell me the truth so I could make my plans to leave town — even though she didn't want me to go. She didn't want me clinging to the hope of Coleman as my reason to stay.

"Thanks for telling me, Tinkie. You're the best friend a gal could have."

She looked down at the table. "You should've left with Hamilton V. Then none of this would have happened. You wouldn't be charged with murder."

I finished my martini and signaled the waiter for another. Tinkie was driving, after all. "I should've done a lot of things differently."

She waited until I had my fresh drink before she spoke again. "I do have a tiny bit of good news."

"I could stand some of that." Now all the laughter around me sounded wrong, harsh. I wanted to belt down my drink and head home, but Tinkie was still sipping hers.

"I spoke with Cece today. She's been spending a lot of time with Gabriel Trovaioli, and she's pulled some interesting stuff from him."

"Like what?" I bit my olive in half.

"Renata started acting really strange about nine months ago. Gabriel said she'd never been all that close to him, but she began to call him almost every weekend."

"Did he say why?" I felt my interest perk up.

She shook her head. "Like she was trying to build some kind of connection is what he told Cece."

In the time I knew Renata in New York, she'd never mentioned a brother or any other family, for that matter. It was as if she'd sprung fully formed from the head of a God — at least in her opinion.

"He told Cece she'd become . . . almost tender toward him."

"Now that is creepy." Renata might be able to play tender on the stage, but I doubted she'd ever felt it. "And when, exactly, did she call and tell him I was trying to kill her?"

"The night before she died. It was after dress rehearsal. She told him you'd stopped her backstage and told her you were going to play Maggie no matter what you had to do to get there."

That was absurd. I wasn't even at The Club for the dress rehearsal. I told Tinkie so. "I don't think I spoke to Renata at all after I ran her errand. I put some flowers in her dressing room, but I didn't see her."

"Renata singled you out, Sarah Booth. She made sure you were the prime suspect in her death. It's like she's reaching out from the grave —"

I leaned forward, suddenly clear on something that I had overlooked. "The person who went into Sheffield Feed Store asking for poison was Renata. She was pretending to be me. She could pull it off, too, with a young girl who was stocking shelves on a ladder."

Tinkie nodded. "I see that. But why?"

That, indeed, was the sixty-four-million-dollar question.

Sweetie's wet tongue licked me awake Wednesday morning, and I sat up and pulled the quilts around me. The temperature had dropped during the night. Dahlia House was cool in the summer, and it could be downright cold in the winter. I looked out the window to see frost glistening across the fields and icing the tree leaves. Sunlight glittered in blinding diamonds, and I jumped out of bed and rushed to the bathroom. In no time at all, I was showered, dressed, and ready for the day. Somewhere in the arms of Morpheus I'd found new hope. For proving my innocence, if not my future with Coleman. Emulating Jitty's latest role model, I would worry about Coleman tomorrow.

While the coffee brewed, I phoned Millie, Cece, and Tinkie. I needed a meeting of the three smartest women I knew. Breakfast at Millie's was just a bonus.

We gathered in the back of the café and waited until Millie had a break in the flow of customers so she could join us. When we were all seated with coffee and our various menu selections, I cleared my throat.

"I don't know who killed Renata, but I do know that she — Renata — deliberately framed me for her death."

"That doesn't make sense," Cece drawled. "If she knew someone was going to kill her, wouldn't she have called the police instead of building a frame?"

During the night my active subconscious had done its work. "In a normal person, yes. But Renata was far from normal. She hated me for reasons I'll never understand. It is hard to swallow that she'd *let* herself be killed just to frame me, so there has to be more to this. This is where y'all come in."

"What can we do?" Millie asked. She was always first on the line to help a friend.

"I think the question that must be answered is why Renata allowed herself to be poisoned. Was someone blackmailing her? There has to be more to this."

"Right." They all spoke in unison, and I saw from their expressions that they were actually buying into what I was saying.

"Tell us your plan," Tinkie requested.

"Cece, can you pump Gabriel for any signs of fear or depression in Renata in the past few months?"

"You got it, dahling. But the order of pumping is somewhat reversed, don't you think?"

I rolled my eyes. "Millie, if you have all those back tabloids, can you go through them to see any gossip that might hint at trouble somewhere in her life?"

"Absolutely. And you're in luck. I have issues that go back two years, at least."

"Tinkie, we need the toxicology report from the sheriff's department, and see if you can weasel any useful information out of Gordon."

"I'm on it." She studied me carefully. "What are you going to do?"

"I'm going to talk to Bobbe Renshaw and Kristine Rolofson. They were both at the theatre the night Renata died. They've been with Renata, in a manner of speaking, for the past year or so. Maybe they saw something."

"And Graf?" Tinkie asked the question that everyone else was thinking. Aside from me, Graf was the most obvious suspect.

"Can you poke around in Graf's financial business? We might find something useful there, and you're the woman for figures."

"Good." We stood up all together, like the four musketeers.

"Let's meet this afternoon at Dahlia House," I suggested. "Millie, can you get off?"

She untied her apron and put it on the table. "Even better. I'm going home right now to start looking through those tabloids. I'll call Annie to come in and take over. I haven't had a day off since last summer, and I'm due one."

My friends were giving up their time to help me. Whatever I might find in Hollywood, it would be no substitute for this.

"Thank you."

Kristine had taken a room at a local motel that allowed pets. Gertrude Strom at The

Gardens had a no-pet policy, and the old bat wouldn't make any exceptions, so it was the Crossroads Motel where I found Kristine, ready to take Giblet for a walk.

The little reddish gold pooch was glad to see me and gave me a warm welcome when Kristine opened the door to my knock. "I'm surprised you're still in town," I said.

"I'm surprised you're not in jail." She opened the door wide. "But any person who might have killed Renata is a friend of mine. Come in."

The room was neat and her clothes were packed, as if she did plan on leaving. "The sheriff asked me to stay in town," she said. "I'm hoping as soon as the show closes he gives us the okay to leave. Now that Renata is dead, I have to get on with my new mission in life. I've spent the last year trying to make her accountable for the hit-and-run." She sighed. "I'm going after the New York state legislature next. Try to get some laws enacted to protect animals."

It was a noble chore she'd assumed. Her attitude told me one thing — she wasn't anticipating that she'd be held here in Zinnia for murder.

"Kristine, I know the sheriff has questioned you, but would you mind talking with me?"

"Not at all. Could we walk while we talk?"

"Sure." My paddock boots were comfortable for walking, and the day, though cold, was sunny and dry. She put Giblet on a lead and we headed out the door at a brisk pace.

"You've followed Renata for the past year," I said. "In the last few months, have you noticed anything different in her conduct?"

Kristine didn't answer immediately. "You know, she did seem to change a little."

"How so?"

"When I threw water on her to see if she'd melt, she did something very strange."

My heart rate increased, and not from the pace Kristine set. "What?"

"She turned to me, and her face was almost expressionless. Normally she had the visage of a Harpy, but she just looked cold. And she said, 'When I'm gone, your life won't have any meaning.' And then she drove away."

I pondered those words, reminiscent of the Richard M. Nixon speech to the press before he resigned as president. So was Renata thinking of retiring, or was it something more sinister?

"What did you make of it?"

"To be honest, I was so delighted at the thought that I'd helped to drive her out of work that I didn't really think about what she said. But now, with her death and all . . ." She turned to me, "Do you think someone had threatened her even then?"

I could only hope that was the case, and that I could prove it. "When was this?"

"In Atlantic City. That's why I've had time to come up with my new plan of action to help protect innocent animals from reckless drivers. Once Renata hinted she was leaving, I set about finding another venue."

"That was smart." I wasn't really thinking about Kristine's venues. I was wondering what might have prompted Renata to say such a revealing thing to a woman she no doubt hated. "Tell me more about your relationship with Renata," I requested.

"After Giblet was released to travel, we loaded up and drove to Atlantic City where the show was being staged. My husband left me very well off financially, so I didn't have to work, and I certainly could afford to pay the $5,000 in veterinarian bills for Giblet. It wasn't the money, it was the principle."

I knew about principles. They made life difficult but also put the spine in people.

"The first night I slipped Giblet backstage, and at the most inopportune time, I let her free on the stage. She went right to Renata and peed on her leg. It brought the house down."

I couldn't help but laugh out loud, though I barely had wind to do it. The pace Kristine and Giblet set was working my butt off.

"I had a stuffed dog made to look just like Giblet, and I recorded Giblet growling and barking. On another night, as the first act closed, I slipped the stuffed dog and the tape recorder into her dressing room. She was terrified to go inside. It delayed the opening of the second act."

I admired Kristine. She was an animal activist of the number one order.

"Did you ever actually talk to Renata about what happened?"

"I did. I asked for an apology. That's all I really wanted. I wanted her to admit that what she did was wrong."

"And she wouldn't?"

She slowed to allow Giblet to water a clump of weeds. "She laughed in my face and told me if my 'ugly mop of fur' got in front of her car again, she'd finish the job."

Typical Renata conduct.

"That's when I vowed to make her life a living hell as long as I could. So I devised guerrilla tactics to thwart her. Giblet and I have picketed every performance of her show since I got to Atlantic City. We give interviews, and whenever possible we get other animals lovers to join us. It's been highly successful."

"And all because she wouldn't say she was sorry for hitting your dog."

Kristine stopped completely. "She wasn't sorry, Sarah Booth. Not a bit. That's what made me so furious. She truly didn't care what she'd done."

I couldn't defend Renata. I was saddened by her complete lack of compassion for a living creature and the human who suffered, too.

"I didn't poison her," I said. "Do you know anyone who might have done it?"

We turned to head back to the motel. "So many people hated her. One night when I was picketing, I heard her get into it with Graf Milieu. Boy, she didn't hold any punches."

"What did she say?"

"She had something on Graf. Something big. And she was holding it over his head, forcing him to do something for her that he didn't want to do."

"Do you remember what?"

"It wasn't clear. It had to do with money and Mexico, but that's all I really heard. I felt sorry for Mr. Milieu. He was always so nice to me and Giblet. He brought treats for my baby."

"Money and Mexico?" I spoke the words aloud, but my thoughts were too rapid to catch hold of for speech. Graf had once talked about a hacienda in Mexico. Perhaps he and Renata had purchased one. It was something to check into. As well as the rest of Renata's will. Who had she left her considerable fortune to? Those who inherit are always up for suspicion. The logical heir would be Gabriel, but he hadn't been in town until after Renata was dead — at least as far as I knew.

"That's all I know," Kristine said. "I hope some of it was helpful."

"Possibly more than you think." I stopped in the parking lot. "Thanks, Kristine. For the information and the walk."

On the way to my car, I slipped out my cell phone and called Cece.

"Can you find out where Gabriel was the entire week before Renata died?" We'd assumed he was a new arrival in town, but assumptions could be deadly in a murder case.

"You bet." She hung up, and I headed back to town.

CHAPTER 12

Bobbe Renshaw was packing her makeup kits when I walked into the backstage area at The Club. A trash can beside her was full of cosmetics she'd tossed, and I noticed they were all Renata's. "I guess the sheriff's office has been through all of that." I pointed to the trash can.

"They've taken samples of everything, tested everything." She picked up the can. "Here, keep it if you want to be certain. I want every last reminder of that woman gone from my life."

"What are you going to do now?" I asked. Bobbe kept her attention on her work and didn't answer. "Go home to your family?"

"For a little while. Danny will go on the road again in the spring, and I might go, take the kid." She shrugged. "It's not as much fun as it was when we didn't have Little A." She saw my puzzled look. "Adam."

"I can imagine." But I really couldn't. Touring in a bus with a bunch of sometimes drunk, sometimes stoned rocksters was a tough life even for a young, single person. For a mom and a toddler, it would be sheer hell.

"No chance at ABC?"

She looked me in the eye. "That's doubtful. Why? You volunteering to write me a letter of recommendation?"

I laughed, and finally, she joined me. "I doubt a letter from a suspected murderer would do you a lot of good, but I'll write one. You've done a great job on my makeup."

She perched a hip on the vanity counter and began to swing a long, shapely leg back and forth. "You know, I got a bum rap hanging out with Danny and the band. Everyone thought I was a drug addict, that I serviced all the guys. It was never like that. Maybe I did too good a job on the makeup, because none of the guys do heavy drugs. None. They drank some, smoked a J now and then. At least that's all I ever saw. Danny grew up with his dad screwed up all the time, and his mom an alcoholic. When I got pregnant with Little A, he stopped drinking completely. Not even a beer, until I got stuck on the road like this." A heavy mark drew her brows together. "That bitch Renata."

This was the most I'd ever heard Bobbe talk. Since she was in the mood to reveal, I asked a leading question.

"How'd you hook up with Renata?"

Her laugh was bitter. "I went to see a play with a girlfriend of mine. We went backstage to congratulate the cast, and I ended up in front of her. Her makeup shade was all wrong, and I just blurted it out."

I could imagine Renata's reaction. She probably belted Bobbe. "And?"

"She was furious. She called security and had me thrown out the stage door. It was all pretty humiliating, but then, I figured I'd opened my mouth and inserted my foot, so I got what was coming to me."

"Until . . ."

"Two days later I got a phone call. She figured out who I was, traced the band, got me that way. She asked me to come and redo her makeup for the show."

"And history was made." I twirled a sable brush that Bobbe used with such artistry. "She looked great in the show."

"She looked great every night. I made sure of that. At first it was a trip, traveling with the show. And my job was so much easier than with the band. I mean, this was regular stage makeup. No special effects, no limb regeneration. It was a piece of cake."

"Until you wanted to leave, right?"

She got up and paced the room. "I got pregnant, and I had terrible morning sickness. I kept working until time to deliver, and that's when I applied at ABC. I was set to take the job when Little A was four months old."

"Renata lied about you."

"In a big, big way. I never so much as stole a salt shaker or a candy bar. It was the meanest thing she could think of to do to ruin it for me. Now, I'm branded a thief."

It was tough to be falsely accused. I was walking a mile in those shoes.

"ABC withdrew the job?"

"With cause. They told me because they're so sensitive about lawsuits. Renata didn't expect that. She thought she'd malign me, and I'd never know."

"How could you work for her all these months?" I was amazed.

"Danny was nearly electrocuted during a show. His guitar was hot, and the nerves in his right hand were damaged."

She didn't have to draw a picture. He couldn't play the guitar if his hand was injured.

"He's been in rehab all this time, trying to

keep it secret from the press. I mean, he's like thirty-two. Virtually over the hill for a rocker. It can't get out that he's injured, even if it's only temporary."

"My lips are sealed." Thirty-two! Over the hill! Yikes. I was practically sitting with my legs dangling in a grave.

"I *had* to hang onto the job, because I couldn't get another with a thievery charge hanging over me. This was the only income we had, and I didn't know where Renata would smear me next."

Renata had held Bobbe by the short hairs and hadn't batted an eye at such unethical behavior. The prima donna got what she wanted, and that was all that mattered.

"The thing that kept me going was knowing the show would close this week. I marked the days off a calendar, like a person in prison. I tried to focus on one day at a time. And then Renata died, and you took the role. It's been a pleasure, Sarah Booth."

"Well, thanks." How hard was it to be nice to someone who was a major talent and made me look good? "Did you notice anything unusual about Renata the last few months?"

"Big time. She would never admit it, but she went somewhere for Botox injections. The last few weeks, she could barely change expressions."

"Did she see a doctor?" I couldn't imagine Renata, with all her bucks, going for black market treatment. I would've figured her for a strictly 90210 doctor.

"I have no idea. I never heard her say, but I didn't keep up with her. All I know is that she couldn't move her eyebrows and the corners of her mouth were sort of . . . frozen in place."

"That's a high price to pay for vanity."

"She was aging. She used to sit and stare at herself in the mirror, pulling at her skin, examining the color of her hair for gray. She was obsessed with it."

I'd spent a few hours searching for gray and lifting my skin up. The first-blush peachiness of youth had slipped from my features, but I was a long, long way from Botox. "Did she have a treatment here, in Zinnia?"

"She must have."

"She never mentioned a doctor?"

"Not to me. I wasn't a confidante. I was the paid help."

Right. I'd forgotten that Renata lived in a class-conscious world that was as bad as anything the Delta had ever concocted. "I'll check around."

There were plenty of plastic surgeons in

Jackson and Memphis, and a few scattered in the Delta. My bets were on Memphis, though. That's where the makeup came from, and that's where Renata probably had contacts.

"Did you ever hear anyone threaten Renata?"

"Only everyone in the cast and crew at some point. Most of it behind her back. She and Graf were going at it like cats and dogs most of the time." She paused. "Keith Watley almost stroked out last week about something she said to him. He told her he was going to kill her with his bare hands."

Renata made people dislike her. Whether it was deliberate or not, she certainly brought it on herself. "Did you notice any strangers hanging around?"

"There was a man in Reno, but she frightened him away with one of her temper fits."

"A name?"

"Buster Long. He was a cute, older man with these amazing muttonchop whiskers. I thought at first they were fake, but they were real. He let me tug on them."

I couldn't help my expression. Bobbe scratched to a verbal halt. "What's wrong?"

"How old was this guy?"

"He looked to be in his sixties, but he had to be younger. I saw him picking up some suitcases, and he was pretty spry."

"He showed up in Reno?"

"That's right. But she ran him off before we came down here."

"You don't remember where he was from?"

She shook her head. "I'm sorry. I wrote him off as a chump, one of those guys who fall for a stage star and live in a fantasy."

"Bobbe, is there any of the original tube of Almond Mocha Retreat left in Renata's makeup?"

"That's what was so strange. I'd been doing her makeup for the whole show and suddenly she has to have this particular lipstick in that particular shade." She threw up her hands. "What a bitch. She'd done all the shows before without it. I'd never heard of the stuff."

I took a deep breath. A lot of things continued to add up — to a very well-planned murder.

While I was at The Club, I went to the bar to talk to the barkeep, Bernard, until I could find Sir Alfred Bascomb. I thought he might be in the dining room for lunch. It was a well-known fact that Sir Alfred liked his vittles, and the chef at The Club was renowned.

"You don't look good, Sarah Booth." Bernard put an icy glass of diet drink in front of me. "How are you holding up?"

"Okay. How's Molly?" Bernard's wife, Molly, was an old family friend and the exceptional seamstress for my gown for the Black and Orange Ball. She'd also been pressed into service to make alterations and repair costumes for the play.

"She's backstage, mending something right now. She saw the play last night." His smile was radiant. "We both did. Sarah Booth, your mama would be so proud of you."

"Thanks, Bernard. Do you really think?"

"Yes, ma'am, I sure do. Your mama had a little bit of the actress in her. She could be dramatic when the need arose. I remember, when you were still in diapers, she taught you to sing and dance. You'd perform these little numbers . . ." His laughter was like a warm kiss. "Folks couldn't help but smile when they saw them. And you loved it! Your mama encouraged you, Sarah Booth. If she were alive, she'd be on the front row every night, clapping herself silly with your daddy right beside her."

The gift Bernard gave me was greater than he'd ever know. I was so young when my parents were killed that I had no real idea how they might view my adult activities. Bernard made me believe they would approve, and God knows I craved their approval. "Thank you, Bernard." I stood on the rungs of my stool and leaned across the bar to plant a kiss on his cheek.

"You take care, Sarah Booth. That mean woman put you in a fine pickle. I heard her in here on her cell phone, planning and plotting."

I eased back down in my seat. "Plotting what?"

"She hated you. She was talking on her cell phone, laughing about her plan. I didn't realize at the time that her plan was to make folks believe you'd killed her." His gray eyebrows drew together in a frown. "She was talking to someone about lipstick and how she'd make sure you picked it up."

I didn't really have to ask, but I did anyway. "Bernard, if it comes to it, would you testify to that?"

"On a stack of Bibles. I already told the sheriff."

"Any idea who she was talking to?"

"It was a man. I was serving her a drink, and I heard him laughing."

"Thanks." I put a five on the bar for the cola and headed toward the dining room.

Sir Alfred was already ensconced in a table

with a view of the garden. The camellias had just begun to bud out, vibrant pinks and variegated blossoms against the dark green of the leaves. These are the winter flowers that grace the lawn of every old plantation home in the South. From the small, pale pinks to the lush, tropical blooms, they mark the closing of winter.

"Amazing that they bloom even in the cold," Sir Alfred said, waving me into a seat. "Ms. Delaney, I'm glad to see you. I've wanted to tell you how greatly I admire your talent."

Sir Alfred wasn't known for his generosity with a compliment, and I couldn't help preening just a little. "Thank you, sir. It's been a pleasure to work with you." I meant every word. The part of Big Daddy was written for him, and though Sir Alfred could be exceptionally difficult, I'd seen none of it during this performance.

"How was it to work with Renata?" I asked.

"She was a terrible bitch, but it's a tough job, performing the same part for years. We were all tired, simply exhausted. The petty bickering that's always a part of a cast and crew had reached gargantuan proportions. We were all looking forward to the conclusion, and none more than Renata. I was honestly amazed when she urged all of us to accept the week here in Zinnia."

"Your contract would have ended in Reno, due to the destruction of the Gulf Coast?"

He nodded as he signaled a waiter. "Bloody Marys for both of us, please." He turned back to me, his thin, aristocratic face puzzled. "It was Renata who insisted we come here. Demanded, actually."

"Do you have any idea why?"

"None whatsoever. It's ironic, isn't it, that she came here to be murdered, and you got the chance to prove yourself a star."

Ironic didn't begin to describe it. "Sir Alfred, did Renata ever mention my name?"

"In fact she did. Not directly to me, but to Graf. Those two seemed to hate each other, and she told him that once we got to Zinnia he could start up his affair with his country bumpkin, that would be you, once again."

"What was Graf's reaction?" I didn't ask for the case but for my own ego.

"He walked away. She called after him, something to the effect that both of you would pay in ways you'd never see coming. How right she was about that."

"Too right to be merely a coincidence," I muttered.

The drinks arrived, and I sipped mine

while Sir Alfred ordered roasted pheasant soup and dill salad for lunch. My appetite was gone. Besides, I was due to meet the girls at Dahlia House.

Millie spread the articles she'd clipped across the kitchen table as Tinkie brewed a pot of coffee and put cream and sugar on the table.

"This is twelve months ago." She pointed at a photograph of Renata coming out of a plastic surgeon's office in Beverly Hills. The tabloid story speculated on the aspect of a face lift or some other procedure. But that's all it was, speculation. Better than a poke in the eye with a sharp stick, though, the article mentioned the doctor's name and with directory assistance, I had his number. Cece placed the call.

"Hello, Dr. Drake, this is Cece Dee Falcon with the *Zinnia Dispatch.*" She made it sound like the *London Times.* "I'm doing a story on the lately deceased Renata Trovaioli. The coroner's report suggests some problem with the use of Botox in Ms. Trovaioli's body, a type of toxic shock that may have come from cosmetic injections and —"

I could hear the doctor shouting.

"When was the last time you saw Ms. Trovaioli?" She wrote in her notepad. "You're certain of that? She never asked for Botox? Never had a procedure? Doctor, I have to warn you, if you're leading me astray, I'll make it my life's goal to document your stellar career to the stars. I'm sure most of your clientele would prefer to remain anonymous."

Cece knew how to threaten, and she had no qualms about doing it.

"I see." She arched an eyebrow at me. "Thanks, Dr. Drake."

She replaced the phone. "Renata never had surgery or Botox, at least from Drake. But he was hiding something, I just couldn't figure out what."

"Too bad we can't get his medical records." I slumped in my chair.

"I'm good, Sarah Booth, but I'm not that good." Cece slumped, too.

"Coleman could order them," Tinkie said.

Her comment fell into a total void of silence. No one looked at me. I got up and poured coffee, trying hard to hide the sudden wash of tears that threatened to ruin my perfect mascara.

CHAPTER 13

We'd finished our second pot of coffee, and I'd avoided an emotional meltdown in front of my friends. I looked around the kitchen table at the faces of the three women who'd become my family.

Tinkie's petite face glowed with all the health money could buy. It wasn't all creams and unguents, though. She had an inner beauty that came through. Somehow in the days since Halloween, Tinkie had found a belief in her own self pure and strong enough to dissolve a breast lump. She'd confronted her anger with Oscar and healed her past. She seemed happy and carefree. Her life had turned around.

Beside her was Millie. Maybe ten years older than the rest of us, Millie's face showed the years of hard work she'd put into the café and the terrible loss of her sister. Mixed with the lines were happiness and the knowledge that Millie's Café was the most thriving diner in the Delta. The tables and booths were occupied from dawn until nine p.m., when she closed the doors. Two women couldn't be more different than Tinkie and Millie, yet they were close friends. Tinkie had grown up with the proverbial silver spoon; Millie had been in the kitchen polishing it. Yet such a thing as class would never come between them, because neither woman acknowledged that it existed.

And Cece. Perhaps the most beautiful of all of us, yet born a man. She'd overcome obstacles that would have stopped a lesser person. She'd triumphed over a body that betrayed her, a family that disowned her, and a town that feared her power in the press yet viewed her as an abnormal outsider. Radiant didn't begin to describe her looks, and her taste was impeccable.

"Are you going to work, or are you going to stare into space like a stoned cowgirl?" Cece asked.

"I was thinking how fortunate I am to have such good friends. Such a wonderful family."

My words brought tears to Millie's eyes. "You girls are my family, too."

"Yes," Cece drawled, determined not to get sentimental. "Dahlia House is where I come when all the bars kick me out."

"Thank you all for standing by me." I held their gazes, unwilling to let the moment pass.

"Sounds to me like a farewell," Cece said. "Is Hollywood beckoning?"

I swallowed. "I don't know what to do about that. It's sort of moot, since I can't leave the county."

"Coleman will let you go." Tinkie was so positive. She got up and began to rummage through the refrigerator. "Don't you have anything sweet to eat? There's nothing in the fridge but molded cheese and something in a bread wrapper that's moving on the bottom shelf."

"Nine-grain. I knew that stuff had life." I laughed at her expression and went to the cabinet to find my last fruitcake from Christmas. I'd preserved it with Jack, so there was no danger it would be spoiled. I opened it and cut thick slices for all of us. The kitchen filled with the pleasant aroma of coffee and Jack Daniel's, the clatter of cutlery on glass, and the laughter of my friends. Could I leave this? I closed my eyes, no closer to an answer than I'd been the night before.

"Gabriel told me some very, very interesting things about Renata." Cece had the floor. "When they were children, they were abandoned by their parents. Renata stole food for them for almost six months before DHR finally got wind of them. They were destined to be split apart and sent to different foster homes, and Renata convinced the people who were taking her to take Gabriel, too."

It sounded almost as if Renata had once had a heart. I wasn't sure I wanted to hear more. It was easier to view her as unloving and unloved.

"She really was his big sister," Millie said, caught up in Cece's story.

"I wouldn't go that far." Cece's eyes sparked humor. "The foster parents were determined Renata would become a secretary. Gabriel they had lined up for a job at the state docks."

Both were good, solid jobs, but neither took into account the aspirations of the two children.

"When Renata hit sixteen, she didn't come home from school one day. She just walked out of their life. Gabriel wasn't allowed to say her name in the house. His foster parents told him she'd been killed on the streets. In effect, Gabriel lost his sister."

After Renata's selfless act in saving Gabriel, she'd shown her true colors and left him to fend for himself while she struggled with her own life. What could a sixteen-year-old do, though? I stopped my own thoughts and listened to Cece.

"Gabriel was nearly twenty when he realized Renata was still alive. He, too, had run away from home. He'd moved to Los Angeles, apprenticed to an architect, and was putting himself through college. He went to a play one night with a friend and saw a woman on the stage who bore a remarkable resemblance to his dead sister. Renata was using the name Selena Zafon at the time, but he recognized her and waited backstage to confront her."

Cece's story had us enthralled. "That must have been hard for him," Tinkie said.

"It was. He was furious. They had a terrible scene, and Renata told him to get lost. He said it took them a decade to get to the point where they could be civil to each other. When Renata hit it big on Broadway, she tried to patch up the relationship with Gabriel. He said it wasn't until just this past year, though, when he felt as if she cared about him. Prior to that, he felt he was an obligation."

"Did he say what changed in the past year?" I asked.

Cece considered. "Renata flew out to LA

to see him. She had appointments with other people. Not movie people. Someone in a medical center on Sunset Boulevard. He assumed she was having some work done, but she never did. She went to half a dozen appointments and then flew back out to New York to conclude *Cat.*"

"Maybe she was making future appointments for Botox treatments?" Tinkie posed the possibility.

"Maybe," I agreed. Renata was certainly vain enough, but she really was only thirty-six or so. Surely that was too young for Botox? "Did Gabriel remember what the doctor's name was on Sunset Boulevard? Since it wasn't Drake, maybe she used someone else."

Cece shook her head. "She wouldn't really talk about it with him, and since he thought it was vanity work, he didn't ask."

"I need a listing of medical practices there." It wasn't a great lead, but I was literally clutching at straws. I had to find out who'd really killed Renata and why. Maybe she was suing a doctor, and he'd sent a hit man to Mississippi. Doctors would know all about poisons.

"Right. Why not ask for all the Chins listed in a Chinese directory." Cece was always droll.

"Cece, you can get that for me, can't you? You have contacts at the *LA Times,*" I wheedled.

"Or you could look it up on the Internet." She arched an eyebrow.

"It would be much faster to go the regular phone book route." I wasn't going to let Cece off so easily.

"Okay. I'll try to get a more specific address from Gabriel. There could be a thousand doctors on Sunset Boulevard, and for all we know Renata was seeing a podiatrist or even a chiropractor."

She was right, but I was determined.

Tinkie cleared her throat. "The toxicology report on Renata was very interesting." She had our attention.

"Renata died of cyanide poisoning. The poison was found in the lipstick and around her lips. She obviously licked her lips and ingested it. There's no doubt she was deliberately poisoned. The lipstick had been dipped into a solution of the poison. Anyone could have done it."

I got up to make more coffee, afraid everyone would see my fear. The noose was tightening.

"There's more." Tinkie grasped my wrist as I walked by and pulled me back to the table.

"Do tell?" Cece was devouring every word, along with the last slice of fruitcake.

"I did a bit of checking on Graf Milieu. His finances are fascinating. For a man who makes a lot of money, he's so far in the red he won't ever see daylight, unless this movie deal comes off."

"Graf never could manage money." At the time I was with him in New York, I didn't let it worry me. I didn't have any money to mismanage. We were both poor and in love. But Graf had become a star in the last year. He was making six, maybe seven, figures. How could he still be so far behind the eight ball?

"It would seem Graf Milieu developed a fondness for Bolivian marching powder." Tinkie watched me closely.

"Drugs?" I couldn't believe it. Graf was too vain to mess with something that might negatively affect his looks. It would be more likely that he'd invested poorly.

"Serious drugs."

Tinkie's words stopped me. "That's nuts."

"I'm not saying he was using them. He was transporting them across the Mexican border and got caught."

"Graf?" He was an idiot about things. He thought he could bluff his way out of serious trouble, and he couldn't. He was just foolhardy enough to do something like try to smuggle drugs. "How in the hell did he get out of prison?"

Tinkie had been waiting for that question. "Renata. She paid off the Federales, got Graf back across the border, and she's been lording it over him ever since."

"No wonder he hated her." I remembered hearing about their backstage fights. It wasn't ego, it was Graf feeling the pinch of Renata's talons. "How much?"

"She paid $300,000 to get him out of jail. There's no telling how many palms she greased on his way back to North America." Tinkie was trying not to grin. "I can't wait to tell Coleman. This is such a better motive than wanting to be on stage."

I was aggravated beyond belief that Graf hadn't told me about this, but I could clearly see why. He was trying to talk me into moving to Hollywood with him. He wasn't going to own up to the fact that he owed Renata a wheelbarrow full of money. Besides, now that she was dead, how would anyone know that he owed it to her? "Was there a record of this debt? Some documentation?"

Tinkie lowered her coffee cup. "There is a record of the debt and also of his payments so far into Renata's account. The reason he owes her the money isn't documented anywhere we could find."

"How did you find it?" I asked.

Tinkie considered whether she should tell me or not. "Harold called someone in New York. Someone who knew the story. He told Harold and Harold told me."

"Then hold off on telling Coleman until we get solid proof."

"You're not trying to protect Graf, are you?" Cece asked.

I shook my head. "Not at the cost of my own skin. Don't worry. If we have to bring this up, we certainly will. But this sounds conveniently like a Renata fabrication to me. Let me talk to Graf. I suspect there's some truth to this, but this may not be the whole truth." It wasn't that I had any illusions about Graf; I just knew Renata's potential to malign people.

I found the three women watching me like cats crouching over a crippled bird. "I'm not defending Graf."

No one said anything.

"I have two more nights to perform. Let's just finish the —"

The doorbell chimed and saved me from some dumb-footed pronouncement of my intentions. "I'll be right back."

Crazy, but my heart lifted at the thought

that it might be Coleman. I knew it wasn't. He was at the hospital with his tumor-producing wife, at her bedside where he'd been for the past year, and apparently where he belonged. The door swung open to reveal Tammy Odom shivering in the afternoon wind.

"Tammy!" I pulled her inside and hustled her toward the kitchen. "You're about to freeze to death. Where's your coat?"

"I was reading the cards for a lady, and I got such a powerful image, I just stood up and walked out the door to come over here."

Tammy was known around town as Madame Tomeeka, Zinnia's resident psychic. Except she was no joke. She had dreams and visions that frequently helped me with my cases.

She stopped dead still in the parlor and turned to me. "We're not alone."

The skin of my lower back rippled. "Of course we aren't. The girls are in the kitchen."

"That's not what I meant, and you know it!"

The one thing I didn't want was Tammy holding a séance and calling Jitty forth so that all four women could harangue me about my life's choices. "It's okay, Tammy. I swear it. The past at Dahlia House is fine.

My problems are in the present."

"You can say that again."

When we got to the kitchen, Tammy was greeted with a hail of welcomes. Tinkie got up and hugged her neck. I got her coffee, and she took a seat at the table.

"I was reading the Tarot for someone else, and I got the strongest sense that I needed to get over here fast. I saw something."

Her words stilled all conversation. Even Cece, the skeptic of the crowd, was listening attentively.

I'd come to have great respect for Tammy and her visions or dreams or telepathic messages from the other side. Normally, though, her dreams and visions were a sign of danger. "What happened?" I asked with some reluctance.

"It wasn't a dream, except that it felt like one, but I was wide awake and looking at my client."

Everyone leaned a little closer.

"I saw you in a dark, dark cave. You were all alone and frightened. You kept feeling along the wall of the cave, trying to find your way out."

"That sounds like Sarah Booth," Tinkie said stoutly. "She's not just going to sit around and be afraid."

I wanted to hug her, but I didn't want to

interrupt Tammy. "What happened?"

"You came to this small spring of water. The surface was perfectly smooth, and there seemed to be a light under the water. You were thirsty, so thirsty you couldn't stop yourself from kneeling down and drinking the water. It was the most refreshing water you'd ever tasted." Tammy's eyes closed as she recounted the vision.

I could almost taste the water, so sweet and quenching. I sighed.

"You were drinking from your cupped hand. You looked down into the water and this body began to float up from the depths of the water. Dark hair streamed out from behind it. It floated toward you, faceup."

Now I was scared. It was only a vision that Tammy had had, but in the past, all of her visions had some tremendous significance.

"The body hovered just beneath the surface, and it was clear this woman was dead."

"Who was it?" Millie asked in a breathless whisper.

"It was Renata Trovaioli."

For a moment there was only the sound of the old kitchen clock that hung over the space heater tick-tocking the seconds away.

"She was dead?" I asked.

"Yes. She was dead." Tammy reached over

and gripped my wrist. "You leaned down to touch her, to make sure she was dead. Suddenly —"

Cece shrieked and nearly fell out of her chair. I glared at her and turned my attention back to Tammy. "Go on."

"Suddenly she grabbed your wrist. She gave a sharp tug and pulled you under the water with her. You struggled, Sarah Booth. You fought to get away from her, but she didn't have to breathe and you needed air."

Tears touched Tammy's cheeks, and when I looked at Tinkie, I saw that she was crying, too.

"Sarah Booth got away, didn't she?" Millie asked.

Tammy sat up and wiped her face. "That was the end of the vision."

CHAPTER 14

Tammy's vision put a darker edge to my performance of Maggie the Cat. While the audience seemed to love it, I was troubled by all the things I'd learned about my co-star. We finished the show, and when Graf asked me for a drink afterward, I agreed. There were things I needed to confront him about.

Because I wanted privacy without the temptation of being in my home, we drove to Cleveland and a small restaurant/bar that specialized in steaks, dry martinis, and quiet. Though I wasn't in a drinking mood, I ordered a vodka martini, dirty and on the rocks. I ate my olives while I watched Graf. He was abnormally quiet, his eyes holding questions and what might be worry.

"Penny for your thoughts," I said, suddenly scalded by another memory when I'd asked him the same thing, wanting badly to hear that he was thinking of me. That, of course, had not been his answer, because at that time Graf had thought only of himself.

"I haven't been straight up with you, Sarah Booth."

Surprise, surprise. "You haven't?" I decided to play it all green-eyed innocence to see where he'd take me. Funny that he was ready to confess — after Tinkie got the goods on him.

"I got in some trouble in Mexico. Stupidity was my biggest sin, but the laws I broke were much more serious."

I sipped my drink, my gaze never faltering. "Go on."

"I was in financial trouble. I had to have some money, quick, or else some of my *friends* had a big desire to rearrange the features of my face."

"You got into loan sharks?" I sat forward, startled despite myself. Graf really was a few brain cells short of a whole package.

"It was before I dated you. I rented a place on Fifth Avenue and bought furniture. I thought if I could live the lifestyle of a successful actor, then folks would view me as successful, and . . ." He finished his drink.

"Perception is everything."

"You've got it." He shrugged and signaled the waiter for another drink. "Anyway, I got in pretty deep before I realized it wasn't going to work. All the furniture was repossessed, and I lost the lease on the apartment still owing a considerable amount in back rent."

"Who owned the apartment?"

He grimaced. "That was the part I didn't get at first. After a guy showed up backstage with a baseball bat, I got the message pretty quick. Then I moved and you came along, and for a while I sort of avoided them."

"And they caught up with you?"

He nodded. "They asked me to bring some stuff back from Mexico. It was either that or they were going to mess me up."

How was it possible that a man with Graf's talent and looks could make such a muddle of his life? "And you got caught?"

He nodded. "I wouldn't tell who the drugs belonged to, so I was held in a Mexican prison. You have to believe me, Sarah Booth, if I'd talked, they would have killed me. Anyway, Renata got a lawyer, paid the fees, paid the court costs, got them to understand I was stupid." He lifted one shoulder. "I was in the process of paying her back. It was a lot of money, though. Half a million."

"Oh, Graf." My tone said it all — disappointment, disapproval, and disbelief that he could be such a fool.

"There's nothing you can say that I

haven't said to myself. Now, if the law finds out about this, I'll be the prime suspect in Renata's death."

Everyone I knew feared being where I was — in the hot seat of accusation for murder. "Did you sign anything, a legal document showing the loan from Renata?"

He shook his head slowly. "No. The movie people were sniffing around my heels, and Renata took a gamble. We made a deal. If I got in at the movies, I'd bring her along. She wanted to be a star. Not just a stage star, but a bona fide movie star."

"I have to say I admire her gambling spirit."

"She really saved my ass. But she always made people pay. If she did the smallest kindness for them, they paid and paid and paid. Renata could never let it go. She was always sniping at me about the drug charges and what would happen if the tabloids got wind of it."

"Why would Renata even take a chance on ruining your Hollywood prospects? If she shot you down, she shot herself in the foot."

He cleared his throat. "Sometimes it seemed that Renata didn't care. Especially the last few months. It was almost as if she was determined to self-destruct and take all of us with her."

I thought about his words. It sounded as if he was telling me the truth. The whole truth, this time. Graf had earned my skepticism, though, and I wasn't about to jump for his story hook, line, and sinker. Like I once had.

"Several people have mentioned a big change in Renata in the past year. You among them," I pointed out. "What would you attribute that to?"

Graf sipped his fresh drink and ordered our steaks. He remembered how I liked mine cooked. There were things that Graf did so well. Out of the corner of my eye, I caught several pretty women simply staring at him, their own dates forgotten as they gazed upon his handsome features. How they must be envying me — and how little they knew of my circumstances.

When he picked up my hand on the table, I felt a chill touch me. He still had power over me, especially in the vulnerable state in which Coleman had left me. "Answer my question, please," I said.

"I was thinking. Renata did change. There were times — just fleeting moments — when I thought I saw something like fear in her eyes. I remember once, she was backstage in Reno, and I walked up behind her as she was staring in the mirror. I would have sworn she was petrified of what she saw looking back at her."

His words chilled me again, and this time it wasn't sexually charged. "What could it have been?"

"I put my hand on her shoulder and asked if I could do anything to help her. She almost bit my head off. That was Renata. She rebuffed all efforts of kindness. It was like she was afraid to allow anyone to see her innermost fears."

Bingo. Graf had hit the nail on the head. But what could she have feared so much? Had she known all this time that someone was trying to kill her? I'd never worked a case where a person had been so aloof. Not one single person really knew Renata.

"Do you have any idea why she hated me so? To the point that she would frame me for her murder."

He gently touched my cheek. "She was jealous of you. There were hints of it when she pushed all of us into coming to Zinnia instead of closing out the contract and going home. She would bring up your name to try and get a reaction out of me."

"Why? I hadn't crossed her path in a year. I hadn't even been to a show as a spectator." I couldn't help that I was whining slightly.

"She somehow viewed you as having something she didn't have, something she wanted."

"You?" I asked.

He shook his head. "I was honorable with Renata until she pulled the plug on our romantic relationship. Sure, then I had some flings. Before that, though, I honored my word to her."

"What could it be?"

Graf's laughter was bitter. "You have friends, Sarah Booth. People who care about you. You left New York, whipped and beaten, and in twelve months, you've turned your life around completely. You're loved here in Zinnia. You're doing a job that makes a difference."

The look in his eyes almost melted my bones. When he looked at me, he saw a diamond. A year ago, I was a lump of coal. No matter what anyone ever told me, this was a satisfying sensation.

I couldn't let my emotions control me. I had to keep pressing if I planned on proving my innocence. "Something changed in Renata's life. Something drastic in the last year."

"You'll find whatever it is, Sarah Booth.

You and Tinkie, and the rest of your friends."

I could only hope he was right.

I awoke the next morning and snuggled beneath the quilts on my bed as I watched the sunshine warm the floor of my room. This was my last performance as Maggie the Cat. Part of me felt relief, but another part, a part I'd thought long dead, wanted more of the stage, more character to bite into. What was I going to do, assuming I didn't go to prison?

Pulling one of the quilts around me, I walked to the bedroom window and looked out over the bare fields. My gaze was drawn to the ten acres of bright winter rye that I'd had planted for Reveler. He was frolicking about in the grass, dancing with his shadow in the crisp morning. I needed a companion for him. I had plenty of land for a second horse, but I'd avoided the responsibility — and the expense. Dragging the quilt, I went to the telephone and dialed up my old friend Lee McBride. She'd bred Reveler and given him to me as part of her fee when she'd been charged with the murder of her rapscallion husband. Some men did need killing, and he'd been a prime example of the breed. Now that she was free of him and of the wrongful murder charge, Lee was breeding some of the finest horses in the nation.

She answered on the fifth ring. "Lee, can I borrow Miss Scrapiron for a while?" She was a lovely bay mare.

"I'm headed to see Dr. Matthews today. I'll drop her off before lunch."

"Thanks." I hung up. Lee knew I'd take care of the horse no matter what. She didn't feel compelled to ask any questions. And I hadn't questioned my impulse. My next call was to Graf.

"How about a ride this afternoon before the show?"

"I'd love it." His voice said he would.

"Two o'clock. Meet me in the barn." I hung up and sat down on the edge of the bed. I'd taken control of my life and wrested it back into forward movement. Coleman had broken my heart. I was charged with a murder I hadn't committed. The future loomed ahead of me, secretive and dangerous, but I'd made a plan for the afternoon. I'd taken a step. It was something.

The telephone rang, and I almost jumped out of my skin. No one would call so early except Tinkie, and I hoped she had news.

"Ms. Delaney?"

I didn't recognize the voice on the other

end of the phone. "Yes."

"This is Brenda Mulholland. I'm Connie Peter's sister." Good thing I was sitting. "Connie wants to talk to you."

"I don't think —" But my words went unheeded. I heard Connie's voice.

"Sarah Booth, Coleman has told me all that I've done to you. I want to apologize."

She sounded lucid and sane. I wasn't interested in getting in a moving vehicle with her behind the wheel, but I could talk to her on the phone. Still, I felt like one of Jacques Cousteau's cameramen being lowered in the metal shark cage.

"I heard you had surgery, Connie. I hope you're feeling better." Damn those Southern manners! Why couldn't I just tell her to screw off?

"I feel like a tremendous pressure has been relieved. But I didn't call to talk about me. I did some bad things to you. I'm sorry, and I hope one day you'll consider accepting my apology. That's all I wanted to say."

"Do you remember what you did?" I couldn't help myself.

"No, but Coleman has given me chapter and verse. I'm not going to try to lay this at the door of a brain tumor. All I can do is promise you that I'm making plans as quickly as possible to get out of your life forever."

I took a breath. "What does that mean, exactly?"

"I'm moving to Jackson with my sister. As soon as I get out of the hospital, I'm dropping my countersuit against Coleman for the divorce. You win, Sarah Booth."

Whatever the genteel response to such an admission might be, I was at a loss to give it. "What does Coleman say?"

"Not much. I thought he'd be tap-dancing in the hallways." There was a pause. "I have to go. I'm scheduled for a CAT scan."

"I hope your health improves, Connie." And I did. Poor health was more than anyone deserved.

There was a click, and she was gone. I pulled the quilt closer and considered flopping back in bed. Connie had taken the starch out of my spine.

Behind me I heard the rustle of many petticoats. Jitty. In antebellum attire, no doubt. I wanted to hide in my quilt. Maybe even my guilt, because for some reason I had just taken a heaping helping of starch-laden guilt, compliments of Connie.

"I hear Connie's cleared the infield and thrown you a touchdown pass."

I whipped around. Jitty hated football. And no one wearing an azure dancing gown of silk should ever talk sports. "You've been eavesdropping. How come you can't do that when I need help solving a case?"

She glided into the room with a movement that sent her hoop skirts swinging. "So Connie's leaving town? Do you believe it?"

"More to the point, what do you believe?" I often let my heart lead me astray, but Jitty was more of a skeptic.

"Why would she call you, Sarah Booth? Connie doesn't owe you anything." One eyebrow arched. "It's something to ponder."

"Thank you, Jitty." I couldn't stop the laugh. Trust Jitty to put things in perspective. Connie didn't have a noble bone in her body. She'd almost accomplished exactly what she intended — which was to make me feel bad.

"Why don't you call Coleman?"

I couldn't believe those words were coming from Jitty's mouth. "Why?"

She fingered a beautiful pearl necklace at her throat. Apparently the jewels in the afterlife were better, too. "He should know about Connie's call, and you can bet she won't tell him."

"I'm not supposed to talk to Coleman. It might taint his murder case against me."

Jitty laughed. "Before you go riding with

Mr. Hollywood Britches, give the lawman a call. Sarah Booth, you've always been an all-or-nothing kind of woman. You're making decisions about your future without all the facts. Truth be told, you might be lining yourself up with a killer."

Jitty wasn't trying to aggravate me. She was serious.

"You think Graf killed Renata?" I truly hadn't given it serious thought. I knew him. He was a convenient liar and a self-centered bastard at time, but not a killer.

"I don't know if Graf killed her or not. But I do know that you didn't. If you didn't, someone else did, and he's high on the suspect list."

Suddenly my afternoon plan for a ride seemed impulsive. Jitty was making sense. I needed a hot shower and some time to gather my emotions. "Thank you, Jitty."

"I only want your happiness, Sarah Booth." Her voice became an echo as she began to fade. "Only your happiness."

I was left sitting in my room cocooned in a quilt made by the hands of one of my ancestors. I jumped to my feet. I had places to go and things to do before the morning was gone.

I picked up the phone and called Tinkie. She answered sounding sleepy and content, though it was nearly nine.

"You okay?" I asked.

"Oscar and I had a late night." I could hear the satisfaction in her voice. Though they'd had their ups and downs, as all couples do, there was still the spark of passion in their marriage. I stamped down the flare of envy. I didn't begrudge Tinkie a single moment of marital bliss. I just wanted to sample a good relationship for myself.

"I'm going to get dressed and head over to the hospital to talk to Doc Sawyer about Renata's autopsy," I said. "Want to join me?"

"Sure." Tinkie sounded suddenly wary. "I talked to Coleman yesterday, too. He's going to try to get Renata's medical records from Dr. Abraham Samen on Sunset Boulevard. Cece came through for us."

I'd never doubted that Cece could get whatever information she set her sights on. She was persuasive. "Did Renata have plastic surgery?"

There was a moment's pause. "No. And I don't want to talk about this over the phone."

Tinkie was sensitive about medical information, and I didn't blame her. "Let's meet at the hospital. I'll pick up some coffee and pastries on the way." We both knew better than to attempt Doc's brew. There was the possibility that it multiplied on its own regenerative power.

"Thirty minutes," Tinkie said before she hung up.

Chapter 15

Doc Sawyer had been trying to retire for the past year, but folks in Sunflower County just wouldn't let him. He maintained an office beside the emergency room in the hospital — allegedly a part-time office — but Doc was there from six a.m. until his work was done.

When I knocked on his door, he opened it and let a smile move over his face. "Sarah Booth, you look more like your mother each time I see you." He leaned over to kiss my cheek. "Congratulations on your acting success. You're a smash!"

"Thanks, Doc. Few people in town are brave enough to kiss an accused murderer."

"Ah, the stupidity of the masses. Remember, these are the same people who push down trees to lay asphalt. What can you expect?"

I held out the bag of pastries. "Tinkie's on her way. We need a powwow."

"Fate is kind to an old country doctor." He took the bag and rummaged until he found a cheese Danish. Doc had the metabolism of a fourteen-year-old basketball player. He could — and did — eat whatever he wanted without gaining an ounce. He'd been my childhood doctor, so I figured him to be in his sixties, at least. Except for the untidy cloud of white hair, he looked younger than that.

"Tinkie got the basic autopsy report on Renata, but I need to ask a few questions."

He nodded. "I knew Coleman would share the facts, but I thought you might be by. I made a copy of the report for you."

"That's great." I checked my watch. Tinkie was never late. I retrieved a cup of coffee from the second bag I'd brought. I offered Doc a cup, but he shook his head and got a cup of black syrup from his own pot.

"Have you tested that coffee for medicinal properties?" To my knowledge, Doc had never been sick a day in his life.

He only laughed. "My coffee isn't for the faint of heart."

There was a light knock on the door and Tinkie stepped inside. She took the coffee I offered and after a brief investigation of the pastry bag, settled on a cinnamon roll.

"Now that we're all having breakfast," I said, "I need to ask a few questions about Renata."

"Shoot." Doc ate the last bite of his Danish and reached for the bag to get another.

"How did the poison get into the lipstick?" I asked. "Has anyone figured that part out? Was the tube dipped in poison?"

Doc's face showed concern. "Yes, a highly potent solution. Whoever did this wanted the person who applied the lipstick to die. It was very clever of them to use a cosmetic scented with almonds to cover up the cyanide. I caught a whiff of it when I did the autopsy, but I couldn't be certain until the tests came back."

"Could this have been an accident?" Tinkie asked.

Doc shook his head. "I'm sorry. I wish I could say otherwise."

"It looks bad for me because traces of cyanide were found in the trunk of my car. I've never bought or used cyanide in my life. I wouldn't even know where to get it." Whoever killed Renata had set a perfect snare for me.

"It's not something you can buy over the counter." Doc considered. "If I had to guess, I'd say whoever tampered with Renata's lipstick understands poisons and reactions. Someone with some medical training. That's where I'd start looking."

"Thanks, Doc. That's a good lead. We'll check it out." I sat back and thought.

"And someone who had access to Renata's things. Whoever did this had to get the lipstick from Renata after Sarah Booth gave it to her."

"I didn't give it to her. I gave it to Graf to give to her." I met Tinkie's gaze without flinching.

"Sarah Booth —" She bit her bottom lip.

"He could have opened it and poisoned it. I know." It looked bad for Graf, but I wasn't willing to believe he killed Renata. Not yet.

"Why didn't you say something?" Tinkie's cheeks were pink with anger. "These incriminating tidbits involving Graf just keep popping up."

"I know what it feels like to have someone jump the gun and make an accusation based on circumstantial evidence. These things look bad in one light, but they don't make Graf guilty." So many things were pointing directly at Graf. He knew Renata better than anyone. He knew her intimately. Yet there was something else niggling at my brain. "Doc, had Renata had any plastic surgery?"

He consulted the chart. "She had a mammoplasty, saline implants. Why do you ask?"

"She went to a doctor in Los Angeles about eight months ago. She made repeated visits. Could you see any reason why?"

Doc frowned. "To be honest, Sarah Booth, I didn't look for cosmetic surgeries other than injections with toxins, such as Botox. The cyanide was obviously the cause of death . . ."

"What are you thinking?" Tinkie asked me.

"I'm not sure. There's just something I can't quite catch hold of here." I stood up. "I want to go to the sheriff's office and see if Dewayne or Gordon can help me pull together a picture of the old man who sold me the lipstick. I think it may be the same man Bobbe Renshaw saw arguing with Renata in Reno. He sold me the lipstick, and he may be the one who poisoned it. If Bobbe can identify him, then we'll have something solid to go on."

"Great idea!" Tinkie was on her feet, too.

We both gave Doc a hug and hurried out of his office and into the hallway beside the emergency room. I was in such a hurry that I barely noticed a large, dark shadow before I bumped into the solid chest of a well-built man. My brain registered the brown uniform, the badge, and as I looked up, the blue eyes of Coleman Peters. He looked as if he'd been gaffed.

"I'm sorry." I stepped back quickly. In that brief moment I caught a whiff of his distinctive aftershave and the starch in his uniform. Coleman managed to look crisp and polished even in the worst of Delta weather. My heart took a painful lurch.

"Sarah Booth." He cleared his throat. "Are you okay?"

His question had nothing to do with our bump in the hall. "As well as can be expected. For a murderess." The sharp words leapt from my mouth. "And tell your wife to stop calling me. I'm not stupid, and she can play the victim for you, Coleman, but not for me. Brain tumor my ass."

I stepped past him and headed out the door, my back so straight my breasts projected like the prow of a ship.

"She's really hurt," Tinkie said to Coleman as she followed me out.

"Don't make excuses for me," I told her once we stood in the weak January sunshine. "He's the one who should be making excuses for his behavior. He and Connie deserve each other."

"Did she really call you?"

I filled her in on the brief conversation I'd

had with Coleman's wife. Tinkie's assessment was the same as mine.

"She's conniving again. I just lost all sympathy for her." Tinkie opened the door of her Caddy. "Want me to go to the sheriff's office with you?"

I shook my head. "Nope."

She slammed the door. "Good. I'm going to see if Doc can't manage to get some medical records on a dead woman. As county coroner, he might be able to get the same thing Coleman can. That way we can circumvent the whole sheriff's department thing."

Connie's behavior had riled her, too. I gave her a big hug. "You got all the brains in this operation."

"Not true. But call me when you get the sketch finished. And you need to take a nap, Sarah Booth. This is your last performance. When I talked to Keith Watley last night, he said several important people will be in the audience."

Keith hadn't said a word to me. "What kind of important people?"

She sighed. "From a couple of movie studios. Graf has been on the phone about you. They've come to look for themselves." She slid her sunglasses on so I couldn't see her eyes.

"It's so nice to be the last one to know."

"They didn't want you to get nervous, but I felt you deserved to know. So take a nap. You need to be rested and ready to wow them."

She walked through the gravel, her tiny red high heels making a scrunching sound that reminded me, for some reason, of the first day of grammar school and the sense of being alone in a large world.

"This computer program isn't as good as a sketch artist, but it's better than nothing." Gordon manipulated the mouse as he talked. "How about these sideburns?"

I sat beside him, trying hard to remember the old codger who'd sold me the lipstick. "Wider at the base. Really tufty."

Gordon cursed softly as he struggled with manipulating the program.

"That's it!" I said, patting his shoulder. "The eyebrows were a little bushier, though."

He worked and I waited. Detail by detail, we created an image of the old man at La Burnisco.

"Do you think this guy was wearing a costume?" Gordon asked.

The question stopped me dead in my tracks. It was so painfully obvious, and yet I hadn't thought about it. Here I was dealing with an actress and a man who looked like he'd just stepped out of a Dickens novel, but it hadn't occurred to me that he might be made-up.

"Well, damn." I sat back, defeated.

Gordon saved the image and turned to look at me. "Even if the whiskers and all are part of a disguise, we'll still have a likeness of the guy."

"And how will that help?" I'd just wasted an hour of my precious freedom. Lunchtime had passed, and I had a date for a horseback ride at two.

"Keep working with me, and I'll show you." Gordon turned his attention back to the computer screen.

I wasn't certain that I liked the kinder-gentler-Gordon, but I wasn't about to complain when someone offered help. We worked on the mouth and chin until finally we had a likeness of the old gent that was very close to the real thing.

"That's him."

Gordon hit print and in a moment we had the black and white sketch in our hands.

"Now watch this," he said. With a few clicks of the mouse, the white hair was close-cropped black, the whiskers and moustache gone. The image on the screen was a man in his forties — a rather handsome man who bore no resemblance to anyone I knew.

"Never seen him," I said.

"Perhaps not. But maybe someone else has. I'll circulate both pictures and see if I get any hits. We'll even fax them to the television stations in Memphis. The media has been all over Renata's murder, so we might as well get some use out of them. I'll put this out as a witness wanted in Renata's death. That might generate some calls."

"Thanks." I rose to go. "I appreciate all you're doing, Gordon."

"No, problem, Sarah Booth. I know you're innocent. It's just a matter of time before we catch the real killer. I'll take one of the pictures by and see if Ms. Renshaw can make a positive identification on the old gent."

"Thanks."

I walked out of the courthouse and stood for a moment in the midday sun. It was nearly sixty, a warm, bright day. I heard a laugh behind me, and Booter walked out onto the steps.

"Tonight's your last performance, Sarah Booth," she said. "I'll bet you'll be a smash star in the women's prison. Once the play is over, Coleman can't continue to let you run free." Her eyes were cold. "No matter how much he doesn't want to lock up his paramour."

"Booter, why do you have it in for me?" I decided to confront her. My impulse was to smack her hard, but if I got in any trouble my bail would be revoked. Words were the only weapons I had.

The question startled her, at least for a second. "I don't have it in for you, Sarah Booth. I wouldn't waste my time."

"That's good to know. I was beginning to think you'd followed me here. Like your life is so pathetic you have to follow me to get some excitement."

"Follow you?" She looked around as if I had to be talking to someone else. "Why on earth would I do that?"

"That's what I'd like to know." Suddenly my gut told me that I'd hit the nail right on the head. Booter had followed me. To what purpose, I couldn't say. "You've been in the café, at The Club, now here at the courthouse. You are following me."

"You're paranoid." She skipped down the steps, leaving me to wonder why I didn't believe a word out of her mouth.

Graf showed up at two on the dot wearing tan breeches, riding boots, and a burgundy sweater that perfectly offset his olive good looks. The wind ruffled his dark hair as he groomed Miss Scrapiron while I readied Reveler.

Lee had been smart enough to leave a saddle and bridle for the bay mare, and Graf tacked her up without any assistance from me.

"She's a lovely animal," he said as he swung into the saddle.

"She is." I watched her move out, so eager. In a matter of moments we were trotting around the barren cotton fields side by side. Reveler occasionally nuzzled the mare beside him, a gentlemanly attempt at paying court. Miss Scrapiron was too much of a lady to acknowledge his passes.

When we left Dahlia House behind, Graf settled his horse to a walk. "Sarah Booth, have you told the law about my adventures in Mexico?"

"No." I hadn't, yet I didn't know why I hadn't.

"Do you believe me?"

It wasn't the right question for a perfect afternoon, but I knew I had to answer it honestly. "I do, Graf. You've always been impulsive. You've always thought that looks counted more than anything else. I believe you could be that foolish."

"You can call me a moron as long as you don't believe I was smuggling drugs for a profit. I just wanted to stay alive, to not be hurt."

I did believe him. Fool that I was. "Okay, but I think it would be in your best interest to go to the police with this yourself."

"So your boyfriend can pop me in jail? No, thanks. He already looks at me like he wants to snap my head off. I don't really want to give him a reason to put me behind bars."

"Coleman can't arrest you for something that happened in Mexico. He can't do anything about whatever deal you made with Mexican authorities. To be honest, it won't interest him. That's not his jurisdiction."

"You're his primary interest, and he views me as someone who might take you away." He slowed Miss Scrapiron until I was even with him. His hand touched my thigh. "Tell me that isn't true."

He spoke with such certainty that I urged Reveler into an extended trot and left him in the dirt. I was no longer Coleman's primary interest. He had a recovering psycho wife to fill that slot. At my whispered command, Reveler stretched into a canter. Graf could keep up or not.

The scenery was a blur as we raced along the edges of the fields. The wind whipped tears into my eyes, and I could feel the sting on my cheeks and lips. Although the weather was clear, it was still winter. Reveler's stride lengthened into a full-out gallop, and I made no effort to check him.

At last I slowed Reveler to a trot. The sound of hooves came fast from behind, and he slowed to a walk. Reveler was blowing lightly, but when an empty bag blew across the path in front of us, he sun-fished, nearly unseating me because I hadn't anticipated his move.

"He's something else." Graf's voice held admiration. "You should have seen you ride, Sarah Booth. I think when we get to Hollywood, we need to do a western. You know, an old-timey adventure of the Old West where the audience can get a full view of your posterior in a saddle."

For just a moment I saw Graf and me on horseback, riding the rolling hills of a studio back lot. It was tempting. I loved westerns.

When I checked my watch I saw it was after three. We turned the horses back toward Dahlia House at a brisk walk. If I was going to get a nap, I needed to do it soon. "Graf, did Renata have any weaknesses?"

His look told me he didn't completely comprehend what I was asking. "She had a weakness for chocolate, like most people. She could be very disciplined. Amazingly disciplined."

"Any kind of chocolate?"

"What is this, Sarah Booth?"

"Humor me. Please."

He shrugged his broad shoulders. "She preferred dark chocolate. She said it was loaded with antioxidants."

"Was she taking any other kind of drugs? Recreational drugs?" I thought of cocaine or ecstasy, the party drugs. There had to be some area in Renata's life that led to her murder.

"I never saw her take anything. She took care of herself, Sarah Booth. Her body was her vehicle to success."

"Did she gamble? Play the ponies?" There had to be something.

"Not to my knowledge."

"Was she afraid of aging?"

He gave this question some consideration. "Yes, but not so much lately. I think the idea of a movie deal somehow eased her mind."

"Who benefits most from her death?" The sun slipped behind a cloud, sucking the color from the day and leaving a sense of nostalgic loss on the air.

"I do. Me and Gabriel, her brother. My debt is forgiven, and Gabriel inherits all of her assets. Of the two, I gain the most."

He was being brutally honest now. "You and Renata were once close. Aren't you sorry she's dead?"

Graf's gaze held mine. "You asked for the truth, and I owe you that much. I'm not sorry she's dead. For the past two months she made my life a living hell. Threats, blackmail, temper tantrums, catching me backstage before I went on and getting one more little dig into me. She changed into a harpy and a shrew. I'm free of her, Sarah Booth. She can't torture me anymore."

"I see." Now all I had to do was get through the last performance with a man who might also be a murderer.

Chapter 16

We got home to Dahlia House in plenty of time for me to take a nap, but I found I couldn't rest. Although I could see it hurt Graf's feelings, I sent him back to his hotel. Alone, I paced the bedroom until I gave it up and went downstairs. Though the idea of a Jack and water was tempting, I avoided the sideboard where the crystal decanter waited. I had my last performance as Maggie that evening. Drinking was a dangerous trap. I wanted to go onto the stage sober and sharp.

By six o'clock, I'd finally settled down. It was with a sense of nostalgia that I drove to The Club and sat down in Bobbe's chair to let her work her magic.

"That deputy showed me the picture of that old fart. He's the guy I saw in Reno," Bobbe said. "I told the deputy so. He thought that might help your case."

I closed my eyes as she applied the

shadow. "Thanks, Bobbe."

"There you go." She tilted the chair up so I could see myself in the mirror, transformed from my everyday Zinnia looks into a glamorous woman. Nothing like my idol, Liz, or my nemesis, Renata — but certainly not the Sarah Booth I recognized. It was fascinating what shadows and the artful application of color could change.

"Did Gordon say when you could leave town?" I asked her.

Bobbe shook her head. "I'll be packed and ready first thing in the morning. I can only hope the law doesn't keep me here."

"Good luck. And thank you." I gave her arm a squeeze as I stepped out of the makeup room.

"There she is, the dahling of stage and film!" Cece's rich contralto made me smile. I was even more delighted when she put a huge bouquet of zinnias in my arms. The vibrant colors were magnificent, a reflection of the town I loved.

"Roses are for your everyday star," she said as she hugged me. "Zinnias are for you, Sarah Booth. Our hometown girl headed for the big time."

"Sarah Booth, there are some people here to talk to you after the performance." Keith bustled up, as usual knocking everyone else out of the way in his hurry to make sure his needs were met. "I told them you'd be available for interviews following the play."

"I'm so sorry. I'm going to a strike party," I said. The expression on his face was priceless. I'd had to give up my idea for a party, but Harold had stepped up to the plate. He was throwing a bash, with candy lipstick as party favors.

"But. But. I —"

"Keith, she's jerking your chain," Cece said, shaking her head at him. "She'll be here after the play. I'll make certain of it." She was edging me away from him as fast as she could without pushing with both hands.

"Thank you, Ms. Falcon. Thank you." Keith caught one of her hands and kissed it. "Thank you."

His gratitude was almost comic. When he was gone, I arched my eyebrows at Cece. "What's the point of killing all my fun?"

"You should be ashamed. Keith isn't worthy of your torment. He's too easy a target."

She was right about that. I shrugged. "Maybe he killed Renata. If it benefited his career, he'd do it."

Cece looped her arm through mine and walked me toward a quiet stretch of hallway.

She let the silence grow between us.

"What did you find out?" I finally asked.

"Not what I'd imagined." She faced me, and her expression was troubled. "The doctor Renata was seeing in Los Angeles was Christian Varik, a retina specialist. He wasn't inclined to give details, but he did imply that there was something serious wrong with Renata's vision."

A cold knot formed in my stomach. "She was going blind?" That could account for a whole lot of meanness. And for her hitting a dog with a car and not stopping. Speaking of which, Kristine Rolofson was strangely absent from backstage for the last performance. I'd halfway expected her and Giblet to come and wish me luck.

"I'm checking out Renata's visual issues," Cece said. "Or should I say Gordon is checking it out. I gave the tip to him. He told me he got an ID on the old geezer that sold you the lipstick."

"Really?" I was amazed that Gordon had achieved such a quick result.

"His name is Morgan, Robert Morgan. He's a New York state licensed pharmacist, a former character actor from a few Broadway productions, and a longtime friend of Renata's."

"She had a friend?" I didn't mean it to

sound as bitchy as it came out. "I mean, Renata didn't cultivate a lot of confidantes." Bubbling in the back of my brain was something Doc had said in his office only that morning. He'd said that if he were hunting the killer, he'd look for someone with a medical background. A pharmacist would have plenty of knowledge of poisons and how they worked and how to administer them. "This has to be the same guy I saw at La Burnisco." Excitement made me want to dance a jig. At last we'd begun to move forward on the case.

"Let's hope this is the same guy. Gordon's got an APB out for Robert Morgan in New York and all around this area. Gordon wants to ask him a few questions."

"So do I." Like how in the hell did he manage to pull off selling me a tube of poisoned lipstick without anyone noticing that he did it? "Did Gordon get an address on him?"

She nodded. "Some of New York's finest went to his apartment this afternoon, and it looked like Morgan left in a hurry. They searched the neighborhood, but he'd disappeared. Gordon says they'll get him, though. What with credit cards and all of that, it's nearly impossible for someone to truly disappear in this country."

I took a deep breath. I had to be on stage in a matter of minutes, and I needed to pull myself together to assume the role of Maggie the Cat.

"I'll see you after the show. Thanks, Cece." I kissed her cheek and walked toward the backstage area where I could have a few moments of privacy. This was it for me, my last performance. I hadn't seen Graf since he'd left the stables, but I had come to trust him — at least on the stage.

"Sarah Booth?"

Coleman's voice stopped me in my tracks. I had to force myself to turn around. The one thing I didn't need was to be upset by my ex-boyfriend. "Yes?" I lifted my chin and dared him to start something as I faced him.

"Break a leg." He turned and walked away.

He was wearing a suit. I could count on one hand the number of times I'd seen him in a suit. I watched him exit the backstage area without ever turning around, leaving me to ponder the multiple levels of the message he'd just delivered to me.

I felt a warm touch on my back, and I turned to find Graf watching me watching Coleman. "Is everything okay?" he asked.

"Yes." Like Maggie the Cat, I could take it on the chin and still function. "Coleman came to wish me luck in the performance."

"Doesn't want his prime suspect out of sight, does he?"

"Thanks, Graf." I walked away from him, angry that he might be correct in his assumption of Coleman's actions. And I'd let myself think the sheriff might have actually come to watch the performance. Would I never learn?

The play went off flawlessly. It was, perhaps, the best performance of the entire run. Sir Alfred kissed me as we took our bows, and Graf used that as a perfect excuse to bend me backwards over his arm and deliver a professional Rudolph Valentino kiss. The audience loved it, and we went back for five curtain calls.

Keith brought me three dozen red roses, and with Cece's instigation, all of my girlfriends in the audience threw zinnias up on the stage at my feet.

I looked out over the audience and saw the faces of people who cared about me, who were proud of me. Bernard had said my folks would've been proud, and for a moment I allowed myself to imagine them sitting in the front row, clapping until their palms itched. I took my final bow and left the stage with tears in my eyes.

The cast was swarmed by well-wishers, and Keith waited as long as he could before he drew me aside to speak with a talent agent from Creative Artists Agency and Federico Marquez, the director of five Academy Award–winning films. The agent, Lester Lee, was unbearable, but Marquez was a modest, intelligent man.

"There's a strike party at Harold Erkwell's," I told both of them. "You're welcome to come, if you'd like."

"We have a midnight flight out of Memphis," Marquez said. "I'm sure we'll be seeing more of each other, Ms. Delaney, when you get to Hollywood. Again, congratulations on a brilliant performance."

When they were gone, I looked at Keith. "You told them I'm charged with murder, right?"

He waved his hands in the air. "Are you insane? Those charges will be dropped by this time tomorrow, and besides, they read the trades. They know all about it. Filmmaking is a gamble, and they're gambling that you'll be free by tomorrow."

He was gone before I could pin him down on his optimism.

Tinkie appeared and whisked me to the party. Harold had pulled out all the stops for this one, and the entire lane up to his home glittered in white lights. Strands of fairy lights were wrapped around the trunks of huge live oaks, spun through the towering azalea bushes, and woven into the decorations that lined the balustrade of his porch.

Harold met me at the door and reenacted Graf's kiss, much to my astonishment and the enjoyment of everyone there. Hoots and whistles followed as he raised me back to my feet. I felt the blush climb my cheeks as Harold leaned close and said in a wicked stage whisper, "If Coleman is out of the picture, I'm throwing my hat into the ring."

"I'm not out of the picture."

The room fell into silence, and I looked past Harold to see Coleman standing with a ridiculous cup of nonalcoholic punch in his hand. He looked like a bear pawing a petit four.

Harold released his hold on me and eyed Coleman. "If I misread your signals, Coleman, I apologize. It's just that when you charged Sarah Booth with murder, I assumed the romance had lost its bloom."

"You know what they say about assumptions, Harold."

Coleman was so angry steam almost came from his head. He didn't hold a candle to my wrath, though. "You don't have any say in what I do or who I kiss," I told him hotly.

Tinkie stepped between us. "This is a

party to celebrate Sarah Booth's success. For those of you here with other intentions, please leave."

She put her arm around my waist and steered me into the front room that had been decorated with cutouts of elegant movie stars. An old reel-to-reel projector was running a film of *This Property Is Condemned,* and Harold had brought in a movie popcorn machine that was going crazy. The smell of hot, buttered popcorn filled the air, and I was suddenly starving. I no longer had to worry about fitting into my mother's dress. I snatched a bag and stuffed a handful into my mouth.

"Your fingers are going to be too greasy to hold a champagne glass." Tinkie disapproved of my eating habits, though pound for pound, she could easily outeat me.

"I'll suck the champagne through a straw." I leaned so I could whisper. "It's my party, and I'll gorge if I want to."

She rolled her eyes. "What are you going to do about Coleman? He's as sore as a wolf with his leg in a trap."

"I'm not going to do a damn thing." I was way too mad to think about Coleman's feelings.

"You should talk to him, Sarah Booth. He's terrified you're going to Hollywood."

"And if I am, it's because of him!"

She hugged me tight. "I know he hurt you."

"That's the understatement of the year."

"Look, Graf is here."

I glanced up to see my costar enter. Every female in the room followed his progress with their gazes. Even Kristine Rolofson and Giblet, who appeared from one of the other rooms. I was surprised to see them, but in some ways they were almost a part of the cast. I gave them a wave.

"Harold invited a dog?" I asked Tinkie in a whisper.

"Kristine overheard the plans. It was awkward. Harold didn't want to hurt her feelings." Tinkie smiled and held up her champagne glass at Kristine, who headed toward us, Giblet trotting obediently at her heels.

"You were marvelous, Sarah Booth. I've seen almost every performance of the play since New York, and this one was by far the best. It was stellar!" She picked Giblet up and the little dog leaned over to lick my face.

"Thanks. To both of you." I gave the dog a pat. "Kristine, when Renata hit Giblet, do you think it was possible that she didn't see the dog?"

"If she was that blind she shouldn't have

been driving." Kristine wasn't going to give an inch.

"Think about it. Renata may have had a problem with her vision."

Emotions played across her face as she thought. "It's possible, but that still doesn't make it okay. She could have apologized, made an effort to show she was sorry for what happened."

"You're right." I didn't intend to challenge Kristine's stand on the hit-and-run. There was no excuse for Renata's behavior. "You've watched every performance of the play. Did she act differently?"

Kristine considered. "You know, now that you mention it, toward the end, she seemed to be . . . brittle. I guess I wanted to believe that I was making her a nervous wreck, that Giblet and I were getting to her. Was it something else?"

I couldn't answer for sure. Instead, I pulled out the pictures of Robert Morgan and showed them to Kristine. "Have you ever seen this man?"

"About a hundred times. When the play was running on Broadway, he was always hanging around backstage. He was some kind of apothecary or something like that." She shook her head. "Like an old-timey pharmacist, is what he said."

My stomach fluttered, and I snatched a glass of champagne from a passing tray. "He told you that?"

She nodded. "He was very angry at me, and he told me if Giblet and I didn't leave Renata alone, he was going to poison Giblet."

"Holy cow." Tinkie's eyes were huge. "He actually threatened to poison the dog?"

She nodded. "He drove this little blue BMW when he delivered things to Renata. Every time I saw it in the parking lot of a theatre, I put roofing tacks under all four tires. I'll bet he had about two hundred flat tires."

I couldn't help but smile. Kristine was not intimidated by anyone, and she had no remorse for her actions. I liked that. "Do you know anything else about him?"

"He showed up all over the place. I thought for a while that he was Renata's lover, but I don't think so. There wasn't that passion between them; there was something else, another kind of bond."

"Thanks, Kristine."

"Do you know when the sheriff is going to allow us to leave?" Her gaze drifted to Gabriel, who was in a corner with Booter hanging on his every word.

I shook my head, but Tinkie answered.

"As soon as he finds the real killer."

"Thanks." She stepped away, her gaze still on Gabriel.

Apothecary was a word that conjured up dark shops filled with herbs and medicines that might require a special incantation. In other words, creepy. Unless Renata was putting curses on people, why would she need a personal apothecary to follow her around the country delivering things? What things? Eye of newt? Toad tongues?

Graf was the only person who might be able to shed some light on this issue, and I saw that he'd joined Booter and Gabriel in the corner. Booter was talking ninety to nothing and pointing in my direction. I was definitely going to have to have a word with Harold about his guest list. Knowing Booter, though, she probably came without an invitation.

"Graf, I need to speak with you." I walked up and edged Booter aside. The expression on her face was priceless — outrage and childish temper.

"Excuse me, Sarah Booth. Mr. Milieu and I were having a conversation with Mr. Trovaioli."

"You're excused, Booter." I took Graf's arm and eased him through the crowd.

Behind me I heard Booter's shrill exclamation.

"Of all the nerve! I can't wait for the prison door to close on your ass!"

"Betsy Gwen isn't one of your biggest fans," Graf said as he hugged me close, "but I think you're winning Gabriel over. He hired Booter to follow you, but he's not impressed with her findings."

"Don't bother with the Betsy Gwen. Those of us who know her and love her call her Booter. It's so much more genteel than ass." I saw the front door open and edged Graf out into the night. "Listen, I need to ask you about Robert Morgan."

"The pharmacist? What about him?"

"What was his relationship to Renata?"

"He compounded some medicines for her. Thyroid stuff, maybe some hormones." He shrugged. "They were thick as thieves. Renata had invested in his apothecary shop in New York, and he hand-compounded all of her medications. He was something of a theatre buff."

I looked him dead in the eye. "Don't you find that even a little strange?"

He blinked. "Well, no. Should I?"

"That he flew around the country delivering Renata's medicine? Yes, that's strange. Why didn't he mail it?"

"There was a cream or something that had to be refrigerated. He brought it on ice." He walked to the balustrade and leaned against it. "To be honest, I didn't pay a lot of attention. I asked Renata about him, and she said he was bringing her medicine and that he was a theatre buff. After that" — he held up both hands — "I just ignored him."

Graf, as usual, was carefully focused only on himself. "The man flew halfway across the country on a regular basis to deliver something that could have been shipped? You didn't even give it a second thought?"

"When you say it like that . . ."

Behind us the soundtrack of the movie echoed sharp and clear on the crisp night air. Natalie Wood was flirting with Robert Redford in that age-old dance of the sexes. It was actually one of my favorite movies.

"What was going on with Renata and Morgan?" Graf asked, pulling me out of my reverie.

"I don't know for sure, but it's mighty damn suspicious that Renata was meeting regularly with a man who compounded drugs and threatened to poison Kristine's dog." I faced Graf. "And he's the same man who sold me that tube of poisoned lipstick."

Graf licked his lips. "Well, hell, Sarah Booth. Let's find him and make him tell us the truth. If he poisoned Renata, we could be on the first flight out to Hollywood to-morrow."

"Let's concentrate on finding him. What I think very strange is the fact that when Coleman and his deputies searched Renata's dressing room and her hotel room, not a single prescription medication was found. Not a tube of cream, not a bottle of pills. Not even an aspirin."

"So where did all of her medicines go?" Graf asked the question that demanded an answer.

Chapter 17

In the silence that followed Graf's at-last astute question, I heard the rising murmur of female voices. The sound grew to a noise resembling a buzz saw. Something interesting was happening in the parlor, and I had a gut feeling that I needed to witness whatever was coming down — maybe a duel between Harold and Coleman.

"Can you call someone in New York to go through Renata's things?" I asked Graf. "We need a prescription from Morgan's pharmacy to connect the two of them. We need physical evidence."

"I'll do it now." He put action to words, pulling his cell phone from his pocket, and I stepped inside to see what all the commotion was about. Gabriel Trovaioli, with Booter at his side, had Kristine cornered, and he wasn't happy. Cece, who was undoubtedly Gabriel's date, leaned against the bar, watching with the interest of a news-hound.

"You made my sister's last months miserable." Gabriel used his six-foot-three-inch-gym-sculpted body to great advantage to hem Kristine in the corner.

"Yeah!" Booter echoed.

"Your sister was a heartless bitch." Kristine wasn't the least perturbed. She lifted her chin and her dark auburn hair shimmered. "The only thing I ever asked for was an apology and for your sister to pay the vet bills. That isn't unreasonable, and she could well afford it. Had she just said she was sorry, I would've let it go." Kristine stepped so that her nose was almost touching Gabriel's chest. "All I wanted was for her to acknowledge that she'd hurt Giblet."

Gabriel's face dropped into lines of sadness. "You're right."

"She is?" Booter looked like she'd been slapped.

"She is. Renata could be a cruel and heartless bitch. I never understood her lack of compassion for animals. It was her worst character flaw."

Like everyone else in the room, I was stunned. It crossed my mind that Gabriel and Renata could not possibly share the same DNA. He was a compassionate, reasonable man.

"Giblet suffered because of Renata, and I tried to make her suffer in return. I never believed she'd die, though." Kristine took a breath. "I'm sorry for your loss, Mr. Trovaioli."

"It takes a woman with a big heart to say that." Gabriel stared into Kristine's eyes. "I'm so sorry for the pain you and your dog endured. I'd like to make it up to you."

Acting as if he hadn't heard the collective gasp in the room, he knelt down and stroked Giblet's silky ears. "I'm sorry for the suffering, Giblet." When he stood up, he looked directly into Kristine's eyes. "I think my sister was afraid to show tenderness. Renata couldn't risk caring for another living creature. She made herself hard so she couldn't be hurt again. In doing that, she suffered more than she ever imagined. And she made everyone whose life she touched suffer right along with her. Especially me."

"You said you were going to give her what for!" Booter tried to step between Kristine and Gabriel. "You said you were going to make all of them pay, especially Sarah Booth. You said —"

"Forget what I said, Booter. I've been a fool. A complete fool motivated by spleen and jealousy. No one in this room hurt Renata. She hurt herself."

"Well, I never!" Booter huffed away.

Everyone in the room stood completely still. Even the popcorn machine had stopped. There was only the sound of the movie, the heartbreak of Natalie Wood as she realizes that no matter how hard she tries, she can't leave behind the person she believes herself to be.

Taking Cece's elbow, I maneuvered her into a dark hallway. Harold's house was old, with magnificent hardwood floors, real paneling, crown molding, and ornamental designs that came off as cheap in newer homes. The past had a death grip on my ankle, even here in Harold's house. The hallway was dark, and for a split second I closed my eyes.

"Sarah Booth." She touched my shoulder. "Are you okay?"

"I am." I took a deep breath. "The play is over, and soon Coleman will have to let the theatrical company return to New York. I'll be the only suspect in town."

"What can I do?"

"Did Gabriel give anything away?"

She considered her answer carefully. "Nothing solid. Since I've talked to him, he doubts you did it, but he wants someone to blame. I told him that it appeared to us that

Renata had deliberately set you up as the killer, and he admitted she had a vengeful streak. But he said she was a fighter. She'd never deliberately let herself be hurt by anyone. That was the only thing he was positive about — she would never play the victim. Whoever did it — she wouldn't cooperate with her or him."

"We have to find the killer, and I believe Renata's past is the key. Someone she knew, something she did — that's going to lead us to the killer."

"Gabriel wasn't much help there. In many ways, he never knew Renata as the big Broadway star. His memories are of a young girl struggling to keep them alive, and some of the things she had to do were unpleasant."

"I can see that."

Cece finished her glass of champagne. "Before this past year, what Gabriel knew of his sister, he disliked. I think it was guilt that made him come all this way to point the finger of blame at you. He didn't love her, and now he feels badly because guilt has convinced him that he should have been a better brother. Someone should have loved her, and he's that logical candidate."

Cece was giving me a real education into the twisted emotions of Gabriel and Renata. "That makes sense." And it did. Guilt and regret are hard companions to travel with. I knew from personal experience.

"Look at that." Cece nodded at Gabriel and Kristine in the other room. The two were standing close, and Gabriel had picked up Giblet and was stroking the dog's head. "If I'm not mistaken, I see sparks of romantic interest between those two."

"Are you okay with that?" Cece had shown a flare of interest in Gabriel when he first blew into town. She wasn't acting territorial now, though.

"Yeah." She shrugged a shoulder. "He's too serious for me. He's a guy looking for a mission to throw himself into — something bigger than he is. The woman he chooses to love will always come second."

"How can you say that?" I put my arm around Cece. "You and Tinkie are the optimists of the group. You always believe in love ruling the universe."

"I do still believe in love, but I also know that my definition of love isn't everyone's. I want that passion that comes from intense connection. I think Gabriel wants a lover who's passionate about the same cause that he's devoted to — a love born out of mutual commitment to an issue." She tugged my hair. "Kristine is the walking embodiment of a person committed to a cause. They're perfect for each other."

For a moment I watched Kristine and Gabriel. Whoever would have thought a man so immaculately turned out would have a soft spot for dogs. In that split second, I saw the future for the two of them — a king-sized bed filled with Gabriel and Kristine and the stray animals they rescued.

"How did you get to be so smart?" I asked Cece.

"I gave up my masculinity for the wisdom of estrogen."

My laughter was impossible to contain. Suddenly, I felt much better. "Thanks, I needed that laugh."

"Anytime, dahling." She kissed my cheek. "I'm going to slip away. Tell Gabriel that I had a deadline. Ask Kristine if she'll give him a ride home."

"Sure." As I watched Cece do a runway walk to the door, I felt pride in my friend who knew herself well enough to walk away. I delivered the messages to Kristine and Gabriel, both of whom seemed delighted.

An hour and three glasses of champagne later, I found myself standing beside Harold as he proposed a toast to me and the show. In a far corner of the room, Coleman glowered, but he lifted his glass and drank to my success. He'd made no effort to talk to me, yet he hadn't left. Curiouser and curiouser.

"Sarah Booth, you revealed a dimension of yourself on the stage that we all suspected but never saw." Harold brushed my hair from my cheek and kissed it softly. "Whatever else happens in your life, you're going to be legend in Delta drama circles."

I smiled and fought back the image of me performing *The Snake Pit* in the prison cafeteria. "Thank you, Harold. And thank all of you who supported me."

Graf stepped forward. "To Sarah Booth, the next Southern star to shine bright in the Hollywood sky."

Everyone cheered and swilled the champagne.

Not to be topped, Tinkie held up her glass. Magically, waiters with glasses of champagne and little candy lipsticks appeared among the gathering. "To my friend and partner, innocent of murder but guilty of stealing all of our hearts." Tears shimmered in her eyes.

I blinked back my own tears, and my gaze was caught by Coleman as he signaled me outside. "Thank you, Tinkie." I gave her a big hug.

As soon as I could, I excused myself from

my friends and slipped to the front porch. The night had grown cold, and I had no jacket, but what I had to say to Coleman wouldn't take long. He stood in the darkest corner, an outline among the shadows. Perhaps he'd always been that and I'd fleshed him out with my desperation and imagination.

"Time for another interrogation?" I asked. "Or maybe playing nursemaid to your wife has grown tiresome so you came here for a break from the routine." My imitation of a striking cobra surprised even me. My anger was an indication of how badly he'd hurt me. Like any other animal, I was fighting back.

Coleman closed the distance between us so fast that I almost yelled. His hand caught my arm in a hard grip, and before I could cry out or fight back, his lips covered my mouth, and he kissed me.

At first I struggled, but my anger dissolved. Time and place fell away, and the only things that mattered were Coleman's lips and arms. This thing that I'd longed for was so much sweeter than I'd ever dared to dream.

His kiss said all of the things that neither of us could express. My response told him my heart and my fears. In my thirty-four years, I'd been kissed thoroughly and with expertise. Never had I been told a story of love by a kiss.

His hands moved over my back, caressing and claiming. I held onto his neck, twining my fingers in his hair, clinging to the strength I felt pulsing through him. An hour or a week could have passed. Nothing mattered except him.

"Tch, tch, tch. Sarah Booth, Coleman, you're out here like two teenagers."

Tinkie's voice cut into my dream and split it wide open. I stepped back from Coleman, my lips and body tingling.

"Half the town is in there." Tinkie's voice was thick with worry and anger. "If Booter or someone else had stepped out here and seen this little display, everything we're doing to help prove Sarah Booth's innocence would have been for nothing."

She had a right to be angry, but I wasn't about to apologize. Coleman took a deep breath. "You're absolutely right, Tinkie. I lost my head."

"You're going to lose your girl if you keep acting like a lovesick teenager." She rounded on me. "And you! After all this work to make it clear Coleman isn't going to be prejudiced in your favor — it's hard to sell that story if you're out here necking in the dark at a party."

"You're right." I spoke softly, not daring to look at Coleman because I knew with one hint of encouragement, I'd be right back in his arms.

"Now, Coleman, you go home. Sarah Booth, get your ass back in there and entertain your guests." Tinkie put her hands on her hips. "Now!"

We scattered like a covey of flushed quail. When I got to the door, I met Booter's sneer. "What's going on out here? Did the sheriff finally decide to get you off the streets for the safety of the town?"

I was just about to stomp her ass when I felt Tinkie's restraining hand on my arm. "Booter, dear, I saw there are only two canapés left. You better grab them so you don't have to leave empty-handed." She maneuvered me so that we both brushed past Booter.

"That was too close for comfort, Sarah Booth." Her fingers gripped my arm. Tinkie was petite, but she was no pushover. "Have you lost your mind? You and Coleman both!"

Apologizing would do no good. "I didn't intend for that to happen. I went out there to cuss him out."

She nodded and turned to face me. "I

believe that."

Something else was bothering her. Tinkie's brows were drawn together in a frown.

"What is it?"

"Gordon ran a background check on Gabriel Trovaioli."

Scanning the room, I saw that both he and Kristine were gone. I had a bad feeling. "He's a successful California architect and . . ."

"He did some time in jail for drugs."

I tried to let the information settle before I jumped to a conclusion. My mind was playing connect-the-dots so fast I felt dizzy for a moment. Graf had been bringing drugs into the United States, according to his story, for an unnamed source, allegedly a New York loan shark ring. And Renata was willing to pay an exorbitant bribe to spirit him back to America without a criminal record dragging behind him. Was it possible that Renata and her brother were drug smugglers? Had a drug deal gone bad ended in her murder?

My face must have reflected all of my thoughts because Tinkie nodded. "How do we know Gabriel arrived in town *after* Renata was dead?"

I gazed around the room, searching again for the handsome architect and Kristine

Rolofson. They were gone. "We don't know that," I said, "and Kristine and Giblet may be in great danger."

Tinkie's thought was to tell Coleman on the spot, but when we looked for him, he'd fled the scene of the crime. "Let's just go check it out," I said. "We can do it without arousing Gabriel's suspicions."

She was still reluctant, but we got our coats and slipped away from the party. It wasn't until I settled into the leather seat of Tinkie's Cadillac that I realized how tense my body was. So much had happened in such a little time, my response had been to tighten every muscle, and now I couldn't make them relax.

"We should at least call Coleman." Tinkie drove like a bat out of hell, but it didn't stop her from thinking.

"Let's see what the situation is." By having the law pull up with sirens wailing, we might put Kristine in danger if she wasn't already.

"How are we going to handle this?" She pulled the Caddy into the motel parking lot and stopped.

Easing out of the car, I stood for a moment in the cold night. The lights of Kristine's room burned dimly, and the curtains were drawn tight — either for purposes of murder or love. “I’m going to knock on the door,” I said. “I’ll act like I need to talk to her.”

“And me?” Tinkie’s look was dubious.

“If Gabriel is in there with Kristine, I want you to leave me here. Head straight to his room at The Gardens and use your charm on Gertrude Strom to get her to let you into his room. Then find whatever you can.”

“No.”

Tinkie was not normally so short-winded in her obstinacy. I took it as a signal that she was going to be truly difficult.

“This is the best plan.”

“It’s the most dangerous for you. What if he’s the killer, and he takes you and Kristine hostage?”

I smiled, even though my cheeks were freezing in the night. “I can handle it.”

Now Tinkie was doubly doubtful. “I don’t like the sound of that.”

“I’ll be fine. This is our perfect opportunity. Tinkie, time is running out. Gabriel, Graf, Bobbe, Kristine, and the elusive Robert Morgan are all suspects. But I’m the one who’s going to be left in Zinnia when all of them go back to their lives.”

“This isn’t safe.” Her chin jutted out, and she refused to look at me.

"If Gabriel's in there, you can call Gordon and ask him to stop by on the pretext of looking for me. That way I can hitch a ride home with Gordon."

"What, exactly, am I looking for in Gabriel's room?" she asked.

"Anything that incriminates him for the murder of his sister."

"Oh, that's all."

I could stand in the cold and argue with Tinkie, or I could put my intuitions to the test. Gabriel was preoccupied with Kristine, and Tinkie and I might never have another chance to search through his things.

Running across the parking lot to the motel door, I eased to the window. There was a tiny crack in the curtains, where I could just make out a body flung nude across the bed. A tangle of auburn hair hid Kristine's face.

My heart started pounding double-time. I couldn't see Gabriel. Was it possible he'd hurt Kristine? I shifted positions to try another angle of the room. Gabriel's bare bottom came into view, and I inhaled sharply. Talk about a room with a view.

Tinkie was still waiting, the motor of the Cadillac sending up a white plume of exhaust in the cold. I waved her on. She hesitated, and I stood and used both arms to signal her to take off.

She eased out of the parking lot, and I knelt by the window again. Gabriel had joined Kristine on the bed. Her moans were those of pleasure, not pain.

They were inside all hot and bothered, and I was outside freezing my butt off. To top it all off, Giblet was somewhere in the room, softly howling what sounded vaguely like "Moon River."

Something about this was very, very wrong! I took one more look and realized that I'd never seen a human body bend like that. Kristine looked like a circus performer and Gabriel was taking full advantage of her flexibility. I tore myself away.

For ten minutes I paced up and down in front of the door, trying to give them time to conclude their encounter before I knocked. At last, when my ears felt as if they might snap from my head, I raised my fist and brought it down on the door.

From inside came the sound of a feminine shriek and male curses. Giblet set up a racket barking. I didn't care. I had to get inside before I turned to ice. I was taking a risk. If Gabriel was the killer, he could hurt Kristine if confronted. He could hurt me, too. As frozen as I was, I wasn't in a position to perform any martial arts action.

The door flew open, and Kristine stood with a sheet wrapped around her. "Sarah Booth." She looked into the darkness behind me as if she would be able to see the reason I'd knocked at her door. "What are you doing here?"

"I need to talk to you." I tried to step past her, but she blocked me. Giblet came to the door to investigate, waiting for whatever cue her master gave.

"I need to talk." I made another stab at entering, but she blocked me again.

"Now isn't a good time."

"Kristine, I need your help, and I need it now. Tonight. Right this minute."

The urgency in my voice did the trick. She stepped back to reveal Gabriel struggling into his clothes. What I'd interrupted wasn't exactly a hostage situation, but it didn't matter. I had to keep Gabriel occupied while Tinkie did her job.

"I apologize," I said. I kicked the door closed behind me as I stepped into the room. I couldn't drag my gaze from Gabriel's naked torso. For an architect, he had a build. His stomach rippled with muscles, and when he turned to get his shirt, his back was a work of art. He was one of the most handsome potential killers I'd ever seen.

"What do you want, Sarah Booth?" Kristine brought me back to reality. I had to fabricate an excuse for being there, and I had to do it quickly.

Chapter 18

"I saw you leaving with Gabriel, and I had to come and check on you." I stepped past Kristine, my gaze on Gabriel. "This man has a criminal record."

Gabriel stopped with his fingers on the buttons of his shirt. "I begin to see why Renata despised you."

"Really, Sarah Booth. That's absurd." Kristine shifted from one bare foot to the other.

"I'm not making this up." I stood with the door at my back. The tension in the room was thick. Even Giblet was eyeing me with suspicion. "The only way Renata's real killer will ever be found involves the truth. All of it. And I'm here to make sure Gabriel tells you about his past." I'd thrown the gauntlet down, but Gabriel didn't seem too interested in picking it up. He looked at Kristine and sighed.

"I might not have a spotless past, but at

least I've never been charged with murder." He finished buttoning his shirt. "Say what you've come to say, Sarah Booth. Then leave. Kristine and I have . . . things to talk about."

"Is it true, Gabriel?" Kristine looked queasy.

He nodded. "It's true."

I thought Kristine was going to say something sharp, but she lifted her chin. "Tell me. Please. I know it can't be bad. You're so kind and gentle. Just tell me the truth."

Gabriel sat on the edge of the bed. "I was going to tell you, but things happened so quickly between us. I saw your love for Giblet, the way that you throw yourself into things with all of your heart. Renata spoke of you — always in a negative way — but I feel I know your heart."

"Cut to the chase and tell her about the drugs." I sounded heartless and mean, but everyone involved in this case had danced around the truth more than once. Gabriel was going to tell Kristine about his past, or I would tell her.

Gabriel cleared his throat. "When I was in my early twenties, I hung around with a wealthy pack of LA kids. We got caught doing cocaine. I pled to a lesser charge, did the minimum time, and went into drug rehab and counseling." He gave a sour look. "It was a long time ago. I was a kid. I changed my life because I saw where I was headed. I see that Ms. Delaney is grasping at straws if she thinks some foolishness from my past is going to paint me as a criminal."

Either he was telling the truth or he had a lot of his sister's talent for acting. "I just wanted to be sure Kristine knew exactly who she was climbing into bed with. Literally."

Gabriel smiled and shook his head. "I have to hand it to you, Sarah Booth. You've got a set of brass ones, coming into a hotel room to throw my past in my face."

This wasn't the reaction I'd anticipated. Without Gabriel to react against, I had nothing more to say. Yet I had to figure a way to keep him occupied. "Are you okay with this, Kristine?"

"Whatever Gabriel did in his past, he's a good man now. I don't want to hear anything more. It would be best if you left, Sarah Booth."

"I don't have a ride." I shrugged. "Tinkie dropped me off because she said I was acting a fool."

"Tinkie is correct, but I'll take you home." Gabriel pulled car keys from his pocket. "In fact, I insist on giving you a ride home. I think my sister unjustly accused you, Sarah Booth. And me, too. I feel I should do my best to make it up to you." He turned to Kristine. "I'll be back as quickly as possible."

I plunked into a chair. "I'm not going anywhere. I have a few more questions."

"Is this really necessary?" Kristine asked, wrapping the sheet more tightly. "We'd like to be alone, Sarah Booth." She went to Gabriel and sat beside him. "He proves to me again and again that no matter what mistakes he made in his past, he's the man I want in my life right now. And Giblet likes him, too."

The dog gave action to her words and leapt to the bed. He snuggled down beside Gabriel.

I felt like the worst kind of heel, but I had to give Tinkie time. "Gabriel, what did you know about Robert Morgan, the pharmacist?"

Kristine touched his arm and looked into his eyes. "If you know something, Gabriel, tell her. This isn't the best timing I've ever seen, but we have to help her, if we can."

Gabriel gave a long sigh. "Robert Morgan was another of my sister's weird admirers. She spoke about him like he was a servant. He ran errands for her, made sure she had her antiaging creams, prescriptions for her migraines, and super vitamins. In return, she badgered people into giving him bit roles in Broadway productions. He was always around, always underfoot." He shrugged. "Renata collected people like that. They told her what she wanted to hear."

"Doesn't it strike you as odd that your sister was poisoned and Morgan is a pharmacist?" Was it just me or was everyone overlooking the obvious?

"He was a friend. He pandered to her ego, but he had no reason to kill her." Gabriel rose and paced the room, his face a mask of determination. "Robert Morgan wouldn't have hurt my sister. In some strange way, I think he loved her."

"Who would have access to poison more easily than a pharmacist?" I asked the question quietly.

Gabriel whirled to confront me. "She told me *you* were trying to hurt her. Why should I suspect her friend when she suspected you?"

It was the question that I had to answer — not just to Gabriel but to everyone. "I don't know why Renata told you that. I never threatened her. I had no reason to hurt her."

"Except for a shot at Hollywood and a career as an actress."

I steadied myself. "You don't really believe I hurt Renata. You've said you don't believe it." I held his gaze and saw something dark in his eyes. "Who do you suspect, Gabriel?"

A tense silence stretched between us until Giblet leaped into Gabriel's lap, demanding his attention. He scooped the dog into his arms.

I pressed on. "When the police searched your sister's hotel room and dressing room, none of her medications were found. Do you know what happened to them?"

"I have no idea." His hands stroked the dog, but his gaze was focused on me. "Renata may have thrown them out. She was prone to tantrums, you know."

The knock that came on the door made all three of us jump, and Giblet begin to bark like a maniac. When Kristine opened the door, Gordon stood there.

"Sarah Booth, the sheriff is looking for you. He has some questions," he said.

"I was just leaving." I stepped through the door and started toward the patrol car. "You two have a nice evening," I said.

Gordon got behind the wheel, and I noticed the smile on his face.

"What's so funny?" I asked.

"You're a regular Darth Vader of love, Sarah Booth. All those two wanted was a motel room and some privacy. Tinkie said you might be in danger." He laughed. "In danger of killing Cupid."

I hadn't realized the depth of Gordon's humor. "That's very funny," I said sarcastically.

He eased out of the parking lot. "Where to, Darth? Maybe we should go up to Opal Lake and roust some kids parking. With you on the job we might prevent half a dozen unwanted pregnancies."

Gordon was having way too much fun at my expense. "Just take me to Harold's, please."

"You got it."

Ten minutes later I got out of the patrol car. Gordon refused my invitation to come in, even though the party was still in full swing. In all likelihood, I hadn't been missed. "Thanks for the ride."

"Where is Tinkie?" Gordon's gaze swept the parking lot for her vehicle.

"She's running an errand."

"Somehow, I don't like the sound of that."

Because I wasn't going to tell him anything else, I slammed the door and ran up the steps. I needed to thank Harold for the party and catch a ride to rendezvous with

Tinkie. Just as I was about to hit the front door, my cell phone rang.

"Sarah Booth!" Tinkie's voice held excitement.

"Did you find something?"

"Renata's will. But Graf already told you Gabriel inherits everything. It's a big estate, and the will is dated this past December."

"I just don't see Gabriel killing his sister." I hated to eliminate him as a suspect, but it felt all wrong. The problem with all of my suspects was that none of them seemed capable of killing.

"That's not all." Tinkie's voice held a secret.

"What?"

"There's a letter from Renata. It basically says that she's retiring from show biz after this play. She says she's going to live in Tahiti. Alone."

"But she was going to Hollywood with Graf."

"Not according to this letter."

"Well, grab it and get out of there."

"Don't you think Gabriel will miss it?"

"Not for the rest of the night. Photocopy it and put it back. Gabriel is busy with Kristine." A mental image of the couple flashed into my head. I was still amazed at his body. "I think you'll have plenty of time. I'm back at Harold's."

As I flipped my cell phone shut, it occurred to me that Renata had told a different story about her intentions to everyone she spoke with. She'd set the stage perfectly for a vanishing act, not a murder.

All of the guests were gone, and I sat in the parlor with Harold sipping a glass of champagne. Tinkie was coming to retrieve me, and while I waited, I took the time to talk to Harold.

"What will you do, Sarah Booth?" He saluted me with the champagne flute.

"About the murder charge, Coleman's tumor-producing wife, or Hollywood?" I sipped the bubbly letting the sparkles dance across my tongue. I generally preferred Jack, but there was nothing like champagne for a celebration.

"All of the above?"

"I don't know." It was such a relief to admit that to someone. Tinkie didn't want to hear it. Neither did Cece or Millie. They expected me to come up with ideas and solutions, plans and strategies. With Harold, I could tell the truth. "Someone set me up, and they did such a good job that I can't figure out who's behind it."

"Who stood to gain?"

"All of us, one way or another." I ran through my suspect list and the things they gained by Renata's death.

"Has Coleman indicated when he'll release the theatrical troupe to go back to New York?"

I shook my head. "Soon, though. There's no reason for him to hold them longer."

"Except that one of them likely killed Renata."

"There's no evidence to that effect. I'm the one that all the circumstantial evidence points to. I bought the lipstick, for which there's no record, cyanide was found in my trunk, Nancy at the feed store heard me ask about poisons, though it wasn't me." I was digging my grave with my words.

"The key word is circumstantial," Harold pointed out.

"I'm the best suspect. If I were sheriff, I'd arrest me." That still didn't let Coleman off the hook. The problem with Coleman was that I couldn't figure out what to feel about him. He'd charged me with murder and treated me like a criminal, yet I'd been making out with him only an hour before.

Harold's eyebrows arched. "So you've forgiven Coleman?"

I shook my head. "I don't know. I don't know what to feel about him."

"He has a job to do, Sarah Booth."

"And he has a wife. Connie is alive and getting well, apparently."

"That's a tough nut," Harold said. He refilled my champagne glass. "Concentrate on proving your innocence. Let Coleman handle his messy marital status."

"Good advice." I drained the glass and stood. The alcohol hit me hard and I staggered a little. Harold steadied me as he walked me to the front door.

"A bit of cool air will revive you."

Cool didn't do the night justice. It was downright cold, but it did snap me out of my stupor. "Tinkie will be here soon."

"Here's a bit of cheerful news. In your absence, Cece managed to spill a glass of motor oil on Booter. She left in a huff." He was smiling.

"Motor oil? Where'd Cece get that?"

"Out of my garage, I presume. She said something to me about Booter's pistons being stuck on bitch so she was felt it was her duty to 'lube her up.' I didn't realize what she intended until it was too late."

My smile was tired. "Cece is incomparable."

"Booter was talking to Graf earlier. They were deep into a discussion for about ten minutes in the backyard. I overheard their voices, but I couldn't hear what they were saying."

I suddenly remembered the night at Harold's when I'd eavesdropped on Hamilton Garrett V. It seemed like a lifetime ago. So many things had changed. "Maybe Graf has a thing for Booter. She has money, and that's bound to be attractive to Graf."

"He'll have plenty once he gets to Hollywood."

"True. If any of that is real."

"Your point is taken. In that case, Booter's bank account would be attractive."

"Graf has financial problems." Harold had been the one who got the information for Tinkie, so I didn't bore him by repeating the litany of Graf's debts.

"Sarah Booth, I know you didn't hurt anyone. But I want you to know, should things go wrong, Dahlia House won't be sold. Tinkie and Oscar and I have discussed this. We'll figure a way."

Caught between fear and gratitude, I kissed his cheek. "I have the most wonderful friends in the world."

"You won't lose your home. Or your hound or horse. So put those worries behind you and prove yourself innocent."

As if his words were magic, Tinkie swung down the driveway to pick me up.

"Thank you." I got into the car and Tinkie carried me home.

When we got to Dahlia House, I turned to her. "Come inside and have some coffee. Will Oscar mind?"

"He's asleep by now." She turned off the car, and we walked across the porch together. Sweetie greeted us with a lick before she ran outside to chase armadillos and whatever else she could sniff out.

"What's on your mind?" Tinkie asked when she'd settled at the table and the coffee was brewing.

"I don't think we have a viable suspect." I could see that my words rang true to her. She didn't even offer a tiny argument. "That concerns me."

"I know." She slumped onto the table. "Graf is so perfect as a suspect, but I don't think he did it."

"I know. And Gabriel is good, too. But it just doesn't hang together."

"Bobbe couldn't do it," she said.

"Nor Kristine."

"So where does that leave us?" she asked.

"Dangerously close to defeat."

She got up and walked to where I stood at the counter. "We've been through a lot worse than this, Sarah Booth. Only a few weeks ago, a serial killer was holding both of us hostage. We'll figure this out and put this murderer behind bars."

"Have we overlooked someone? Someone right under our noses?"

Tinkie tilted her head as she thought. "Who? Sir Alfred Bascomb?"

"We haven't checked him out thoroughly."

"You don't sound all that enthusiastic."

"It doesn't feel right. Sir Alfred really has nothing to gain."

"That we know of." She got the heavy whipping cream from the refrigerator and poured it into two cups. I added the coffee.

"Someone from the audience?" I thought again of Booter and Graf. We'd ruled Graf out as a suspect, and Booter had no motive.

"What did you learn about this Robert Morgan?"

I filled her in on what Gabriel had told me, none of it adding up to serious suspicion.

"He's the best we've got. I say we go for him."

We settled in at the table to drink our coffee. The clock showed two a.m., but the next day was Saturday, and I didn't have a single thing I had to do. The show was over. I could collect my mother's dresses from The Club and resume my life as a murder suspect. My moment of glory was passing, and even if Graf went to Hollywood, I wouldn't be allowed to leave Sunflower County.

"Cheer up, Sarah Booth, we'll —"

She didn't get to finish her sentence. The phone rang. I picked it up, checking the caller ID to see that the call came from The Gardens. "Hello."

"Sarah Booth, it's Graf. I just got a call from Morgan. He's in Memphis. He says he has to see me. You and Tinkie want to come along?"

"You bet." I signaled Tinkie with excitement. "What does he want? Did he say?"

"He said he had to talk to me. He said the cops are on his tail, and he has things he has to get rid of before they catch him."

This sounded like the most promising turn of events since Renata had died. "Tinkie and I'll pick you up."

"No! I'm going alone. You two follow. I'm meeting him in the bar of the Peabody Hotel. I told him I'd be there in an hour."

"We're right behind you." I was undressing as I spoke. I wanted my black jeans, boots, and my all-purpose leather jacket.

"Do you have any jeans in the Caddy?" I asked Tinkie.

"I'm not going horseback riding at two in the morning. Not even for you." She walked to the coffeepot and poured another cup.

"We're going to Memphis. Graf is meeting Robert Morgan."

Her eyes widened, and then she bit her lip. "You can't go, Sarah Booth. You can't leave the county."

"Watch me."

She frowned. "I'll go. You stay here."

"Not in this lifetime."

She signed. "I have some khakis and hiking boots in the trunk. I'll get them."

"Hurry. I'll fix a thermos of coffee for the drive."

Chapter 19

No one followed us out of Sunflower County, but as a precaution I slid down into the seat so that only Tinkie's head was visible. Well, partially visible. She's pretty short.

Once we cleared the Sunflower County line, I sat up and poured us both more coffee. My body ached with exhaustion. Tinkie had to be tired as well. All of the details of the production had fallen on her shoulders for the past month, and on top of that she was worried to death about me.

"I'll be glad when this is over," I told her.

"Me, too." She hesitated. "What do we hope to gain by going to Memphis?"

I didn't have a ready answer — at least not one I wanted to give. "Graf said Morgan had some things he needed to get rid of before he was picked up by the authorities. Morgan knows he's a wanted man. If he's a killer, Graf may be in trouble."

"And we're going to protect Graf? And do a better job than Coleman could do?" She was dubious.

"We have surprise on our side. And no one will suspect you. And I told Graf we wouldn't notify the law unless he was in danger."

"Sounds like Graf has something to hide."

Ever astute, Tinkie went to the heart of the matter. "You know he does. But even knowing all that I know, I can't see Graf hurting Renata."

"Is this a smart decision?"

"I have to see Morgan. To be sure he's the man who sold me that lipstick. If he is, then we'll figure out a way to get Coleman to nab him." The truth was, Coleman was hamstrung by legal procedure, and I wasn't. I'd taken no oath of public office. I was a free agent, in a manner of speaking. "It's just that we can be more subtle than Coleman."

"We can?"

I rolled my eyes. "Well, duh, Tinkie. We don't have to wear a uniform."

"Should I call Coleman and at least tell him what we're doing?"

I wanted to answer yes, but I didn't. I was violating my bond, and no matter how worthy the cause, Coleman would have to uphold the law. "It's best to leave him out of it. He'll have to arrest me."

"What if this Morgan is dangerous?"

"We'll cross that bridge when we come to it. I just want to see him. To see if he's the guy. Bobbe identified him as the man hanging around the show all the time, but if I can hook him into that lipstick . . ."

Tinkie gave up the argument as we entered the parking garage. "We can hang out in the ladies' room until we figure out what's what." Tinkie tossed the valet her keys and headed in.

"Keep the car available for a quick getaway." I gave the valet twenty dollars and hurried after my partner. For a short person, she could cover some ground when she set her mind to it.

Like all of the Delta belles, Tinkie knew the Peabody lobby like the back of her hand. High school and college graduation spawned dozens of parties in the grand old hotel where ducks waddled through the lobby each morning and afternoon on their daily march to the pond. The Peabody retained the grandeur of a South long gone, and it was revered in planter families like an old and glorious family member.

We skirted the lobby, which was almost empty at nearly four a.m. The hotel employees, who'd seen rich people do all kinds of crazy things, paid us no mind. Finally we slunk into the ladies' room, which featured a sofa to recline on, hot and cold washcloths, a drink machine, and ashtrays for those women who'd failed to give up the habit but didn't smoke in public. Just the sight of the porcelain designer ashtrays made me want to light up.

"Wait here. I'll do surveillance." Tinkie was out the door before I could protest. It was the best plan, too. Morgan might recognize me, but he had no reason to know Tinkie. Unless, of course, he'd been lurking around Zinnia and knew she was my best friend and partner.

I almost went after her, but I forced myself to wait. Tinkie was capable. She'd fought a long, hard battle the last few months to prove that to herself and to me and Oscar. She'd willed or prayed or chanted a breast lump away — with both Oscar and me sniping at her heels to go to a surgeon. The least I could do was trust her enough to spy around a lobby.

It was a long five minutes, but when she returned, she had information. "Graf is in the bar, alone. He saw me, but he only arched an eyebrow. He acted like he thinks he's being watched."

"Excellent." I gave her a hug.

"You were worried about me," she accused.

"Damn straight."

She hugged me back. "That makes us even. So what's the game plan?"

"You bribe the bartender to let you work the bar. I'm going to" — I shook my hair loose and quickly worked it into a French braid — "pretend to be a janitor." Somewhere I'd find brooms and cleaning supplies. There might also be a shirt with the hotel insignia. "At this time of night, it won't be odd to see someone cleaning, and once he comes in and sits with Graf, I can get a good look and then get out of there."

Tinkie's expression showed her doubt, but she kept her lip zipped about it. "Okay, and then what?"

"When Morgan gets there, you can eavesdrop. See what they're talking about. Just mix Morgan's drink really strong."

"What are you going to do, jam him in your clean-up cart and abduct him? Maybe break his kneecaps to make him talk?" She put her hands on her hips.

"If I have to." I wasn't kidding. I was charged with murder. This man might be able to prove I'd bought lipstick already coated with a deadly poison. A deadly poison that he'd likely applied to the lipstick.

"He's not going to say anything that would incriminate himself."

She had a point. "At least I can identify him."

"It might be smarter if we tailed him. Maybe then we could find out where he's staying, what he's up to. Then we can call Coleman and he can call the Memphis police and they can grab him. He's wanted as a material witness in this case, you know."

She was right. "Good thinking, Tink! I'll go talk to the valet and find out what kind of car Morgan is driving."

"I'll take over as bartender. I know you trust Graf, but I'm not totally there yet. I want to keep an eye on him as well as Morgan."

In the lobby we parted ways. Tinkie went to the bar and I found the valet talking to a desk clerk. He gave me his full attention when I palmed another twenty to him.

"Dude with strange whiskers?" he asked when I questioned him about Morgan.

"That's him."

"Pulled up in a Tahoe. Navy Blue. Told me to keep it close, he wouldn't be long."

"I need to follow him when he leaves."

He nodded. "He cheating on his wife?"

His grin was wide.

"Something like that. When he starts to leave, could you give me a signal?"

"I'll do more than that. I'll hold him up at the booth until you can get behind him."

His name was on the tag on his lapel. "Thanks, Anthony."

"All in the name of justice." His grin was infectious, and I was smiling when I took up my station behind a potted palm. It annoyed me that I could do nothing but wait, but that was the role I needed to play. At least for a little while.

Twenty minutes later Tinkie brought me a cup of steaming coffee and some news.

"He and Graf have been talking. A couple of times, I thought Graf might hit him, but Morgan calmed him down. Whatever's going on between them is intense."

"Could you hear anything?"

"Not much." She glanced over her shoulder. "I think they're almost finished. Are we set to tail him?"

"We're ready."

"Good. I'm going to turn the bar back over to the bartender. She's getting antsy."

"Thanks for the coffee."

She hurried back to the bar, and I sipped the strong Colombian brew. Just as I put my cup down, a tall man came out of the bar and walked straight toward me.

I eased back into the indoor shrub as much as possible, but it was unnecessary. Morgan was preoccupied with his own thoughts. I got a good look at him as he passed, and I felt my heart begin to thud. It was the same man from the cosmetic shop in Memphis. He'd thrown away the white, muttonchop whiskers, which had obviously been a disguise. Instead, his sideburns, while still oversized, were salt-and-pepper, like his hair. He was younger, fitter, and his mouth was a long, self-satisfied slash.

He passed me by and headed for the parking garage.

Graf was a minute behind him, as was Tinkie. I grasped her hand and squeezed it. "It's him! He was behind that counter at La Burnisco! He's the one who sold me that lipstick." I finally took a good look at Graf. He didn't look good. "Are you okay?" I asked him.

He sank down on one of the sofas. "He's a real bastard."

"What's wrong?" I touched his shoulder.

"Renata sold my debt to him. He came to tell me I owed him $350,000 at the interest rate of seven percent. I've got until midnight to make my first payment or he's going to the tabloids and tell them all about my Mexican drug experience." He looked up at me like a kicked dog. "My Hollywood career will be over before it even starts. No one wants a drug-crazed actor on location."

"Renata sold him the debt?" I was astounded. This sounded like something from indentured servitude.

Graf rose abruptly and began to pace. "I thought I'd gotten out from under it. Imagine that. I didn't kill Renata, but I had this completely idiotic idea that I'd finally bested her. I was wrong." His laughter was bitter. "Renata always wins. Even from the grave she's reached out to hurt me."

"If you get the Hollywood deal, you can pay that off in no time." Tinkie was the pragmatist, and I could clearly see she wasn't overly concerned with Graf's financial whine.

Graf looked at me. "I'm not sure I can get the movie deal without Sarah Booth."

Anthony opened the door and windmilled his arm at me in a get-going signal. I gave Graf a quick hug of support. "We have to go."

"I'm just going to sit here a little while." He plopped back down. "When I'm feeling better, I'll drive back to Zinnia."

He looked completely undone. I felt a

pang of remorse as I walked away from him. He was in a financial pinch, but I was charged with murder, and the man who might be able to prove my innocence was about to leave town.

To my surprise, Morgan headed south, taking I-55 down toward the Delta. That would have been the last place I expected him to go. As far as I knew, he was a man without a place to stay. The police in New York were looking for him, and Gordon and Dewayne had alerted the counties around Sunflower to be on the watch for him. He would eventually be caught, but how much better if we could herd him right into Sunflower County where Coleman and the gang could snatch him up. Now that I knew he was the same man that sold me the lipstick, I knew he held my future in his hands.

Tinkie kept behind him a safe distance, but she chanced a glance at me. "We should call Coleman. Or at least Gordon. I'm serious, Sarah Booth. We need official intervention here. If Morgan slips away from us, we might not find him again. Coleman can set up roadblocks and take him into custody. We can question him then. If we can get him to admit he sold you that lipstick, then you're off the hook, Sarah Booth."

To the east, the sun was creeping up the horizon. Another day was beginning, and for most people I knew, their lives would fall into the normal rhythm of a Saturday morning. "You're right. We have to get him into custody." We were exhausted.

I pulled my cell out of my purse, then thought better of it. We were still a ways from Sunflower County. "You should call."

She slipped her hand in to her purse, digging around for the phone.

"Want me to hunt?" Tinkie's bag was almost as big as she was. She had all of her cosmetics, credit cards, checkbooks, Blackberry, and God knew what else in there.

"Sure."

Just as I took the purse, I heard her indrawn breath. I looked up to see that Morgan had floorboarded his Tahoe. "I think he might have realized we were following him."

I didn't know how that was possible. We were a hundred yards back and the cruise control was set on seventy-four, a respectable four miles over the speed limit. Just like he was. But something had spooked him. Some bee had gotten into his bonnet.

"Should I follow him?"

"We can't afford to lose him now." I dialed the sheriff's office number on her cell phone and handed it over to her. She gave Dewayne the statistics in rapid-fire sentences. When she snapped her phone closed, she shook her head. "He's flying, Sarah Booth."

And he was. He was doing at least 120 on that straight, empty Delta highway. While the Caddy could handle the speed, the SUV had a different center of balance. A couple of times it wobbled on the road as a wind current swept over the empty fields and buffeted it.

"Did Dewayne say they'd stop him?" I asked.

"He was calling Gordon and Coleman to set the roadblock. I'm supposed to call back if he turns off the main highway."

"I wonder what spooked him."

The answer came from behind us. The silver Porsche buzzed past us as if we were standing still. I barely caught a glimpse of Graf behind the wheel before he was gone, blistering down the highway toward the Tahoe.

"Damn!" Tinkie had the pedal to the floor, but the Porsche was created for speed. The Caddy was a luxury vehicle.

"What is Graf trying to do?" I had no idea what he hoped to accomplish by chasing Morgan.

In the early morning light, the little silver

car had blended into the gray highway. It was like he disappeared. The Tahoe was still visible, and far in the distance a truck pulling a tractor waited on the side of the road. When I saw it, I had a bad feeling.

Tinkie's grip on the wheel tightened, and she eased off the gas. We both saw the farm truck edge forward onto the highway in the path of the Tahoe. It was almost like a movie. The truck and trailer pulled onto the Interstate, the Tahoe swerved into the left lane to avoid it, the Tahoe wobbled slightly, ran off the road, swerved back on and slammed into the side of the trailer, then bounced away, veering off the road and into the ditch.

Morgan didn't have a chance. The Tahoe flipped three times, all sorts of things flying out the openings as the doors were wrenched free. Finally the vehicle settled on its roof, dust roiling all around it. The explosion that followed felt like I'd been kicked by Reveler, and we were still a quarter mile away.

I saw the Porsche then. Graf passed the wreck without even slowing. He disappeared in the distance, swallowed by the highway that faded into nothing.

In the carnage of Morgan's wreck, it didn't

matter to me that I was outside Sunflower County. Tinkie and I waited, unable to do anything except watch the Tahoe burn. The farmer, shaken but uninjured, sat with us as we listened for the sirens that marked the arrival of the deputies and an unnecessary ambulance. There was no way Robert Morgan could have survived the wreck and then the fire.

Tinkie didn't say anything. We both sat mute, watching the flames. The one person who could have proven my innocence was dead. Perhaps he had killed Renata for his own reasons. Most likely, we'd never know. Morgan had died and taken his secrets with him.

Coleman gave me a look when he arrived, but his primary focus was on the safety of other drivers who were beginning to fill the highway now. He took a statement from the farmer, and then Tinkie, and finally me.

"You're out of Sunflower County," he said.

"I realize that." I couldn't read his expression.

"Why don't you and Tinkie head home? Get a couple hours sleep. Then I want to talk to you. At the sheriff's office at eleven."

I couldn't tell if he wanted to talk or if this was a plot to get me close enough to the jail so he could throw me in and lock the door. I honestly didn't care. I was beaten down. My last hope at exoneration had been cremated in the Tahoe.

I got in the car and slumped against the seat.

"I'm sorry, Sarah Booth." Tinkie touched my arm. "We were so close."

"When I feel better, I'm going to kick Graf's ass all the way back to New York." Why had he done that? Why had he given such hot pursuit to Robert Morgan?

My head spun with fears and rationalizations, and none of them changed the fact that I was in serious trouble.

Chapter 20

I felt at least a hundred years old as I tossed beneath the hand-sewn quilts on my bed. Winter sunshine danced in the windows, and if I looked out, I'd see Reveler and Miss Scrapiron playing in the paddock. They'd become the fastest of friends, and though I should have called Lee to come and fetch her mare, I didn't. As long as I was free, I wanted Reveler to have his lady friend. If I went to prison, Lee would take Reveler and care for him. She was that kind of friend. Tinkie would take Sweetie Pie.

But what of Jitty? Would she wait for me here? Tinkie and Harold would stop the bank from foreclosing on my mortgage as long as they could. But in reality, they couldn't pay off the debt if I were sentenced to life. Dahlia House would fade and decline without love. And though my friends had true-blue hearts and money, the bank had rules and stockholders to account to. It wasn't a personal charity fund that those three could dip into whenever they felt the need to rescue a friend from financial ruin. And if this happened, what would become of Jitty?

As if I'd called her, she shimmered into being at the foot of the bed. She wore a floor-length cotton gown, with pale pink ribbons woven through the bib, and her hair was braided and hung on her shoulder. If she'd had a candle in one hand, I might have thought she'd stepped right out of time and into my bedroom.

"Mr. Sandman must have an appointment with you," I told her. "I'm glad one of us looks like she's going to get some sleep."

"I don't need it. You do." She sat so lightly on the foot of the bed that I couldn't feel her body weight. Then again, she was a ghost. How much did she weigh? I'd heard the weight of a soul was twenty-one grams. Jitty, I was sure, would be only a fashionable nineteen. "Why aren't you snoozin'?" she asked.

"I can't sleep. I'm worried."

Her smile was sad. "Me, too."

That scared me. Jitty hadn't been her normal sassy self since this whole thing had started. She'd been melancholy, and that was my modus operandi. "Am I going to prison?"

"You know I don't tell the future. That's the province of your friend, Madame Tomeeka."

"The last vision Tammy had wasn't a good one. Renata reached from the world beyond and grabbed me." I thought again of Graf and how he'd said almost the same words — that Renata had reached from the grave to punish him.

"This woman has a long reach for a corpse."

That was a statement I couldn't argue with. No matter that I'd bested her on the stage — my talent was at last acknowledged. Renata was still the superior . . . enemy. The word surprised me. I'd considered Renata an adversary, a bitch, a dangerous acquaintance. Never an enemy. Until now.

"There is reason in all things, Sarah Booth. You may not see it right this minute, but one thing will shift into focus, and you'll see the truth."

"What makes a person an enemy?" I couldn't let go of the idea.

"Jealousy, competitiveness, revenge, covetousness." Jitty said each word with care. "Back when Alice was alive, she had a young friend by the name of Bethelyn Carlisle James. Her cousin was someone you might have heard of, Jesse James."

I remembered this old story, but I fluffed my pillows to listen again. It had been years since anyone had told me a bedtime story, and I was ready to listen. "The legendary outlaw, Jesse James."

"That was him, but it's not a simple story, and what I'm goin' to talk about really has nothin' to do with outlaws. Only in-laws." Jitty crooked a leg up on the bed, and the thin winter light struck her skin, rendering it the most perfect shade of golden mocha I'd ever seen.

"Bethelyn had a younger sister, didn't she?" I knew the story, but Jitty always added a detail that I'd forgotten.

"Her name was Karalyn. She was a year younger, a child born too soon, before her mother had fully recovered from the birth of Bethelyn." Jitty's eyes had gone unfocused as she walked the dirt roads of the past.

"Celestine James died a month after giving birth to Karalyn, and Luther was destroyed. He loved his wife more than anything else in his life. More than his children. But it was his good fortune that Bethelyn grew into the spittin' image of her mother. It was truly uncanny. Some said that the spirit of Celestine James had lingered in the old plantation and slipped into the body of her eldest daughter while the girl slept."

I didn't bother to point out the irony of a ghost telling me a ghost story. I listened with rapt attention.

"Luther loved Bethelyn beyond reason. She had the finest ball gowns for the parties of the day, and two maids to attend to her grooming and toilette. Alice, who was the same age, told me later that Bethelyn never let the attention spoil her. She tried to be a mother to Karalyn, who would have no part of it. Abandoned and neglected by her father, Karalyn grew to hate her older sister and view her as the source of all of her unhappiness."

"Couldn't Luther see what he was doing?"

"He was blinded by love for a woman long gone. By trying to recreate the past and have his beloved Celestine, he never really knew Bethelyn, and worse, he drove Karalyn away."

"Do you ever tell stories that aren't sad?" I suddenly didn't want to hear any more. I'd asked the question about enemies. The answer Jitty was giving me was making me very uncomfortable, because I couldn't help but draw a parallel between Luther James and Graf Milieu. Both men found themselves caught between two women, and

Luther had paid a terrible price.

"Stories aren't interestin' if they don't have drama." Jitty's smile was fleeting. "This all happened back in 1855, six years before the war. Alice and Bethelyn were just teenagers in a world doomed to die a brutal death. Those were days of grand parties and weekend-long barbecues. I'd been born on the Caldwell Plantation, Mossy Oak. The Caldwells had a son, Jacob, they hoped to match up with Bethelyn for marriage. Talk was that it was a true love match — that the couple had fallen deeply in love. Alice was excited for her friend, and she was thrilled to be goin' to one of her first grown-up parties, a barbecue to be followed that evening by a ball with musicians from New Orleans. It was quite a do.

"As I said, Alice and Bethelyn were good friends, and they'd traveled down to Mossy Oak together, gigglin' and carryin' on the whole way."

There was a portrait of Alice in the music room wearing a magnificent midnight-blue gown. She was fifteen, little more than a child, but considered a woman in her own right at that time. The dress had been made especially for her to wear to the Caldwell Plantation ball, and somewhere in the attic, the dress was wrapped and stored in a cedar trunk.

"Bethelyn and Alice got to the party. I remember when Alice stepped out of the carriage, I knew I had to be in her life. She was something special, Sarah Booth. She had a light about her that came from within. And Bethelyn looked as if she'd been released from prison. She was free of her father and her sister. Karalyn was arriving later, with Luther. Karalyn was fourteen, too young to attend the party, but she'd wrangled Luther into letting her go to the barbecue, if not the ball."

The way Jitty told the story, I could see it all unfolding. The girls arriving with trunks and maids. It had been March, as I recalled the story, when spring touches the South with such kindness and grace. The dogwoods would have bloomed white against green lawns and towering masses of bright purple and pink azaleas mingled with the long branches of bridal wreath creating private alcoves where an ingenious couple could meet for a kiss.

Jitty's voice spun the spell. "The barbecue was almost over when Karalyn and Luther arrived. No one took much notice of the younger girl. It wasn't until the women headed into the house to take a nap in the afternoon that Luther noticed Karalyn was missing. Also missing was Jacob Caldwell."

"No one took the absences seriously. At first." I picked up the thread of the story. "Luther searched the yard, moving on to the stables, then the cow barns. By then he was worried. If not in physical danger, Karalyn risked her reputation if she was off with Jacob, her sister's intended."

"Those times, a girl's virtue was her most prized possession." Jitty threw me a look that said a lot about my tarnished virtue. "Luther went back to the house and got all the men to help, and the servants. Because I loved to fish and spent a lot of time along the creek, they sent me to hunt there."

Jitty's hands were folded in her lap, but as she recalled the details of the story, I could see how it still unsettled her, even after all these years. Her fingers laced and held, as if she could grip the past and change it.

"I found him first. Jacob. He was facedown in the creek. He'd been struck in the back of the head with a tree limb, and I remember how his hair waved so gently in the water and a stream of blood flowed out behind him like a kite tail. Lord, I started screamin' and draggin' at his body, tryin' to pull him up the bank and make him breathe. Mr. Luther came up and helped. There was nothin' to be done, Sarah Booth. He was gone."

I closed my eyes, but I couldn't stop the images.

"Mr. Caldwell found Karalyn. She'd hanged herself in one of the beautiful oak trees beside the creek. She had a note pinned to her dress. It said, 'You can't have everything, Bethelyn. You don't get to have it all.' "

"And that's the story of how two sisters became mortal enemies." It was a bitter tale, and I saw Jitty's point — there is a seed of unreason in the bond of enemies.

"Jealousy can twist a person's mind, Sarah Booth." Jitty rose to her feet.

"What happened to Bethelyn?" I knew the short answer — she'd never married but had tended her father until his early death from a heart attack only five years later. She sold the Jameses' land in Mississippi and moved to Missouri to join up with the rest of the James family. "Did she ever recover?"

"She wrote Alice, a lot before the war, then a few letters after the South was defeated. That's when her cousin came home from soldierin' and got caught up in his life as an outlaw. When she died of typhus, she was writing the story of Jesse James's life. Alice believed that Bethelyn rode with the James gang on some of their raids."

"Did anyone have an easy life during those times?"

Jitty walked to the doorway and turned back. "Not then. Not now. Close your eyes and try to nap. Life's gone come knockin' on the front door before you know it."

This time when she left, she walked out the open door like a regular person would do.

I had two hours before I had to be at the courthouse. I shut my eyes and fell into a deep sleep.

Getting to the courthouse on time proved a bit more difficult than I'd anticipated. The entire block around the courthouse was a circus. Media lined the street. Some enterprising fool had set up a funnel cake booth, and I could smell the sugary confection cooking.

Word had spread about Robert Morgan's fiery death — another twist in the tabloid special of "the diva murder." I ignored all the questions and was immensely glad when Cece appeared at my side. One look from her and the other reporters crept back. I was clearly her story, and they'd better not dare to try to get a piece of me.

"Coleman has run that pack of wolves out of the courthouse several times. He's put two photographers in jail, but it hasn't dimmed their bloodlust." Cece looked at them admiringly.

Right. And the blood they lusted for was mine. Suspect numero uno. "Why don't you become my press agent?" I asked her.

"That's the most insulting thing you've ever said to me!" she huffed. "I'm a journalist."

"When did journalists move from omnivores to pure carnivores?"

"Very funny." She slammed the courthouse door in the faces of a herd of her fellow reporters. I watched in amusement as she slid the lock home. "Hurry up, Sarah Booth. It'll take them a couple of minutes to run around to the other doors. We can be in Coleman's office by then."

Glad of the reprieve from the flashguns popping in my face, I followed her into the main sheriff's office and straight past Dewayne to Coleman's inner office. He was on the telephone and didn't look up.

"Brenda, I can't come and sit with Connie. Either you'll have to do it or get another family member."

There was a long silence. Coleman looked down at his desk and rubbed the deep furrows in his forehead with his left hand.

"I'm sorry. My number one suspect in a murder case was killed this morning. I'm a little busy. If Connie's able to use the telephone, she's able to stay by herself. She can call one of you to help her." He replaced the receiver on the hook even as I could hear Connie's sister, Brenda, talking angrily.

Coleman looked at Cece and a strange message seemed to pass between them. At last he turned to me. "I should put you in jail."

If Connie had a tumor, Coleman was a freaking schizophrenic. Dr. Jekyll-slash-Mr. Hyde. He was all kissy and loving one minute, and the next he was the Iceman. I wasn't about to apologize or explain. I gave him look for look.

"Where's Tinkie?" he asked.

There was a sharp knock at the door, and Tinkie came in. She looked refreshed and glamorous. I felt like an old gym suit. "Looks like a happy crowd," she drawled as she closed the door.

"Tinkie, you and Sarah Booth have some explaining to do." Coleman looked only at her.

"I guess I'm here to play secretary and record the minutes?" Cece asked.

"You're here as a journalist," Coleman

said. "The story about Robert Morgan is going to get out, and I'd just as soon that it comes out correctly."

"I think that's a compliment," I said to Cece.

"What the hell were the two of you doing in Memphis?" Coleman asked Tinkie.

"Memphis?" Cece gave me a disapproving look. "Your bond —"

"Hush," I snapped.

"It was my idea," Tinkie said. "And I needed Sarah Booth's help. We got a call from Graf that he was meeting Robert Morgan in the Peabody. I wanted Sarah Booth to positively identify Morgan as the man who'd sold her lipstick at La Burnisco. She did. We were tailing him home and he took off doing about 200 miles per hour. A farm truck pulled back on the road. Morgan lost control and flipped. End of story."

Cece was scribbling madly as Tinkie talked. I thought Tinkie had done a brilliant job. Just the facts, ma'am.

"Why was Graf meeting Morgan?" Coleman, who was nobody's fool, asked.

"You'll have to ask Graf. The important issue is that Sarah Booth identified Morgan. He'd dressed in a disguise and sold her the lipstick. He's a pharmacist with access to all kinds of drugs and poisons. Now

Sarah Booth isn't the main suspect." Tinkie took a deep breath.

"No, Sarah Booth isn't the main suspect any longer," Coleman answered slowly. "She's the only living suspect. I'm cutting the theatre company loose today. I can't hold them any longer. Watley left yesterday, all excited about an offer he had to get to New York to investigate. Bobbe Renshaw is packing, and Kristine Rolofson is heading out to Los Angeles with her dog and Gabriel Trovaioli."

"You're letting all of them leave?" A terrible pang in my stomach made me hug myself. Coleman's blue gaze told he me was dead serious. All the other suspects were leaving. "Even Graf?"

"Graf has already left town, Sarah Booth." Coleman's tone was gentler, but he was still angry. "He blew through Sunflower County without stopping, headed south."

"Where did he go?" I couldn't believe he left me in Zinnia to face all of this alone. I'd begun to believe he'd changed. At least a little.

"Where do you think he went?" Coleman asked.

"Hollywood?"

"Would you have a specific address?"

I shook my head. "Call Federico Marquez.

That's the director who was interested in Graf for a movie." I looked at Tinkie. Her blue eyes were misty as she saw my dream begin to crumble at my feet. "If Graf is missing, that's where he's gone."

Now that Robert Morgan was dead, chances were good that Graf's debt would be forgotten. He could go out to Tinseltown and live the good life, the life he'd offered to share with me.

"Any other possible places he might go?"

I shook my head.

"Well, you can console yourself with the fact that he hasn't gone to Hollywood. And he won't likely be going. I took a statement from the driver of the farm vehicle, one Calvin Rogers. Mr. Rogers said the driver of a silver Porsche was obviously in pursuit of Robert Morgan on the highway. We have a warrant out for Graf's arrest for vehicular homicide and leaving the scene of an accident. He won't be going to Hollywood or anywhere else."

I felt the pain in my stomach tighten. "Graf didn't kill Morgan. Coleman, that's just not fair. Graf might have been chasing him, but it was Morgan who drove an SUV like it was a sports car. You can't blame Graf for Morgan's stupidity."

Coleman stood up. "Oh, but yes I can.

Graf Milieu is somewhere in the state of Mississippi. If he tries to buy a plane ticket, I'll have him in custody in nothing flat. There's an APB out for him from here to California. We'll have him before the weekend is out."

"Can I print this?" Cece asked.

"Every word of it." Coleman walked to the door and opened it. "You're all free to go. For the moment. Sarah Booth, if you leave Sunflower County again, you'll be in jail without even a chance to explain. Tinkie, you'll be in the cell beside her."

When we'd all been evicted from his office, he closed the door and I heard the lock slide into place.

Chapter 21

Tinkie blazed a trail through the reporters, and I followed, abandoning the roadster and diving into the front seat of the Cadillac for the moment. When the journalists and paparazzi cleared the square, I'd go back and get my car.

"Imagine what it must be like to be a celebrity every day," Tinkie said. "This is what life in Hollywood will be like."

"The difference between celebrity and notoriety is vast." I shielded my face from a hundred flashes as Tinkie drove slowly through the crowd.

"Coleman was really pissed." She stated the obvious.

"Too freaking bad." I was really pissed, too. He had no right to act so high-handed. Connie was nibbling him to death, but that didn't give him cause to mood-swing all over the place. I had nothing to do with the complications of his life. I was only trying to save my butt from going to prison for something I didn't do.

I sat up taller as we left the reporters behind.

"Where to?" Tinkie asked.

We couldn't go to Millie's. The café was crawling with journalists. They'd found good coffee and a place to set up their laptops, and they weren't going to budge. "Tinkie, what are we going to do? With Morgan dead . . ."

She headed out of town toward the wide-open spaces of the Delta. "We're going somewhere quiet where we can think for just a minute."

We were a long way from Scarlett's moment in the Georgia clay, but there was truth that the land sustained us. Whenever I was down, if I went back to the earth, that rich dirt that grew crops in such abundance, I found momentary peace. As we drove deeper into the land down poorly maintained farm roads, I felt my body relax. I didn't care where we went.

Careful not to cross the boundary of Sunflower County, Tinkie pulled into the driveway of the old Maxwell Plantation. Treacherous buck vines with half-inch thorns grew out of the untended azaleas and climbed the old oaks. The house itself seemed to slump. I closed my eyes, suddenly overcome with a desire to cry. The place retained an elegance that's hard to describe in the middle of decay, but time had worked hard magic. Vines wound around the columns that supported the second story. The old bricks, baked by slaves, had begun to crumble. The massive oaks that lined the drive held Spanish moss that wafted in the gentle breeze and told a story of past lawn parties and laughter.

Tinkie and I had grown close enough that I could speak my thoughts. "Dahlia House will look like this if I go to prison."

Tinkie's hand found mine on the car seat. "No, Sarah Booth. It won't. I'll buy Dahlia House, if it comes to that. Harold and I have discussed it. Your home won't be sold or razed. You have our word."

The tears slid down my cheeks. I hated to cry in front of anyone, but Tinkie was more than just anyone. She was the sister I should have had. "I'm sorry," I said. "I just can't help feeling sorry for myself."

She hugged me to her, and I felt her own tears wetting my hair. "It looks bad right now, but it isn't over. You know that. The fat lady hasn't sung yet."

"Do you really think Graf has left for Hollywood without me?"

She looked at the Maxwell place. The processes of nature were at work even as we sat and watched. "Graf doesn't take action, Sarah Booth. He reacts. If he has gone to Hollywood, it's not because he didn't want to take you with him. It's that he fled in such a hurry, he couldn't wait."

I saw that, but it didn't make me feel better. "Everything he said was a lie."

"Probably. But did you really expect it to be different?" She smiled at me. "I think not. You always knew him better than the rest of us. We saw that gorgeous exterior, and we thought the outside was a preview of the inside. We were just wrong."

How to explain to her that I'd really felt that Graf was different? The first time I'd fallen for him, I'd been inexperienced and unprepared for a man who believed his own lies. I'd allowed myself to be swept up in his powerful beliefs. This time, though, I hadn't. Yet Graf had played me again and made me believe in him. Or at least in his innocence.

"I wonder where he is."

"Coleman will find him. Eventually. But Graf can't really help us, Sarah Booth. We need someone who can corroborate your identification of Morgan as the man that sold that lipstick."

"And in the meantime, I'll have my preliminary hearing and then be indicted by a grand jury for murder. That's going to be a great recommendation for your future clients. 'Oh, yeah, my former partner's doin' time for murder.' "

"Let me worry about my future," Tinkie said. "Why don't we go for a ride? You have Miss Scrapiron over at your house. I could ride with you."

I sat back and felt Tinkie's forehead to see if she had a fever. She didn't ride horses. She didn't like to get dirty. I didn't think she even owned a pair of breeches, much less paddock boots.

"Oh, pick up your jaw," she said. "I took lessons at summer camp each year. And I dated a boy my freshman year at Ole Miss who owned a breeding farm in Lexington, Kentucky. I used to help him breeze the racehorses."

"You what?"

She laughed. "See, there are still some good surprises left in the day, Sarah Booth." She started the car and backed out of the driveway. "If you mess with me, I'll have to race you, and then you'll be humiliated when I win."

Surprised, yes. Humiliated, never. "You're on." I covered a big yawn. I was tuckered out.

She pulled up at the courthouse so I could get my car. The reporters had moved on, sharklike, looking for new stories. "Why don't you grab some lunch and take a quick nap. I'll give you a call to wake you up and be at Dahlia House at three, ready to ride. Then I'm going to make you eat my mud."

Food and nap, in that order. Tinkie was a genius. "I'll be ready at three."

I watched her pull away before I drove home. Once inside I fell into bed, asleep before I could even slip out of my clothes.

I dreamt of vines and old houses that moaned as each brick fell from the foundation. Behind the houses was a small black spring that whispered darkly of the future.

"Look deep, Sarah Booth. Don't back away. Look deep to see what's hidden." The spring called to me. Though I knew better, I was drawn there to gaze into the slick black surface.

Renata floated up, hair streaming around her pale face. Her eyes were wide open, her expression frozen into victory.

When I backed away from her she reached for me.

"From the grave, Sarah Booth. We're coming from the grave for you."

I looked deeper and saw Robert Morgan

floating up behind her. His hands had talons for fingers and he snatched at me.

I awoke at the sound of my own scream. Sweetie Pie was frantically licking my face, and once I sat up, I realized it was nearly five o'clock. I'd slept away the entire afternoon. Dusk was settling over me, and Tinkie had stood me up. I could only smile. She'd tricked me into focusing on a horseback ride so I could sleep. Pretty clever, my old friend. If the dreams had left me alone, I would have slept through until the next day. As it was, I awoke with a sense of dread and no plan for the afternoon.

I scouted the house for Jitty, but she was nowhere to be found. Not even up in the attic, where I sometimes found her in Alice's old rocking chair. The old rocker, armless and designed for nursing mothers, was covered in dust. No matter how much I knew about the past, or how much I cared, I couldn't maintain the weight of it, as well as the present. The future was a dark spring that dared me to look deeply. My goal was to find that place of balance in the present.

I tried Tinkie's cell phone, but she didn't answer. Cece answered but said she was on deadline, that she'd call me back. Millie sounded frazzled, but she told me she was bringing a boxed dinner and a stack of old tabloids for my entertainment.

"There's another big story about you, Sarah Booth. It's in *The Galaxy.* They've got a great photo of you and Graf kissing, and they've drawn prison bars — like the two of you are locked up together. Very sexy, I have to say."

Great. Now some maniac was drawing me into prison. "Do they say I'm guilty of murder?"

Millie's chuckle was amused. "Honey, they don't care if you're guilty or not. It's the romance of two stars locked up together. It's a great story, even if it isn't true."

"Right."

"I'll be by in fifteen minutes. And I have a doggie bag for Sweetie Pie."

"You're the best, Millie." Sweetie had been reduced to dry dog food for the past several days, and the food from Millie's would be a real treat.

I fed the horses, whistled up my hound, and made a Jack and water while I waited on the porch for Millie to arrive. True to her word, she was there before my butt had frozen. We went inside and I made her a wine spritzer. Millie wasn't a big drinker, but she liked a light drink.

The stack of old tabloids she'd brought was impressive. Maybe it would keep my mind off my woes. I picked up an issue while Millie opened the go-box and changed my dinner to a china plate. "No sense in eating out of Styrofoam," she said. "I hate the way it sounds when a fork touches that stuff." She shuddered.

The plate she set before me included all of my favorites — fried chicken, fried okra, turnip greens, purple hull peas and a corn muffin. My mouth watered as I looked at it.

I saw that Sweetie, too, had a treat. Millie had brought her a half-dozen chicken tenders, broiled, and a dollop of homemade macaroni and cheese, one of Sweetie's all-time favorites.

"This is wonderful."

"Tinkie said you might be hungry."

"Speaking of Tinkie, where is she?"

Millie looked chagrined. "I shouldn't have mentioned her name."

Now I was really curious. "Where is she?"

"She went to Memphis, Sarah Booth. She knew you couldn't go, but she said she had something she had to do."

"What?" I lowered my fork.

"She was going to that cosmetic shop. And she was going loaded for bear."

It was eight o'clock when Tinkie finally called me, and I could tell from her voice that she was both jubilant and tired.

"Meet me at the sheriff's office," she said. "I'm about ten minutes from town. I've already called Coleman."

I didn't argue, I just loaded into the car and drove. I took Sweetie Pie along. She liked to ride, and she enjoyed a visit to the jail, where she'd once spent several days — falsely accused of biting.

The reporters had cleared out of the town square, leaving only the wind to whistle down the empty streets. It seemed much later than it was as I parked and walked along the sidewalk. A piece of litter skittered across the sidewalk in front of me, and Sweetie nabbed it. She carried it up the steps and into the courthouse where I put it in a waste can.

The sheriff's office was quiet, and Coleman was nowhere to be found. Gordon met us. "Coleman can't make it," he said. "Connie went into some kind of seizure. He's at the hospital."

I didn't believe a word of it, but I also didn't feel the need to comment. Tinkie had plenty to say, though.

"Gordon, I have a sworn statement here from Carlotta La Burnisco saying that Robert Morgan was in her shop the day Sarah Booth bought the lipstick. Carlotta turned the shop over to Morgan." She produced a paper with a flourish and slammed it onto the counter.

Gordon and I both peered at the paper, which was typewritten and signed by Carlotta La Burnisco. It was exactly as Tinkie said — a sworn statement attesting to the fact that Morgan had taken over the shop that day, that he'd torn a page from her ledger and that he'd paid Carlotta five grand to be absent and to lie to anyone who asked.

"Well, looks like Ms. Carlotta La Burnisco has some serious questions to answer." Gordon keyed the radio and called Dewayne. "Sarah Booth and Tinkie are up here at the sheriff's office. We're going to need some help from the Memphis PD to pick up Carlotta La Burnisco. Then you're going to Memphis to pick up that cosmetic woman and bring her here to answer some questions."

"The bitchy one?" Dewayne asked, his voice loud on the radio.

"That would be her." Gordon turned back to us. "Good work, Tinkie. How'd you break her? We couldn't get her to admit to anything."

"Oscar helped me," Tinkie said, giving me a hug. "It was a financial thing. It took some digging around, but Oscar discovered some irregularities in the mortgage payments on the cosmetic shop. La Burnisco was about to go into default, and suddenly, the balloon note on the mortgage was paid in full." Tinkie had our full attention as she talked.

"Money was coming in from somewhere, but Oscar couldn't get a clear picture. The bank was reluctant. It took him several days, but he finally traced the money back to Renata. A week before she died, Renata wrote Carlotta a check for nearly fifty thousand dollars, essentially buying in as a stockholder in the company."

"Damn." I was ready to spit nails.

"Why?" Gordon asked.

Tinkie was triumphant. "Sarah Booth is innocent. She was framed, and she was framed by Renata herself! Renata is behind every move in this game."

"It still doesn't make sense." Tinkie was slugging back a strong cup of coffee though I'd begged her to go home and get some rest. "The facts don't lie. But why? Gordon asked the right question. Why did Renata do this? Why, if she knew someone was going to kill her, did she spend her time pinning it on you instead of trying to stay alive?"

We sat at my kitchen table, and I pulled

out the stack of tabloids Millie had brought. I'd noticed something in one of the stories from the past summer. I found the place again and scanned the story more closely.

Photos of Renata, barefoot and wearing a sarong, showed her on a beach in Tahiti. She was walking alone down the beach, her smile resplendent. The reporter quoted her as saying, "My dream is to simply slip from the public eye and live out the rest of my days in an island paradise like this." There were other pictures of her in a villa with a distinctive Mediterranean look, the surf pounding in the distance.

I pushed the paper to Tinkie. "Read this. I think Renata was going to disappear. But not before she fixed it so that Graf and I would suffer."

Tinkie quickly read the article. She looked up at me. "Remember the letter she sent her brother? It said something about how she was going to vanish." Her voice was threaded with caffeine-induced excitement. "Sarah Booth, that finally makes perfect sense. Renata intended to set up an elaborate frame to snare you and Graf, and then she was going to disappear. She didn't intend to be killed, but she fully intended to make it *appear* that she was dead. So you and Graf would pay the ultimate price."

She pulled out her cell phone. "Gordon, have you heard from the Memphis PD?" She arched both eyebrows at me and whispered, "Carlotta's in custody, and she's agreed to tell everything she knows. Her lawyer is on the way so she can give a statement." She turned back to Gordon.

"That's excellent, Gordon. Now I have something else. Was there anything left of Robert Morgan's belongings in the car?" She paused. "Uh-huh. Can you check the Memphis airport and see if he had a ticket booked anywhere? Some far-flung getaway." Her smile told me Gordon was willing to comply. "Thanks, Gordon, you're the best."

She was about to hang up when I heard Gordon call out to her. She listened again, a furrow drawing between her eyebrows. "Okay, I'll tell her."

She hung up and didn't look at me.

"Tell me what?"

"Never mind. It'll only piss you off."

"So tell me."

"Connie has stabilized. They're transferring her back to Jackson, and Coleman is headed down there, too. Graf's been taken into custody."

CHAPTER 22

After Tinkie left, promising to go home and sleep, I found that I couldn't unwind. Maybe it was the coffee, which I'd made mega-strong. Or maybe it was the idea of Coleman rushing off to Jackson. Or maybe it was the pure vindictiveness of Renata and her efforts to destroy my life. Her actions were shocking, and no matter how I examined them, I couldn't really grasp what might have motivated her.

I was completely out of her world. I'd left New York and acting. Yet she'd finagled the theatre troupe to come to Zinnia. She'd spent weeks and thousands of dollars to set me up as a murderess. She'd put equal energy into punishing Graf. But at least she and Graf had a relationship. I had nothing with Renata. Why had she settled on me as the scapegoat? And what had gone wrong with her plan to disappear?

I could see the grand design. The poisoned

lipstick had been left at the shop for me to buy — with all records destroyed by Robert Morgan. Then Renata left the lipstick message smeared on the mirror of her dressing room, alluding to the fact that someone wanted her dead. Renata had carefully maligned me to her brother and all who would listen, saying I wanted her dead. But she'd meant to disappear. What had happened? How had she actually applied lipstick that she knew to be poisoned?

My footsteps echoed emptily in the house as I walked from room to room, seeking some place of comfort. Of safety. I wandered the office of Delaney Detective Agency, straightening my desk so that it looked like Tinkie's, imposing order out of chaos because I'd lost control of my life.

The music room held Alice's portrait, and I went there to study my great-great-grandmother's likeness. She'd been such a child, but she held herself with the composure of an adult. No one lingered in childhood in those days. At fifteen, she was a woman of marriageable age. Soon she would be married, and soon after that delivering her first child, a son. I touched the canvas, feeling the texture of the paint.

"You look like her at times, Sarah Booth." Jitty's voice was dark and rich. "The two of you, side by side, I see it more clearly. 'Course Alice was a lady, which is a label no one can put on you."

"The label I'll be wearing is 'convicted murderer' if I don't shake some evidence loose." As I sat at the grand piano, I found Jitty sitting in a chaise lounge near the wall. Her huge skirts took up half the room, and the vivid pink reminded me of the frilliness of azaleas. Why Jitty had chosen a time period when women had fewer rights than cattle, and blacks had no rights at all, I couldn't begin to comprehend. Jitty was a law unto herself, and when she was ready to reveal the master plan behind her clothing, she would.

I pressed middle C on the keyboard. Long ago, I'd taken lessons. The memory of my mother, sitting beside me on the piano bench as we played that beginner duet, "Heart and Soul," almost made me cry out with pain. "I'm glad Mom and Dad aren't around to see me charged with Renata's death."

"Shoot. You think they'd bat an eye? Your mother would be picketing the sheriff's office and threatening to shoot Coleman." She laughed. "Your pa would be digging through the evidence, looking for the one thing that everyone else has overlooked."

She walked to the cabinets where so many of the family albums were kept. "Might want to look over some things from the past, Sarah Booth. Seems to me that whatever grudge Renata held against you, it would have to come from that year you were in New York. You've already figured out you didn't have anything in common in the present."

"But —" It was pointless. Jitty had taken herself off to the past or the future or wherever the ghostly cocktail hour was being held.

I found myself reluctant to pull out the photo albums, but I did it anyway. What else was I going to do? I couldn't book a flight to Tahiti to find Renata's hideaway, because I was still under my bond. I hoped that a search of Robert Morgan's New York apartment or his credit card charges would give us Renata's ultimate destination, but someone else would have to do the legwork to prove that. What I could do was examine the past.

I found the New York album, which I'd begun with such great expectations. I'd gone to the Big Apple fresh from three years of success in regional theatre. Reviews of my work were terrific from San Diego to Boston. I'd played vixens, killers, beguiled daughters, comic harridans, angry mothers — the widest variety of work I could get. I was ready to take New York.

The first picture shows me standing outside a sixth-floor walk-up apartment on the upper east side of Manhattan. The boxes containing all I'd need for my new life are on the pavement around me and a moving crew hustles them up the stairs.

My fingers traced the features of my face as I tried to connect with the young woman I saw in the photograph. The picture was taken only a couple of years earlier, yet I found it difficult to believe I had once been that woman. She was touched by sadness, but there was also an optimism that I'd lost somewhere along the way.

I went through the preliminary photos quickly, stopping only when I got to the snapshots I'd requested at *'Night, Mother.* There I'd been Renata's understudy, and I had met Graf backstage after the show.

I'd given all the members of the crew disposable cameras and asked them to document the backstage moments. It was a goofy, naïve thing to do, but the photos had given me great pleasure as I'd dreamed of my coming success. Renata had been a perfect bitch to me, but that hadn't dampened my enthusiasm. I'd thought I could learn something from her, and I'd endured her petty cruelties with that in mind.

I came to the photographs with Graf and studied them. We made goo-goo eyes at each other right from the start. Looking at the photos, I could see that I was helpless before his charm.

Within a week, we were inseparable. He was the male lead in *Same Time, Next Year,* and we were backstage at one or the other of the theatres. Even though I didn't have a part, I was living the theatre life, just like I'd dreamed it. Hearing the applause for Graf was almost as good as hearing it for myself. Or so I'd thought at the time.

I flipped the album pages, sinking deeper into the past. One photo stopped me. Graf and I are kissing in the foreground. Renata is on stage, but she's looking at us. The pure hatred aimed in our direction almost made me drop the album. Funny, I'd looked at the photo numerous times, but I'd never noticed her. I'd only seen Graf.

Was it possible that jealousy from so long ago could motivate her to concoct such a plan for revenge? It just rang hollow. The bottom line was that Renata had no reason to vent her jealous rage on me.

I picked up the phone to call Tinkie and stopped. With any luck at all, Tinkie was asleep. My questions and concerns could wait until morning.

But other things couldn't. I got my jacket and my hound and headed to the motel where Kristine Rolofson was staying. I could only hope that I could catch her before she left town. I needed to talk to her.

The manager told me that she was still checked in, and I went to her room, praying she'd forgotten about my last visit. My luck wasn't that good. She opened the door to my sharp knock, but as soon as she saw me, she tried to slam it shut.

"I need your help. Please."

She eased back off the door. "Gabriel thinks you're insane. He's gone to get his things and then we're leaving. Together."

"Please, Kristine. I need to ask a few questions."

"The sheriff said Gabriel and I could leave Zinnia."

"I know, but I need some answers before you go. Please."

She stepped aside and let me in, taking a wary stand between the bed and the door. Giblet sat on the bed. His tail wagged, but his gaze never left me. If I tried anything, he wasn't going to let me get away with it.

I gave a low whistle and Sweetie Pie came bounding into the room. With a few sniffs and growls, the two dogs became the fastest of friends.

"Oh, Sarah Booth," Kristine said, "you know how to win me over. Giblet has been so lonely. That hound is a perfect playmate."

"Sweetie is great. But I need to ask about Renata."

She sighed and sank into a chair. "I've told you and the sheriff everything I know. I've been over it again and again."

"This hasn't been asked." I sat on the end of the bed, ignoring the dogs as they tussled and romped. "You saw Robert Morgan at different theatres, right?" I pulled out the sketch I'd gotten from the sheriff's office to show her. "This man."

"I saw him in New York, Atlantic City, Reno, and here. Yes, he's been in and out. I had the impression he wanted a part in the play."

"Maybe. But I think he was Renata's . . . friend." I wasn't sure if their relationship was romantic or symbiotic. Somehow they were linked. "I'd like to determine what kind of friend he was. How he fit into her life."

She rubbed between her eyebrows with an index finger as she thought. "I only saw them alone together once."

"And?"

"It's hard to say. It didn't seem romantic." Her eyes widened. "They were talking about you. I remember it now. She said something like you wouldn't be able to resist coming to the show as her understudy."

"And what did Morgan say?"

"I can't remember," she said. "I wasn't paying close attention."

"When was this, Kristine? It's important."

"New York or Atlantic City. Before Reno. I can't be certain, but it was after the hurricane that hit the Gulf Coast."

"Did you ever hear her say anything about Graf? About hurting him?"

"She was always muttering threats, but not just about Graf. Once, though, she did tell him to be careful what he wished for because those were the things that came true."

I felt a little deflated. Kristine bolstered my theory, but she hadn't given me anything to help prove it.

"Thanks," I told her as I called Sweetie to my side. "I'd like to speak with Gabriel before you leave."

"I'll tell him. He's at The Gardens packing his things. We have big plans, Sarah Booth. We're going to start a foundation to fight for legislation in each state to help protect innocent animals. Gabriel is a good man. It's hard to believe he and Renata shared the same blood."

"Good luck, Kristine."

"And good luck to you, Sarah Booth. I wish I could help you clear your name." She reached over to stroke Sweetie's long ears. "I wish this had never happened. Not even Renata deserved to die like that. And Gabriel said she was coming around, at least toward him. He said that the last time he saw her, he could see that her meanness came from fear."

"Gabriel is a lot more forgiving than I am." I shook Kristine's hand before Sweetie and I took our leave. I wasn't finished for the night. Bobbe Renshaw was staying at The Gardens, too. Maybe I could get both of them in one fell swoop.

Gertrude would never allow Sweetie Pie in her B&B — if she saw her. I had to talk to Bobbe, and it was too cold to leave Sweetie in the car. Ergo, Sweetie was going in with me.

I parked down the driveway, and Sweetie and I crept through the shadows toward the front window of the B&B. Certainly Gertrude had to sleep sometime. She couldn't always be sitting at the desk, and if the coast was clear, I'd just have a look at the guest register and find out what rooms Gabriel and Bobbe had taken.

To my aggravation, I saw Gertrude's copper-wire hairdo behind the counter. I'd have to find Bobbe's room on my own. Sweetie and I slunk along the back gallery of the rambling old house, listening at doors, prepared to duck into the shadows at the first sound of footsteps.

I caught the sound of Bobbe's voice clearly raised in agitation. I couldn't make out the words, so I moved closer to the door. The Gardens dates back to pre–Civil War days, and every room has a door on the interior hallway and a door on a gallery. Even though it was January and cold, the door to Bobbe's room was cracked and cigarette smoke seeped out. Gertrude would have a hissy fit if she knew Bobbe was smoking amongst her priceless antiques. I peeked inside and saw Bobbe's bags stacked on the floor. She held her cell phone as she paced in her jacket and boots, a cigarette between her fingers.

"I don't care how you do it, just get that stuff back in his room." Her tone brooked no arguments.

"Danny, you went into a dead man's apartment. You took things that the law will be looking for. I don't care why you did it, I only care if you're caught, I'll be the one charged with murder. Put that stuff back exactly where you got it."

She paced silently as she listened.

"Just do it. No excuses. Just get it done. I've got a midnight flight out of Memphis. I'll be home by six a.m." She snapped her phone shut and then opened it to dial.

Sweetie Pie's growl came from deep in her throat. The hair on the back of my neck stood on end, and I pivoted on my toe just as something hard slammed into the back of my head.

I tried to brace myself on the door of Bobbe's room, but it flew open and I felt myself falling onto the faded Oriental carpet. Then there was only blackness.

Strong arms lifted me, and I curled against the warmth of someone's chest. I was very content until I felt something wet and warm moving over my face. That's when I heard Sweetie Pie's worried whines.

I forced my eyes open to find Graf holding me and Tinkie advancing on Gertrude Strom.

"I thought she was a burglar," Gertrude said. She held a rolling pin in her hand and I was able to put two and two together. I reached up to touch my head. The goose egg was impressive, but there wasn't any blood. Gertrude had cold-cocked me with a baking implement.

"Gertrude, you know Sarah Booth. You did this out of pure damn meanness." Tinkie was very put out.

"I don't allow dogs or snoops on my premises." Gertrude was completely unrepentant. "Isn't she charged with murder? How is it that she's out running around, peeping in people's rooms?"

"Ms. Strom, are you going to file charges against Sarah Booth?" Gordon asked. He held a notepad in his hand.

"I hardly think so," Tinkie said. "Because if she does, Sarah Booth will file assault charges against her."

"Help me up," I said. Graf set me on my feet. Though I wobbled a moment, I regained my balance and walked over to Gertrude. "File charges. Please do it. I'm going to sue you until the cows come home." I felt the angry blood thud in the lump on my head.

"Oh, posh! Just get off my property and take that mangy dog with you." She stormed back inside, swinging the rolling pin with each stride.

I was still a little confused. Especially about Graf. Last I heard, he'd been taken into custody. "What happened?"

"I was up at the jail bonding Graf out when Gordon got the call to come here. Something told us the reported burglar might be you, so we came, too."

"You bonded Graf out?" I was still confused.

"Oscar says I might as well open my own bonding business." She smiled. "Not such a bad idea."

I suddenly remembered why I was at The Gardens and the conversation I'd overheard. "Bobbe Renshaw." I started toward her room.

"She's gone." Tinkie looked worried. "We saw her pulling out of the parking lot just as we were coming in. Coleman told her she could return home."

I felt a wave of weakness, and as I stumbled, Graf caught my arm to give me support. "We need to stop her."

"Why?" Tinkie asked.

"I think her husband may have taken something from Robert Morgan's New York apartment. Something that may prove my innocence."

"How does Bobbe's husband know —" Graf started to ask, but Tinkie cut him off.

"Then we need to stop her." Tinkie put her words into action. She started toward the parking lot. "Gordon, you've got the patrol car with the siren and lights. Can you catch up to her?"

"She's headed to the Memphis airport," I told him.

Gordon wasted no time. He was across the porch and running to the patrol car. "I'll stop her before she gets out of Sunflower County."

"We'll be at the sheriff's office." Tinkie opened the passenger door of her Caddy for me. "Give Graf your keys, Sarah Booth, so he can drive your car."

I did as I was told, as Tinkie opened the back door for Sweetie. In a matter of minutes, we were en route to Zinnia.

"Why in the world didn't you call me if you were going to snoop around The Gardens? You know Gertrude hates you."

"She hates you, too," I pointed out.

"Right. But she's afraid of me because of Oscar and the bank. She would never have struck me with a rolling pin."

"I didn't call you because I thought you were sleeping."

"That coffee you made was strong enough to wake Lazarus. I tried to sleep, but I couldn't. Then Graf called, and I went to make his bond."

"How did Oscar feel about that?" Somehow, I'd never thought Oscar would be so tolerant of Tinkie's new lifestyle.

"He's not thrilled, but he realizes that I'll do whatever I have to where you're involved."

"Thanks, Tinkie, but how is Graf's bail tied to me?"

"If Renata meant to disappear and frame you for murder, then she had to have a reason. That reason has to be tied to Graf. Don't you see? Otherwise why would she have chosen you to frame? I think we need to have a long sit-down with Graf, and we couldn't do it in the jail."

"That makes perfect sense." My head was throbbing, and my temper was short. "I get the distinct impression that nobody has told the complete truth. Not Graf, not Kristine, not Bobbe."

"And the biggest liar of all was Renata." Tinkie pulled up to the curb at the courthouse. We stopped behind Coleman's truck.

"I thought he was in Jackson." The one person I didn't want to see was Coleman Peters.

"Sarah Booth, whether you feel like it or not, I think tonight's the night to clear up any misunderstandings. This business has gone on long enough. On all fronts. Coleman is going to come clean. So is Graf, and so is Bobbe."

"Throw Gabriel in there, too. We need to find him and bring him up here."

"That's an excellent idea." She whipped out her cell phone. "Coleman, it's Tinkie. I need you to bring Gabriel Trovaioli in from The Gardens so that Sarah Booth and I can talk to him. I realize you don't have to do this, but I think you should. It's time to put a stop to all of this suspicion. We both know Sarah Booth is innocent. One of these people killed Renata, or one of them knows who did. I want answers, and I want them now."

I could hear the weariness in Coleman's deep voice, and for a split second, I felt sorry for him. Then I reminded myself that pity ran only one way with him. He had done what he felt he had to do. Now Tinkie and I were going to do what we had to do. And the end result was that my name would be cleared before the clock struck midnight.

Chapter 23

Coleman arrived with a sputtering Gabriel about the same time Gordon returned with a very unhappy Bobbe. She was complaining loudly about missing her flight when she stepped into the sheriff's office and saw Graf, Gabriel, and me.

Sweetie Pie wagged her tail, but that was the only bit of welcome Bobbe got. I called Sweetie to my side, and she sat down, uncertain about all the tension in the room.

"What's going on?" Bobbe asked, but I wasn't paying that much attention to her.

My gaze had settled on Coleman, and I wasn't prepared to see how worn he looked. He'd lost at least ten pounds since I'd seen him last, and the lines around his eyes and mouth were not put there with smiles. The gauntness made him seem angry.

"What's this about?" Bobbe's hands trembled, and I wondered what she really had to hide. I'd felt sorry for her, thinking about how she'd been forced to be away from her husband and baby. She'd played on my sympathy — and then she'd tampered with evidence, leaving me to face a murder charge.

"It's about the truth," Coleman said. "At last. We've come to the part in the investigation where someone is going to tell me exactly what's going on here."

He walked past Gabriel and Graf at the counter and on to Bobbe, where she stood by the door. "I suggest you all take a seat. No one is leaving until this is finished and the truth is told."

"You can't hold us. You have absolutely no reason to detain any of us." Gabriel started toward the door.

"Gordon, put the cuffs on him and read him his rights." Coleman's voice was calm and deadly. "Charge him with obstructing justice. We'll hold him as a material witness until the trial."

"You can't do that!" Gabriel looked around at us but found no help. "Kristine is waiting for me. We have plans. We —"

"I have plans, too, Gabriel." I spoke with a certain edge. "Like living the rest of my life free because I didn't do anything wrong."

"Really, Sarah Booth, it's not my fault this

has come down on your head." He glowered at me.

"Wrong." I really looked at him. Perhaps it was the lighting, but I thought I caught a glimpse of Renata in the depths of his eyes. "You came to town accusing me, saying that Renata was afraid of me, heightening the suspicion that I hurt her. And you did this without any evidence. You took the rumor that someone deliberately planted and helped to grow it until I stood accused in my hometown."

Gabriel wasn't one to back down. He met me glare for glare. "I came to Zinnia for justice for my sister's murder. Which I haven't received yet." He gave Coleman a contemptuous look. "I'm beginning to wonder if I'll ever find out the truth."

"You had one goal in mind when you came, Gabriel." I thought of his very public accusation in Millie's Café. "And you set Booter on me like a bloodhound. You wanted me to know you suspected me, and you fed that suspicion in Booter and anyone else who would listen. You led her on and sicced her on me like a mad dog."

He shrugged. "So what? So sue me. I thought you killed Renata, and I devised a small way to make your life unpleasant. I admit that. But so what?"

Tinkie lifted her chin. "So what is that Sarah Booth didn't do a thing to Renata, and she's suffered all this time. So what is that you've just admitted to slandering Sarah Booth in front of witnesses. You should be ashamed of yourself."

"Who did kill my sister?" Gabriel looked around the room. "If not Sarah Booth, who? Are you any closer to answering that question?"

"Maybe." Coleman glanced at Tinkie, then at me. "With Sarah Booth as a named suspect, I'd hoped to draw the real killer out."

"Gee, thanks." I felt blood rush to my face, and my head, where Gertrude had bonked me, started throbbing again. "Does the word scapegoat ring any bells here?"

"I never believed you harmed Renata. Of all the people who were suspects, I knew you hadn't hurt anyone." Coleman's tone was gentle, a little sad.

"Could you have mentioned that to me?" I could hear my heartbeat in my ears, a very bad sign. If I started crying, it would all be over with. I only cried when I was so angry that there was no undoing the damage. If Coleman made me cry, in public, in front of these people, I would never forgive him.

"It had to play out the way it did, Sarah

Booth. Trust me."

"Right. That's exactly what I want to do — trust you."

Graf moved up to stand beside me. "That's a rotten thing to do to anyone, Sheriff, but especially to someone you say you love."

"Stay out of it, Milieu." Coleman's tone was murderous. "You don't have a clue about any of this."

"I have enough of a clue to know that no one deserves to be accused of murder. Not only accused, but charged and put in jail. This is the woman you say you love. How, exactly, does love figure into those actions?"

For once, Graf got it right. "If you don't believe that I killed her, who then?"

"That's something the night will tell." Coleman pointed at Gabriel. "You, come with me. Gordon, take Milieu to a cell."

"What about me?" Bobbe asked.

"You've got some explaining to do. And Sarah Booth and Tinkie have some questions for you."

While Graf and Gabriel were shifted out of the room, Bobbe turned to me. "You have to help me. My husband and baby will be at the airport to pick me up. You have to —"

I shook my head. "No, I don't."

"I didn't do anything," Bobbe wailed.

"What was taken from Robert Morgan's New York apartment?"

All of the color faded from her face, leaving her lipstick a dark umber slash. "How did you know?"

"I overheard you on the phone just before you took off for Memphis."

"But —" She looked away. "You heard me telling Danny to put what he'd taken back."

"That's right." I'd been bonked on the head, but my memory was still intact.

"It isn't like it sounds. It was just a medical report."

"What kind of medical report?" Tinkie asked.

"Renata's."

I sat up. "And what did it say?"

"Nothing of any importance to anyone but me." Bobbe bit her bottom lip and one lone tear traced down her face. "Honest, it was about makeup. She showed me the report and said she was keeping it for future reference."

Coleman stepped back into the room. He stood near the door to his office, listening, allowing Tinkie and me to conduct the interview.

"What kind of report about makeup is worth stealing?" Tinkie asked.

"One that says that Renata's makeup wasn't pure." Bobbe's voice was barely a whisper. "After Danny was nearly electrocuted, we came very close to losing our home. Renata used this incredibly expensive makeup." She looked at me. "You know that. The stuff was hand-concocted especially for her. Her lipstick was a hundred and fifty dollars a tube. The liquid foundation she wore cost nearly three hundred. She'd give me the money to order it for her. Renata liked to have people run her personal errands. I think it gave her a sense of real power."

To quote Johnny Cash, I could see the train a'comin'. "So you bought cheap makeup, put it in the expensive bottle, and kept the money."

She nodded. "I know it was wrong, but I was desperate. I figured it couldn't hurt. The makeup was excellent, but so are a lot of less expensive brands. No one could tell the difference, and for the most part that was true."

"Except . . ."

"Except Renata's face broke out. She had the makeup tested and discovered the switch. She thought the company had screwed her, so she was raising hell with them, threatening a lawsuit."

"La Burnisco?" I guessed.

"Right. Renata has used their cosmetics for years. They worked it out somehow."

I knew exactly how. The money Renata gave Carlotta was only part of the deal at La Burnisco. The other part of the bargain was when she dropped the threat of a lawsuit. No wonder Carlotta had jumped into the fire with the devil.

"You got your husband to steal the report because it would show a history of tainting her makeup." I wasn't certain how much of Bobbe's story I believed now. It was possible she'd worked with Robert Morgan to poison the lipstick.

"I knew how bad it would look if Renata died of tainted makeup and then it was discovered that someone had tampered with her makeup once before. I knew it would all be traced back to me, so I called Danny and asked him to steal the report."

I remembered how freaked out Bobbe became when I wanted to call Danny and ask him to come to Zinnia to support his wife. Now I knew why. She had him busy on a breaking-and-entering errand in New York. "So Danny got the report."

Bobbe nodded. "Then when the sheriff said I could go home, I realized that it was wrong to take the report. Danny was going to put it back."

"A day late and a dollar short," Tinkie sniffed.

"It was only a skin rash. It wasn't a serious problem." Bobbe's voice cracked.

"When did this happen?" I asked.

"In Reno."

"Why did Renata send the medical report to Morgan?" The connection between those two held the answer to a lot of unexplained things.

"I don't know. They were friends. He came up with some cream to soothe the rash." Bobbe shrugged.

"Tampering with evidence in a murder case is a serious thing." Coleman walked over. "And it does look bad, Ms. Renshaw."

She sighed. "Ever since Renata came into my life, things have looked bad. I did a bad thing, but I didn't hurt anyone. Neither did Danny. Let me call him and if he still has the report, he can fax it to you."

Coleman nodded and handed her a telephone.

Bobbe fought hard to hold onto her composure as she placed the call. She spoke hurriedly with her husband and gave him the fax number for the sheriff's office. When she hung up the phone, she took a deep breath. "I'm glad you know. I'm glad all of this is over. I just want to be free of this nightmare."

It was a sentiment I could clearly echo. The fax machine in the corner whirred into life and began producing pages.

Coleman examined the report and passed it to me. It showed exactly what Bobbe had said. The makeup contained nothing unusual, but it didn't match the composition of La Burnisco's magic formula. Bobbe hadn't harmed Renata in any serious way, but my eye was caught by the name of the doctor that Renata had gone to for the skin rash. Albert Samen. A copy of the report had also been sent to Dr. Varik, the retina specialist. Why would Renata send a report of a skin rash to two medical doctors in Los Angeles?

I pointed this out to Coleman. "Did you ever get Samen's medical report on Renata?"

He shook his head. "First thing tomorrow, I'll make another call." He looked around the room. "As for tonight, Milieu, Trovaioli, and Ms. Renshaw will be guests of Sunflower County."

Coleman was calling a halt to the questioning. I was surprised to find that it was nearly midnight. Tinkie was dead on her feet, and Coleman didn't look good either.

Gordon had taken a seat at the radio, but he looked done in, too. I could only assume that I was in a similar state.

"We'll be here bright and early," Tinkie said as she took my arm and led me into the hallway. Sweetie fell into step beside us, seemingly glad to be leaving the courthouse.

I turned back. Things with Coleman were not good, and I wanted to finish it. At the thought of what he'd done, my anger bubbled up again. "I want to have a talk with Coleman."

"Not now," Tinkie said, tugging on my arm. "Let it go for tonight, Sarah Booth. We're all about to drop."

"But —"

"No buts! Get some sleep and see how you feel in the morning." She dragged me down the hall and out into the cold night. I shivered until I thought my bones would rattle. She was right. I had no reserves left. There wasn't anything I had to say tonight that wouldn't wait until morning.

When I finally woke up the next morning, I felt as if I'd been away from home for a long, long time. I'd dreamed about Hollywood. The dreams had been fragmented, split with images of orange groves, the ocean, windswept hillsides. The scenes I'd witnessed had contained big-finned Cadillac convertibles, blondes with dark sunglasses and cinch-waisted dresses, martinis and palm trees. It was as if I'd flown over the state of California, sampling different places, different times.

Now I was in my own bed in a cold bedroom with late morning sun pouring through the windows. When I checked the bedside clock, I was shocked to see it was nearly eleven. No one had called, or knocked on the door, or licked my face. I'd been allowed to sleep for a solid eleven hours. And I felt much better.

I got up and called Tinkie. "Where are you?" I asked her.

"At the bakery. I'm picking up some Danish and coffee and one tall society reporter."

"Cece?"

"That's right. She called about thirty minutes ago. Seems like she finally turned up something on those Hollywood physicians."

"What about Coleman and Graf and Gabriel and Bobbe?"

"Coleman was called out of town. Gordon said he'd be back after lunch, so I thought we'd wait until then to go talk to Graf and Gabriel."

I didn't disagree with her logic, but I

wasn't prepared for the sense of betrayal that came with the knowledge Coleman had left Sunflower County. Again. No doubt involving Connie. I wasn't going to ask, though. Whatever convoluted schemes Connie had trapped him in were his business. I could wait to talk to him later, when my name was completely cleared, and I could tell him exactly what I thought.

"Are you bringing Cece here?" I asked, forcing my voice to remain bright and cheerful.

"If that's what you'd like."

"Or I could meet you at the paper?" I looked around the room to see clothes scattered everywhere. Surely I had clean jeans in the closet, and a sweater. How hard could that be to find?

"Then meet us at the paper. Cece's on her morning deadline, and that'll be easier on her. Then we can go on to the courthouse."

"Got it." I was already out of bed, digging through the closet. I came up with an old pair of worn blue jeans and a perky red sweater. Perfect. In three minutes I was lacing my paddock boots and dashing downstairs as I ran a brush through my hair.

I stopped long enough to feed Reveler and Miss Scrapiron, and then I was in the roadster headed to the *Zinnia Dispatch.*

As soon as I walked in the newsroom, I was blinded by a flashgun going off inches from my face.

"Gavin, you moron." Cece stalked across the newsroom and snatched the camera from the photographer's hands. "What are you doing?"

"She's news. Indicted, unindicted, out on bail, in the slammer. Sarah Booth Delaney is news. I can get five hundred dollars a pop from the *National Snout* for a picture of her."

"Gavin, we're going to hold you down and wax your legs." Cece's threat was serious. "We'll pull the wax off slowly, so that you feel each screaming root as it lets loose."

"Hey, that's not right. You can't threaten me."

"Oh, dahling, that's not a threat. That's a promise."

Gavin backed away, leaving his camera in Cece's clutches. "I'm going to tell the publisher on you."

"Do that." Cece dropped the camera in a trash can as we walked to her office. "Sorry, Sarah Booth."

"It's okay. He's only trying to make a little money on the side."

She arched one eyebrow. "Tinkie told me you were struck on the head. I see it was serious."

I shook my head as we walked into her office and she closed the door. Tinkie was already there, and she held out a cup of coffee for me. I sipped the brew and waited until Cece was sitting at her desk, an envelope in her hand.

"I got this by FedEx this morning. One of my colleagues at the *LA Times* did some legwork for me." She dumped the contents of the envelope on her desk. There were several photographs, which she passed to me. They showed a middle-aged man, shoulders hunched, as he walked into a glass and steel building with the words Samen Clinic on its facade. Right behind him was Robert Morgan.

"What's going on?" I asked. "Why was the photographer taking pictures of this clinic and Morgan?" I accepted the pastries that Tinkie passed and selected a cheese Danish.

"Essentially, Samen is an internist with a very particular speciality. He's been experimenting to help stop the aging process. That's why the photographer had him staked out. Word on the street is that a number of aging stars have been seeking his unapproved treatments." Cece was grinning like a Cheshire cat.

"You think Morgan was setting up a treatment for Renata?" I could see all sorts of new motives to murder Renata and put the blame on someone else. Maybe it wasn't personally directed at me — maybe I was just convenient as the sacrificial murderess.

I handed the photographs to Tinkie. She studied them a moment before she spoke. "Morgan looks a little furtive, doesn't he?"

"Yes." Cece and I spoke in unison.

"What if something this guy Samen gave Renata had begun to cause serious problems for her, health-wise? What if one of the experiments went awry?"

"And the two men, caught in what could potentially be horrific publicity and monetary damages, decided to end the problem simply." Cece popped the last of the Danish in her mouth. "Renata provided the perfect suspect, because she was constantly talking about you. Her jealousy set you up like a lamb to the slaughter."

Tinkie bit into a cream puff. "We're going to have to get Dr. Samen's records."

Chapter 24

With Cece's help, we'd inched closer to uncovering what might be the truth. The note Tinkie had found in Gabriel's room could be evidence to support our theory that Renata never intended to die. She had intended to stick me with a false murder charge while she frolicked away her middle years on the sandy beaches of Tahiti. Except something had gone wrong.

"Let's stop at Le Chic," I suggested to Tinkie as we left the newspaper office.

"Are we going shopping?" Tinkie perked up instantly. "You're in desperate need of something new, Sarah Booth. It'll take your mind off a lot of things."

My intention wasn't to shop, but Tinkie was so excited that I couldn't crush her enthusiasm. "I can shop for an hour. That's it. An hour. I already owe you money for the bail, so I'm not buying anything, but I'll talk while you shop."

We walked the two blocks to the cute little boutique that fronted Main Street and had been renovated between an old drugstore and a toy store. Zinnia had a good bit of charm, and Mitzy Mercer had made the most of it with her shop. The dress in the window was dazzling — a perfect winter white sheath sprinkled with shimmering crystals and a ruffled skirt that started at the upper thigh and ended about six inches above the knee in front and trailed to a V in the back. Va-va-voom. That was a dress to wear to a screen test.

"That says Hollywood to me," Tinkie said. "You've got the perfect skin tone for that warm white. With your hair and eyes . . ."

I tore myself away from the dress and the temptations that danced in my head. Even if Hollywood called, I couldn't go. I couldn't leave Sunflower County.

"Tinkie, do you think all along Coleman knew I was innocent?" The bell over the door tinkled merrily as we entered the shop.

"I don't think he ever really believed you'd harmed Renata." She greeted Mitzy with air-kisses to each cheek. "Sarah Booth wants to try that dress on." She pointed to the window. "She's going to Hollywood for a screen test."

Mitzy didn't even try to hide her excitement. "Sarah Booth, I saw the play. You were incredible. I mean I was simply transported out of time and place. I was right there with you and Brick and Big Daddy."

"Thanks, Mitzy." She was always nice when I came into the shop, but she'd never been effusive. I couldn't tell if it was Tinkie or my work on the stage.

Mitzy went to the back of the shop and brought out the dress in my size. "I only got two of them. This and the one on the dummy, which is Tinkie's size 2."

I took the dress and held it. Suddenly, I didn't want to see how I looked in it. I was tempting a fate that could end up breaking my heart.

"Go on." Tinkie pushed me to the dressing room. "I won't take no for an answer." She followed me in but stopped at the door of a booth when I entered.

As I took off my clothes, I tried to think of a way to ask my question that wouldn't make Tinkie think I was throwing a pity party. "If Coleman never believed I did it, why would he charge me? Why would he destroy my life?"

"First of all, your life isn't destroyed. Think about it, Sarah Booth. You got international attention on the stage *because* you were charged. But you're asking me to fathom the dark recesses of male thought processes, which I'll try." She took a breath. "I think it was two-prong. He knew everyone else would think you guilty, and if he didn't charge you, the doubt would linger. Forever. And I also think that he had a plan in mind. If you were charged, then the real murderer might grow careless."

"Yeah, that worked great." I slipped the dress over my head. The material was silky, and it settled over my hips like a lover's touch. I reached around and zipped it most of the way up. It fit like it had been made for me. I was almost afraid to look in the mirror.

"Are you done?" Tinkie's fingers gripped over the edge of the door.

I turned the knob and stepped out. I could see from her face that the dress was perfect. Mitzy walked back with a pair of sling-back heels in her hand. She stopped. "My God, Sarah Booth, you even look like a movie star, and you don't have on a stitch of makeup."

I turned and looked in the full-length mirror. The two weeks of torture had worked as the most effective diet I'd ever tried. I was thin. Movie star thin. Which made my eyes look larger, and sculpted collarbones showed near my throat. I simply stared.

"She'll take the dress." Tinkie snapped out of it first.

"I can't." I stepped back into the stall to take it off. When it slid to the floor, I picked it up and put it on a hanger. When I walked out, I went past Tinkie and Mitzy.

"I'll give you a discount," Mitzy said, hurrying after me. "Sarah Booth, it's perfection on you. No one else can wear it the way you do."

I smiled at her. "Thank you, Mitzy. If I get my name cleared, and I get some money, I'll be back for it."

"I'll put it up."

"No, don't do that." I couldn't make any promises when I would be back, if ever. "Don't hold it for me. Thanks, Mitzy. It's a great dress." I signaled Tinkie that I was leaving.

I heard Tink's high heels tapping after me, and when we were on the street again, she fell into step beside me in silence.

We walked several blocks. I had no real destination. I needed to talk to Coleman, but at the moment, I had no stomach for it. My emotions were too volatile. Still, we were going to have to go to the courthouse to see what he'd gotten out of Graf and Gabriel. Maybe a night in the slammer had cleared Bobbe's memory, too.

"Tinkie, do you still have that letter Renata wrote to Gabriel?"

"I made a copy of it, like you said. I put the original back in Gabriel's room." She slowed so that she could rummage around in her purse until she brought out several folded sheets of paper.

I took them, and we walked to a small park between a restaurant and a music shop. Long ago, a car dealership had been in the empty spot. I remembered it because I'd been fascinated by the glass bricks used for one entire wall. It had been highly innovative architecture for Zinnia in the '70s.

We settled onto a bench in the sunshine. The day was warmer than it had been, and several small wrens had taken up a chirping residence in an Indian hawthorn. The town had removed the poinsettias that had been planted in the huge pots on the corners. The first pointed leaves of daffodils, tulips, and bearded irises were breaking the soil. Soon the spring flowers would be in bloom. Time was passing quickly.

Tinkie handed me the letter she'd found, and I read through it quickly. It was exactly as she'd said. Renata was telling Gabriel that she was leaving the stage and Graf and the United States for an "island paradise" in an undisclosed location. "Don't try to find me," she said. "You're well and healthy and should lead a happy life. I was never really part of it, so let me go. We parted ways long ago when I was sixteen and forced to leave you behind."

I read the letter again, noting that the date was in November, only two months before she died. She had to have been in Reno. She could have canceled the Mississippi leg of the production, yet she'd been the one to insist on coming to Zinnia. Why, if she was so eager to get to her "island paradise"? The answer was simple. Because she intended to set me up.

"Who do you think killed Renata?" I handed the letter back to Tinkie for safekeeping. It might prove to be valuable evidence in my trial.

"I think Robert Morgan had a hand in it. If we're right, then one of her doctors is also involved. Someone who is unscrupulous. I mean, that's not unheard of in a world where beauty is bought and sold in a doctor's office. There's no telling what Renata might have signed up for, or what went wrong. Sarah Booth, do you realize some women are ingesting tapeworms to stay thin? How sick is that?"

Tinkie had finally done it. She'd rattled me out of my self-involvement. "What?"

"They put the tapeworm in a gel capsule and then swallow it. The tape grows and grows, eating a lot of calories in the process. Then they kill it with wormer and start over again."

I liked my newly acquired thinness, but not at the expense of swallowing worms. I'd had too many dogs, cats, and horses — and the attending parasite issues — to be enthused about the dietetic properties of tapeworms. "Can't the worms do permanent damage?"

"My point exactly. This kind of madness bolsters your theory that something went wrong during a medical procedure."

"This is all great, Tinkie. But we have no evidence of any of it."

She stood up. "So why are we sitting on a park bench like two old-timers? Let's shake the lead out and get after this."

I had no choice but to follow her. When we passed Le Chic, I noticed that the mannequin in the window was stark naked. At the sight a shiver ran through me. Someone had bought the dress in Tinkie's size. That's how easily a dream could be stolen, and Renata had done a thorough job of stealing mine.

As Tinkie hurried up the courthouse steps,

I lingered for a moment to pay my respects to Johnny Reb. The statue, symbolizing the dead Confederate soldiers whose bones were scattered across the entire South, looked more worn than usual in the winter sunshine. Johnny's hat was rumpled, and a stain at the corner of his right eye made him look as if he'd been crying.

I turned away and ran up the steps. Tinkie was already at work. It was time for me to get busy, too.

"What do you mean they're gone?"

I heard Tinkie long before I opened the door of the sheriff's office. Everyone in the courthouse's lower floors heard her. She was furious, and she wasn't hiding it.

"What's wrong?" I stepped inside and pushed the door closed. I looked from Tinkie, whose face was beet red with a pulse throbbing at her temple, to Dewayne, who fondled the microphone on the radio and refused to look up.

"What happened?" I asked again.

"Coleman let all of them leave." The words exploded from Tinkie's mouth.

"Since you weren't up here earlier, he cut them loose about ten o'clock. Look, he didn't really have any grounds to hold them. He interviewed them and he cut them loose." Dewayne spoke to the microphone.

"We had no idea he was going to let them go." Tinkie leaned against the counter and glared at Dewayne. "He could have called us."

"Coleman's not obligated to call you." Dewayne's jaw was setting into a stubborn position. One thing about Coleman's deputies — they were loyal to a fault.

"Why did he do that?" My question was asked softly, and both Dewayne and Tinkie looked at me as if I'd declared that I was going to fly.

"Because he talked to them and had no reason to hold them longer." Dewayne rose and came to the counter. If he'd been chagrined before, now he was testy. "So that's that. You can yell at me all you want, but it won't change a thing." He directed that at Tinkie.

She'd managed to gain some control. "I'm sorry, Dewayne. This isn't your fault. But what in the world possessed Coleman? Why would he do that when he knew we were counting on talking to Graf and Gabriel?"

"You'll have to ask him that." Dewayne wasn't going to take any more of our questions. "Now I've got work to do." He picked up his hat and a set of keys to a cruiser and headed out the back door.

"You can't leave the sheriff's office unattended," Tinkie said.

"Watch me." He closed the door on his retreating back.

"Well, I never." Tinkie looked at me. "Why would Coleman do this?"

"Because they had nothing useful to add." A better question, from my point of view, was where had Graf gone? Had Coleman dropped the charges on him about the wreck where Robert Morgan had been killed or was Graf still tied to Sunflower County by a bail bond, like I was?

"I wonder where Coleman is," Tinkie said.

I wasn't going to lie and say I didn't care. But I also wasn't going to speculate and spend my time thinking about him. Either he was on the case or not. Nothing I thought or said or did would make a difference.

"When Doc did the autopsy on Renata, he said he hadn't found any unusual substances like Botox in her system." There were things that just didn't add up, and my brain kept going back to Renata, the doctors she'd visited, and her plans to move to Tahiti.

"That's right. Except for being dead, she seemed fine."

I rolled my eyes at Tinkie. "Very clever." But something she'd said stopped me. I pulled out my cell phone and dialed Doc Sawyer.

"Doc, can you talk to me and Tinkie? Right away."

"Are you two tailing the sheriff, or do you want to talk to me about something serious?"

"Coleman is there?" Was he really on the case?

"He was. Been gone about two minutes. Left here in a hurry, too."

"We're on our way."

We jogged back to Main Street, where we'd left our cars. The roadster was closest, so we took that, buzzing through a quiet downtown on the way to the hospital.

We turned to go to the hospital when I noticed a silver Porsche on our tail. The car zoomed up close, giving me a clear view of Graf behind the wheel.

He hadn't left town. Whether it was because he was still on bond or because he was waiting for me, I didn't know. But the fact was, he was here. Despite all my internal monologue about how Graf wasn't a man to pin my hopes on, I felt my spirits lift. While everyone involved with the play was now undoubtedly gone, Graf had remained behind.

"Snap out of it," Tinkie said grumpily. "I

see him, and it means nothing except he's as desperate as you are to clear his name."

My answer was to pull into a parking slot and get out. Graf parked beside us. When he stood, tall and handsome in the noon sunlight, I walked over and gave him a hug.

"Why are you following us?" Tinkie asked.

"I went to Dahlia House, but no one was home. I tried the sheriff's department and no one was there." He shrugged. "Like a good junior detective, I found your cars on Main Street and waited."

"That's the *how.* What I asked is why." Tinkie gave no quarter.

"Coleman dropped the charges against me. I'm free to go. I told him the truth, that I intended to get ahead of Robert Morgan and force him to stop. But I didn't cause the wreck. I did leave the scene. Because I was scared. But I turned myself in at the Jackson, Mississippi, Police Department. He believed me and cut me loose." His arm dropped over my shoulders. "But I'm not leaving Zinnia without Sarah Booth. So why I'm here has to do with helping to prove her innocence. I'm available to do whatever you need done."

"What about Hollywood and Federico Marquez? You had a screen test scheduled. You —"

He pulled me against his chest. "We have a special magic, Sarah Booth. I'm not going without you. Sure, I could be a leading man on my own, but with you at my side, I can be a star."

I saw Tinkie roll her eyes, but that wasn't my reaction. I heard the self-serving portion of Graf's statement. But I also heard the fact that he was putting his bright career on hold to help me. Perhaps it was partly for selfish reasons. I didn't care. He was standing tall beside me, and I so needed that.

"Where are we going?" he asked.

"You're not going anywhere." Tinkie put her hands on her tiny hips and tapped her alligator shoe on the asphalt.

I was caught between the two of them, a position I'd felt for the last two weeks. I sighed. "Graf, do you know where Gabriel went?"

"To get his things from The Gardens. He was picking up Kristine and Giblet and they were going to leave after lunch."

"Could you find them and ask Gabriel if he'd be willing to talk to me?"

"Sure." He didn't hesitate or question my reasons. He opened the door of the Porsche and got in. "Do you have a cell number?" He whipped out his phone, ready to install my pertinent data for instant communication.

I give him my number and, for good measure, Tinkie's. As we watched him drive away, she turned to me. "I still don't trust him."

"Tinkie, the only person I trust is you." I wasn't normally a touchy-huggy kind of person, but I put my arm around her shoulders and gave her a squeeze. "Don't worry about Graf."

"It's just strange that he'd hang around when the whole world is waiting for him to explode from the silver screen."

"I know." Graf's taillights disappeared. "He isn't our biggest worry, though."

"Who is?"

"Renata."

"I realize she's set up an elaborate frame, but she is, after all, dead."

"She may be dead, but she's still clinging to this world. Today, I'm going to put the stake through her heart."

Chapter 25

Doc had Renata's file open on his desk when we got to his office. "Before you ask, I'll tell you exactly what I told Coleman. In fact, he asked me to tell you." He let that sink in while he adjusted his glasses and perused some papers. "A preliminary autopsy showed Renata to be a healthy female of the age of thirty-seven. There was no cancer, no life-threatening disease."

"The toxicology showed no drugs in Renata's system?" I asked.

"None. The only thing unusual I found was some elevated levels of CoQ10."

"The health food stuff?" I'd never have taken Renata for an advocate of eat right, feel right. She was carnivore down to the bone.

"CoQ10 is being evaluated in a number of studies." Doc shrugged, "I'm not up on my research like I should be, but the journal articles I've read show promise in a lot of different areas. Stroke, Alzheimer's, mental acuity. Renata may have been taking it as a boost to memory, or it could be something else. There's no way to tell, because it's an over-the-counter product, and we have no one to ask about the dosage or why she was taking it."

"Memory?" That triggered a thought. Graf had said Renata was having trouble remembering her lines, even though she'd done the play a thousand times. "Like absent-mindedness or what?"

"CoQ10 is beneficial to memory, or so some studies show. A lot of people without any serious medical conditions take it to improve their memories."

Tinkie shook her head and pointed to Doc's coffeepot in the corner. "Maybe you should figure a way to get your coffee into a gel cap and use it for health enhancement. Heck, looking at you, I think that stuff may be the fountain of youth."

"Was Renata showing any signs of illness? Anything at all? Clogged arteries, anything?" There had to be something.

"Her liver showed a few irregularities, but nothing life threatening or even indicative of permanent damage. Of course I didn't do a genetic screen or anything like that." Doc rubbed his chin. "She was poisoned, so it was obvious what the cause of death was. Maybe I should order some additional tests."

"This is all so vague." I wanted to kick the wall. I needed to find answers, but Doc couldn't get the answers I needed from a corpse. Dr. Samen's records might hold some useful information, but I didn't know how to get them. Renata had to be involved in something worth dying over. I just had to figure out what.

"Doc, I know Coleman requested Renata's medical records from Dr. Samen in Hollywood. If he gets them, he'll probably ask you to interpret."

"If he's a smart man, he will. Coleman couldn't read a medical chart if his life depended on it." He looked over his glasses at me. "And neither could you."

"Will you call us?"

"I will. If Coleman says so." He cleared his throat. "You haven't even asked me to snoop into the charts about Connie Peters. That's not like you, Sarah Booth."

I stood up. "And I won't. I can't keep going back and forth like that, Doc. I never believed Connie was sick. Coleman continues to believe whatever lies she tells. That's his choice. I'm finished."

Doc rose and came over to me. His arm

went around my shoulders, and he gave me a hug that brought tears to my eyes. "Sarah Booth, I don't know a finer man than Coleman Peters. But he is a man with obligations."

"Coleman loves her." Tinkie rose slowly, looking from Doc to me. "That should count for something. He truly loves her."

"I realize that." Doc put his other arm around Tinkie and drew her close. "In a perfect world, Tinkie, love would transcend all other things. Evil would bow before love. Death and disease would flee in its presence. But love isn't enough. Not nearly enough. I've watched Sarah Booth pass up several good men while she waited for Coleman to set his house in order. I'm with her. She's waited long enough."

Tinkie was smitten silent. "Thanks, Doc," I said, working hard to control the quaver in my voice.

"I'm only telling you what I think your folks would say. There comes a time when walking away is the only answer that makes sense."

I kissed his cheek. I'd taken that first step in ending what now seemed like a lifetime of love. In high school, I'd always noticed Coleman, the football hero, the kid who worked after-school jobs to get his college degree in horticulture, the young adult everyone respected. We'd never dated, because Connie had always been on Coleman's arm. And she was still there, one way or another.

I couldn't look at Tinkie. I had to walk out the door and keep walking before I dissolved in tears. My hand was on the knob when she spoke.

"You both make it sound so cut-and-dried." Tinkie refused to let it die.

"If it were cut-and-dried, I'd be Coleman's date and not his prime murder suspect." I took a deep breath. "Now let it go. I have to, so please let it go."

I walked quickly out the door, down the corridor, and into the winter day. The sun had been replaced by clouds that scudded north, as if the troubles from down on the Gulf Coast had blown Renata into our midst and now promised more bad news.

"Sarah Booth! Sarah Booth!" Tinkie called out to me as she ran to catch up. "You don't mean that. You aren't giving up on Coleman, are you?"

How to explain this? It was difficult to think of a way to say it. "Coleman is who he is, Tinkie. That's why I love him. Because he takes his vows seriously and does what's right instead of what's easy. But I can't be the part of his life that's wrong any more. I have to find a place where I'm what's right. For me and the person I fall in love with."

She grabbed my hand and slowed me so that I faced her. "Is that Hollywood and Graf?"

I didn't know. I had no answer for her, because a broken heart doesn't mend with the promise of a screen test. "I'm not in love with Graf."

"Could you be?"

"I was, once. But that was a million years ago." I forced a smile. "I was a different person then with different dreams and ambitions."

"Those dreams are close enough to touch now."

I nodded. "But I have to figure out if I want to touch them."

Tinkie started to ask something else, but she changed her mind. "We need to know more about Robert Morgan. Let's go by the junkyard and see if there was anything in his Tahoe."

Abel's Junkyard was an amazing place. Kudzu had grown over the thirty acres of wrecked cars, creating clumps of vines, now wintery brown, that sometimes took on the shapes of animals. It was like a crazy, deformed topiary on Planet Mars. And the proprietor looked like something Stephen King might have dreamed up. He was a tall, slender man with a stoop and a long, asymmetrical face marked by profuse hair growth. Abel Cain had parents with a twisted sense of humor and just enough Biblical reference points to be vicious.

Tinkie made the introductions, handing the junkman one of our business cards.

He looked at it for a long moment. "What can I do for you little ladies?" he asked, his bushy eyebrows jittering around on his forehead. I couldn't tell if he had a nervous twitch or if he was trying to wink at Tinkie.

"We need to see that blue Tahoe." Tinkie pointed it out, a burned and twisted heap.

"Pulled that off the highway myself. Man died in it. Lost control." He clapped his hands so suddenly and loudly that I stepped back. "He burned up fast."

Tinkie cleared her throat. "Fascinating. Could we take a look at the vehicle?"

"Why?"

"We're investigating the accident. Insurance purposes." She leaned forward, showing off her assets in a scoop-necked sweater. "It's possible fraud is being perpetrated upon our Fremont Insurance, and they've hired us to find out."

Tinkie was smart not to disclose our true purpose. Abel Cain didn't look like a man who wanted any part of a murder investigation, but insurance fraud was undoubtedly something he heard a lot about in his line of work.

He shrugged. "From what I heard the guy was speeding and lost control. Sheriff got some eyewitness reports. The driver didn't make it to tell anyone anything."

"You didn't happen to find anything at the scene, did you? Maybe a bottle of liquor, or something more interesting." Tinkie gave him a knowing look. "Wouldn't be the first man got tanked in Memphis and tried to drive to Jackson."

Abel shook his head, and I thought of a St. Bernard. "Wadn't nothin' left in the car to find, but the good Lord saw fit to give me some excellent peepers. I found somethin' a little interestin'. Might appeal to two insurance ladies."

"Something you didn't show the sheriff?" Tinkie winked at him.

"Wadn't a reason to involve the law. Legal prescription." He frowned. "Thought there might be somethin' there, but I did some searchin' around and discovered there's no market for what he was takin'. Unless it's the insurance market."

I wanted to tie this guy in a knot. "Where is it?"

"Where's what?" He gave me an innocent look.

"Ignore her," Tinkie said, kicking me in the shin. "What did you find, Abel? You could help me pop this case wide open, and if that happened, I'm sure you'd be rewarded." She reached into her purse and brought out a hundred-dollar bill. Who walks around with hundred-dollar bills in their purses?

I opened my mouth to tell her that Abel Cain was scavenging drugs from wrecked cars and trying to sell them. He was little more than a petty drug dealer, capitalizing on the misfortunes of others. I didn't even get the first syllable out of my mouth when Tinkie clipped my shin bone again. I despised those pointy-toed shoes of hers.

"Show me what you got, Abel," she said, taking his arm and moving him away from me.

I was about to follow and make a few unbiased observations about the character of her latest male conquest when my cell phone rang. I answered while trying to keep up with Abel and Tinkie, who seemed determined to outdistance me.

"Miss Delaney, it's your attorney, Harry

DeLa Bencher, Esquire."

I almost groaned. "Yes?"

"I need you to come into my office immediately. Drop whatever you're doing and come now."

I slowed my steps. "What's wrong?"

"I can't discuss this over a telephone line that isn't secure. That's not in your best interests. I am, after all, looking out for you."

"That's comforting."

"Miss Delaney, sarcasm doesn't serve you well in this instance. I'll be waiting. And by the way, I'm putting my bill in the mail."

I started to protest, but it wouldn't do a bit of good. I'd fallen into the court system of America, and even though I was innocent, I'd still have to pay my lawyer and forfeit the money given to the bondsman. Neither whining nor threatening would lower the freight of this experience. "I'll take care of it."

"Very good. And may I say that I hope your adventures in Hollywood prove profitable and shine the light of success on your home town."

No point in arguing my future, either. It was obvious that Bencher had an inside source on gossip. "Thank you."

I closed the phone and started toward Tinkie and Abel. They were deep in conversation, and I saw the junkman reach into his pants pocket and bring out a pill bottle. Tinkie had what she'd come after.

"What's up with Bencher acting all John Grishamy?" Tinkie asked as we sped back toward Zinnia and her copy of Physician's Desk Reference. Our intention was to look up the drug and find the reason Renata had been killed. Just because Abel Cain didn't recognize the little pink pills didn't mean they weren't some kind of power-punch drug. It was possible Renata had been involved in some kind of drug scam — Graf certainly had been. Or it could be the prescription was for something else entirely. Something that might spell murder for a different reason.

"I can't begin to fathom Bencher," I said, "and I can't wait to find out what STD Renata was passing around New York." I opened the prescription bottle and dumped the little capsules in my hand. I'd never heard of the drug before, and though the prescription was in Robert Morgan's name, I didn't believe it for a moment. This was Renata's medication. If only we could figure out why she was taking it.

"We're almost to the end of this case," Tinkie said. "We're going to find out what

Renata was up to and why she was killed. Then we're going to clear your name, Sarah Booth."

We pulled into Hill Top, screeched to a halt, and ran into the library. In a moment we'd found what we were looking for. The particular drug in the bottle was new — just approved by the FDA for use in the treatment of progressive pseudobulbar palsy, among other things.

"What, exactly, is progressive pseudobulbar palsy?" Tinkie asked.

I picked up the phone and dialed Doc Sawyer's number. He answered on the sixth ring, sounding as if he'd been asleep.

"Doc, what is progressive pseudobulbar palsy?"

There was a pause. "So you talked to Coleman."

"No." I hesitated. "We found a prescription for Robert Morgan, but we think it was actually for Renata."

"That's what Coleman came to discuss with me. It seems Morgan was the front man for Renata's illness. Coleman got Renata's chart, and the prescriptions, written by Dr. Samen in Los Angeles, were for Renata under Robert Morgan's name. Renata simply couldn't afford for the news of her illness to get out."

"What kind of illness?" I almost couldn't wait to hear it. Tinkie and I had been on the right path. Renata had gotten involved in some kind of medical mess.

"She was diagnosed with PPP, a form of ALS. It's a tough disease, Sarah Booth. Paralysis of the facial muscles, vocal cords, throat. For an actress, it would be the worst possible thing. It would eventually have taken away her ability to express emotion, then to swallow. Another aspect of the disease is unbalanced emotions. Rage, hatred, despair. Someone suffering from PPP could go from one extreme to the other at the drop of a hat. It's amazing she stayed on the stage as long as she did without coming apart in front of an audience."

I sank onto a sofa, feeling as if the air had been let out of me. "Is there a cure?"

"No. CoQ10 is being studied, and there are new drugs, but no cure."

After all of this time, I was shocked at what we'd discovered. I'd anticipated finding that Renata had undergone some devious medical technique to hang on to her youth or that she'd contracted some form of an STD that might bring shame on her and someone in the White House. I'd never considered that she faced a serious illness, an illness that struck at the heart of who she was.

"Where did Coleman go?" I asked.

"He didn't say, but he left about thirty minutes ago."

"Thanks, Doc." I hung up the phone and relayed the information to Tinkie.

"Where the hell is Coleman?" she asked as she slumped beside me on the sofa. "We know that Renata was sick, but that still doesn't tell us who killed her. Or why."

No matter how hard I tried to shake the feeling of doom, I couldn't. Renata, on the stage, was vital and alive. Yet she'd been stricken with a terrible disease —

I sat up. The truth came like a clap of thunder.

"What's wrong with you?" Tinkie asked, concerned.

"Damn it." I jumped to my feet and began to pace. "Damn it all."

"What's wrong?" Tinkie was really worried.

"It's all right there. Right in front of me. I just didn't see it."

"See what?" Tinkie was growing impatient. She stepped in my path and grabbed my wrists. "If you don't slow down and tell me what you're so rattled about, I'm going to kick you in the shin again."

That was threat enough. "No one killed

Renata."

Tinkie took a deep breath, realization dawning hard and fast. "Because she killed herself."

"Exactly."

"And in one last act of malice, she framed you."

I nodded. "I think she wasn't rational toward the end. The disease was so awful for her. She focused on me, because there had to be someone to blame."

"And Graf cared about you."

I swallowed. "My God, Tink, can you imagine what it must have been like for her?"

Tinkie grasped my arms and held them firmly. "How can we prove this?"

My cell phone rang again and I answered, hoping in my heart that it was Coleman calling to tell me the charges against me had been dropped.

"Miss Delaney, it's your attorney, Harry DeLa Bencher. I'm still waiting."

And I knew then that Coleman had no intention of telling me. That was the message Bencher was meant to deliver — that at last I was a free woman.

Chapter 26

"The charges are formally dropped, which means there'll be no record." Bencher stroked his tie as he talked. His manicured hands were impressively clean.

"Thanks, Harry." I was ready to leave. I had places to go and things to do. Finding Coleman and confronting him was right at the top of my list. He'd taken the coward's way out — leaving Bencher to tell me that the two weeks of torment had been for nothing.

The case of Renata Trovaioli's murder was closed. Doc had changed the cause of death from murder to suicide. Tinkie had gone to tell Oscar, and I stood on the porch of the old home Harry had converted into his law office, trying to figure out what to do next.

I heard the honk of a horn, and Graf glided into a parking space, the Porsche a glint of silver in the gray light. We were going to have a storm. A big one. And I wanted to be home when it struck.

To my surprise, Gabriel got out of the passenger side. Both men walked toward me. "Gabriel . . ." I faltered. How to deliver the message that his sister had taken her own life? How much worse not to tell him? "I'm sorry. It seems Renata was very sick. Her death has been ruled a suicide."

He was stunned. He stopped, his expression hardening before he controlled it. "Suicide? Renata? That's impossible."

I was the worst person to deliver the news to him, but it was done now. "I am sorry. You can check with Doc Sawyer at the hospital, or with the sheriff. They have all the details, and once you hear them, I think you'll understand."

"I'll bet." His anger was back in place. "Renata would never have taken her own life. This is some plan that redneck sheriff cooked up to make sure you didn't go to prison."

"Gabriel." Graf put his hand on Gabriel's arm as if to restrain him. "Hear her out." He turned to me. "Why would she do such a thing?"

I told him about the palsy she'd been diagnosed with, about the effects, and the ultimate conclusion. "Renata didn't want to die like that, Graf. And I don't blame her.

Everything she'd worked so hard to become was going to slide from her grasp, degree by degree. She couldn't have swallowed food. She —"

"She never mentioned she was sick. She said she was going to retire and live the good life on an island paradise. She said —" He turned away. No matter how hard he tried to deny it, the truth had finally caught him.

"One of the aspects of the disease is that it makes the person irrational. For some reason, Renata wanted to punish me, and to some extent, Graf, too. She set it up to look like I'd killed her. Robert Morgan helped her do this. I think he must have loved her very much." As I spoke those hard words, I suddenly wondered how much of an accident Morgan's death might have been. Had he, too, simply chosen not to live? "I am sorry."

I had no desire to hurt Gabriel more, or to malign Renata. Had I walked in her shoes, no telling what I might have done. But I wanted him to know the total truth, so that my name would be cleared completely in his thoughts. Doubt and bitterness can ruin a person's life, and I didn't want Gabriel to shoulder that in regard to me.

Graf came and put his arm around me. "How did she get this disease?"

"No one knows. Like so many other unfair things in life, it happens to someone out of the blue. Or at least the medical experts don't know the reason yet."

Gabriel leaned against the fender of the Porsche. He was pale, and when he rubbed his forehead, his hand was shaking. "That doctor she was visiting in Los Angeles. He wasn't doing plastic surgery, was he?"

I shook my head.

"She was sick, and she didn't tell me. She made me believe she was abandoning me yet again, going off to her secret place on Tahiti. So I'd hate her. She did that because she knew she was going to die, and she didn't want me to know."

It may have been the last act of kindness Renata was able to perform. "She was trying to protect you, Gabriel. She was your big sister."

"You could have gone to prison for something you didn't do." He sat up taller. "That's terrible."

"That didn't happen. I'm okay." Now who was lying to the man?

A cold wind gusted down the street and dead leaves swirled around us. The storm was getting closer. The leaden sky promised cold rain and the howling of wind. I desperately wanted to be at Dahlia House. "I have to go. There are things that must be done, and I have to get busy."

"What about the screen test?" Graf asked.

"I don't know." I couldn't make that decision right then. I couldn't.

"I'll check on you later tonight."

I nodded and walked away before I couldn't contain my tears.

Lightning forked across the dark sky and I stood in the barn with Reveler and Miss Scrapiron. Sweetie had caught the scent of a rat in the hayloft and was busy tunneling her way through the sweet-smelling bales I'd stored.

Reveler arched his neck and leaned across me to gently nibble Miss Scrapiron's mane. He was grooming her, a gesture of friendship. The animals were unperturbed by the thunder and lightning that signaled the impending rain. When it hit, it came with a roar, echoing off the tin roof of the barn and creating an ear-ringing din. Rain sluiced from the roof like waterfalls.

The storm was wonderful, fresh and clean. I loved the smell and the sound, especially when I was safe and dry and standing between two horses that munched hay in such a comforting manner.

Sweetie set up a howl, and I hoped the rat escaped. After my experiences, I had pity for all creatures trapped by fate.

Reveler lifted his head, ears pricked forward. Something outside the barn had caught his attention. I strained to see into the darkness, and I caught my breath when a large form stepped from the shadow into the light.

Coleman threw back his rain slicker and walked toward me.

If I'd had a gun, I might have shot him. Since my only weapon was words, I chose to hold my ammunition.

"I owe you an explanation," he said. "And a lot more."

I'd waited two weeks for this, but suddenly I didn't want to hear it. I'd made my decision. I'd stepped down a path that no longer ran parallel to Coleman Peters. Right or wrong, I wasn't turning back. I shook my head. "You owe me nothing, Coleman."

"Connie is —"

I held up a hand to stop him. "Please don't say another word. I don't want to hear it. I can't. I can't consider the many factors that go into your behavior. I can't think about Connie's tumor and your obligation to her. I've been a fool."

If I'd shot him, the effect couldn't have been more painful. He took a breath. "Are you sure?"

"I'm sure." Oh, I would doubt myself in the future. I would question this decision, and my truth would shift and skitter around in my heart. But I hung onto what I'd come to feel was my truth. Doc was right. Love couldn't save anyone, least of all me and Coleman.

"Sarah Booth, you're breaking my heart."

One look at his face, and I knew he wasn't lying. Coleman wasn't a man who spoke the words a person wanted to hear. "I know. I'm sorry." I swallowed anything else I might have added.

"I only want you to hear one thing. I charged you with the murder because the district attorney was making noises about calling in the Mississippi Bureau of Investigation. I charged you to keep the case from being snatched out of my hands. Had the case gone to them, I wouldn't have been able to investigate properly. I was afraid you'd end up in jail for weeks while they put together a case based on emotion and supposition. I had no faith they'd get to the bottom of it."

"Why didn't you tell me?" One sentence. One brief phone call could have helped me guard myself from the hurt that had finally broken my heart.

"It had to look like I meant it. If there'd been one glimmer that we were in collusion of some sort . . ."

"Yet you risked it all at Harold's party."

He took two short breaths. "I saw you up on that stage, and I knew I'd lost you. You're too fine an actress not to give it your best shot. You were born to act, Sarah Booth. The realization that you were gone — I lost my head. I thought if I could make you understand how much I loved you, somehow, magically, things would change."

I didn't try to stop the tears. We'd been star-crossed from the first. Only a fool would have given us a chance, but it didn't stop the pain. I turned into Reveler's neck and sobbed. When I looked up again, Coleman was gone.

The phone was ringing when I walked inside. Caller I.D. told me it was Tinkie, so I picked up.

"Are you okay?"

Somehow, she knew. Tinkie had that radar that comes with close friendship and love. "I am."

"I got a call from Graf. He's worried about you."

"I don't want to see him right now."

"I understand. And he does, too. You know, he loves himself a lot, but I think he has big feelings for you, too."

A smile pulled at my mouth. Tinkie had a way of putting things. "Feelings aren't always good things, Tinkie."

She hesitated. "I'm meeting Bobbe and her husband the rock star, Kristine, and Gabriel at The Gardens for a drink. Would you join us?"

"They're all still in town?" I figured they'd all be far from Zinnia.

"They decided to stay until you were cleared."

I found another reason to tear up. "That's amazing."

"You're amazing, Sarah Booth. Whatever happens, I'm right beside you. I'll swing by and pick you up, if you'd like."

The storm had passed. Sweetie was in the kitchen eating broiled chicken tenders. The only thing I really wanted was a long hot bath and my bed. "Can we meet for breakfast tomorrow with Cece and Millie and all of them?"

"It'll have to be early. Bobbe has a morning flight out of Memphis and Kristine and Gabriel will head out on that cross-country drive."

"And Graf?"

"I get the impression he's not leaving Zinnia without you."

"In the morning then. Bright and early." I loved her even more because she didn't ask about Coleman. She accepted that I knew what was best for me, even if she might disagree with my decision. "I love you, Tinkie."

"Right back at you."

I climbed the stairs and went straight to the bathroom to draw a tub. I was leaning over the old claw-foot bath when I noticed a second reflection in the water. Jitty looked like she was going to a ball.

I turned slowly, taking in the beautiful dress and the elegant way Jitty wore it. She looked as if she'd stepped out of a picture from the past.

"Another ball?" I asked.

"Hard to give up the habit once it grabs you. Nothing like a Virginia Reel to set a girl's heart to going pitter-pat." She sat down on the toilet, her skirts rustling and crowding me back against the wall.

"You knew all along that Renata killed herself, didn't you? That's why you told me the story of great-great-grandmother Alice and Bethelyn Caldwell." I'd given that story some thought after Coleman left me in the barn.

"I suspected."

"Couldn't you just have come out and told me?"

"You knew all along, too, Sarah Booth. You knew Renata had grown forgetful and erratic and bitter. Bobbe told you that her expression had become brittle, that she didn't show emotion when Kristine threw water on her. You knew. You just didn't want to believe that someone so young and vital could be dying."

"Death is no respecter of age. I know that. My mother was only a few years older than I am now when she died."

"Intellectual truth isn't nearly as real as heart truth."

I got up and went into my bedroom. Lying across my bed was the beautiful white dress from Le Chic. Beside it were the sling-back shoes and a beaded white purse. Tinkie had been at work.

There was also a note, and I picked it up and read it.

"Good luck in Hollywood, Sarah Booth. Knock 'em dead, and then come home to your family. Love, Tinkie, Cece, and Millie."

Beside the note was an airline ticket,

booked for the day after next into LAX. It was open-ended on return.

I picked up the dress, and the light from the bedside lamp caught the tiny crystals embedded in the material.

"That's a mighty fine dress to sashay around Tinseltown in."

"Tinkie has exquisite taste." I couldn't look at Jitty. I hung the dress in the closet and felt the pressure of tears. "I don't think I can leave."

Jitty's laughter was gentle, like the rustle of leaves in the sycamore trees on a bright summer day. "You're not leaving us behind, Sarah Booth. We're all in your heart."

"Jitty, if I go out to Hollywood, and I really need you, will you come?"

She pondered my question. "This is my home, Sarah Booth. My bones are out there in the cemetery with the rest of your family. I don't like to be too far from my bones."

I caught the glint of the devil in her eyes. She'd never cared about bones before now. "You'll come. If I really need you, I know you'll come."

She shimmered, translucent as she began to fade. "Remember, you set out to let go of the past."

"Why is it that life never turns out the way I think it will? I did set out to let go of the past. I meant to leave behind all the sadness of loss, but all I've done is lose Coleman."

"And found a dream."

"Maybe. Maybe not. Only time will tell, Jitty."

"Give my regards to Halle Berry. I think we look something alike, don't you?"

Her laughter echoed softly from the walls of my bedroom. I undressed, sank into the bath, and let the warm water wash over me. There were decisions to make, details to attend to, and dreams to spin.

But for this one night I was going to sleep in the bed of my childhood in the room where I'd once been safe from all dangers and bogeymen. For one more night, I'd pretend that the past was alive, and it was a place where I could hide. In the morning, I'd deal with whatever I had to.

ABOUT THE AUTHOR

A native of Mississippi, **Carolyn Haines** lives in Southern Alabama on a farm with her husband, horses, dogs, and cats. She has been honored with an Alabama State Council on the Arts literary fellowship for her writing, a family with enough idiosyncracies to give her material for the rest of her life, and a bevy of terrific friends.

She is a former photojournalist.

Visit her at www.carolynhaines.com.

The employees of Thorndike Press hope you have enjoyed this Large Print book. All our Thorndike and Wheeler Large Print titles are designed for easy reading, and all our books are made to last. Other Thorndike Press Large Print books are available at your library, through selected bookstores, or directly from us.

For information about titles, please call:

(800) 223-1244

or visit our Web site at:

www.gale.com/thorndike
www.gale.com/wheeler

To share your comments, please write:

Publisher
Thorndike Press
295 Kennedy Memorial Drive
Waterville, ME 04901